Scorned Lover

Luci O.

ISBN: 979-8-9933009-0-0
Cover Design: [Daracomics]
Printed in [United States of America]

First Edition

Thank you to my husband for always believing in me and thank you to new friends who have helped boost my confidence in not only life but the confidence to put my dream onto paper.

Glossary

1.Prologue

2.Chapter 1

3.Chapter 2

4.Chapter 3

5.Chapter 4

6.Chapter 5

7.Chapter 6

8.Chapter 7

9.Chapter 8

10.Chapter 9

11.Chapter 10

12.Chapter 11

13.Chapter 12

14.Chapter 13

15.Chapter 14

16.Chapter 15

17.Chapter 16

18.Chapter 17

19.Chapter 18

20.Chapter 19

21.Chapter 20

22.Chapter 21

23.Chapter 22

24.Chapter 23

25.Chapter 24

26.Chapter 25

27.Chapter 26

28.Chapter 27

29.Chapter 28

30.Chapter 29

31.Chapter 30

32.Chapter 31

33.Chapter 32

34.Chapter 33

35.Chapter 34

36.Chapter 35

37.Chapter 36

38.Chapter 37

39.Chapter 38

40.Chapter 39

41.Chapter 40

42.Chapter 41

43.Chapter 42

44.Chapter 43

45.Chapter 44

46.Chapter 45

47.Chapter 46

48.Chapter 47

49.Chapter 48

50.Chapter 49

51.Chapter 50

52.Chapter 51

53.Chapter 52

54.Chapter 53

55.Chapter 54

56.Chapter 55

57.Chapter 56

58.Chapter 57

59.Chapter 58

60.Chapter 59

61.Chapter 60

Acknowledgements

About the author

Follow me for updates

Trigger Warnings

Physical Abuse

Mental Abuse

Verbal Abuse

Mental health

Mild SA

Trauma

Flashbacks

Depression

Playlist

Bad Girls Club – Falling in Reverse

Pray – Jessie Murph

King For A Day – Pierce the Veil

How Could You – Jessie Murph

Black Magic – Little Mix

Don't Talk About it – Skydxddy

Deep End – IPrevail

Cyclone – Baby Bash

Buy You A Drank – T-Pain

My Boo- Usher

Rock That Body – Black Eyed Peas

CHARACTERS

Liora Morgan [Lee-or-ah]

Malrik Rose [Mal-rick]

Ryder Jackson [Ry-der]

Jasper Evans [Jas-per]

Trixie Beam [Tricksee]

Delilah Morgan [Duh-lie-lah]

Lilthe [li-lthe]

Daemous [Day-miss]

Jupiter [Ju-pi-ter]

Aurelius [Ah-rue-lee-us]

College name: Rosepin University based east Texas
(Rose garden that green witches take care of and any color you can think of is there.)

Sport: Squashball (paranormal soccer) when score there are holes and that have to squash the ball down the hole. Can also mean to squash your opponents to score.

Team name: Rumbling Buds

Blobball=dodgeball

Ingredients

—-- moonshade rose- blooms different at night and when brewed correctly can reveal true magic but brewed incorrectly will cause horrible tremors to body and if dose is lethal enough can cause a cancellation of your magic and you go mad

—--- glimmer mothix- shed scales of relaxation but too many in one place can be an omen and powerful storm coming

—--- light fox- can help lead you where needed if lost. Tail glows like a beacon

—--- dark fox- opposite of light fox. Impish and will lead you to death if not careful they look the same other than ones tail glows and the others does not.

—--- celestialscales- massive sea dragons that if scales are harvested can grant visions but if mixed with moonshade rose will cause you to descend into echo sickness

—--- echo sickness- can mimic depression but if not careful will cause the person to go mad and harm themselves because of angry voices

—--- ground eclipsed seed- only grows in soil tainted with blood. Can cause user immense power but too much or continuous use with sap ones soul away and they become a shell of themselves

—--- beetrootrot- looks like a beet but when prepared right can cause powerful healing magic that boosts a healing spell. Because true healers are rare/extinct this is how healers do as much as they can. However eaten raw will kill someone next time they fall asleep

—---- drownedsorrow- berry like fruit that can be tasteless. Eating will make you relieve you're worst memories and can cause you to descend into madness

—---- ghostbrat- an almost translucent root than can cause invisibility for a short time but only if ground into a powder if mixed into potion before being ground into powder will cause everyone to forget you

—---- mystix herb- found in a nighttime hidden meadow that grows under moonlight that when used in a potion can cause severe psychosis. Mostly used as a way to change the way one thinks and acts.

—---- melodic herb- the counterpart to mystix herb. Melodic herb grows in the same meadow but grows from the sunlight. Can be used to relax you and help with any pain.

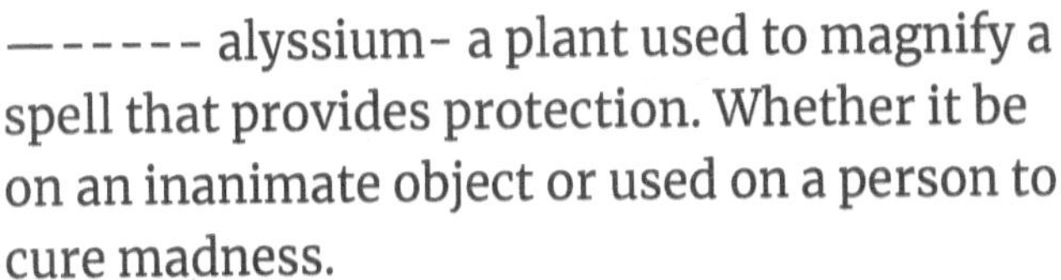

——----- alyssium- a plant used to magnify a spell that provides protection. Whether it be on an inanimate object or used on a person to cure madness.

——----- Starlit Safeguard – birth control potion that lasts 3 months and if brewed incorrectly will be ineffective.

Prologue

Liora

It was cold and wet when I opened my eyes. Ugh, why does my head hurt so much?

My mom must have hit me harder than I thought.

Opening my eyes, a little more as I take in my surroundings. Asphalt? Why am I outside?

The last thing I remember is falling asleep in my bed listening to the sounds of her drinking and laughing at her new boy-toy.

It wasn't always so bad. We used to be a happy family, and she used to be an awesome mom. That was before Dad passed away and everything around me fell apart.

I had to leave behind my best friends when my mom took me and disappeared without a trace, I didn't even get to say goodbye. It's been 9 years. They probably don't even remember or care about me anymore.

Groaning as I sit up and look around, I see that I am 3 houses down from mine.

Wtf?

Glancing at my surroundings there's a scary looking motherfucker leaning against the light post staring at me like I am the bane of his existence. Why is he so pissed? I'm the one who has no idea what is going on.

You know what, I don't care why he's pissed, I am going to demand some answers.

As I jump to my feet I have to pause because holy shit the world is spinning; deep breath Liora you are not a weak ass bitch, breathe through the nausea. Once my head isn't so fuzzy, I continue my mission of demanding some damn answers. Mystery douche quirks his eyebrow when he sees me coming like this is all funny to him. As I get closer, I get a better look at him, and can I say holy shit he is fine as hell.

He chuckles and in a deep, gravelly voice says, "You are not bad on the eyes yourself, mami."

I smack my forehead because obviously my mouth does not know how not to word vomit. His lips twitch like he is trying not to smile or laugh at me.

"And what the hell is so funny?" I demand with my hand on my hips, trying to look intimidating. Although I must look ridiculous because I'm 5 foot 2 and barely coming up to his chest as he towers over me. This sets him off laughing, and I do not mean a chuckle; no, he bends over laughing so loud it echoes in the dark of night.

"You're not scary at all; it is almost like a Chihuahua standing guard for a Cane Corso," he explains.

"Chihuahuas can be fierce as hell, don't doubt them just because they're smaller, they can still do damage!" I gritted out.

He puts his hands up almost placatingly, "OK, ok, yes, they're just as scary and can-do damage if needed."

I huffed out a breath, "Thank you."

Sitting in silence as we stare at each other, I notice he has a small scar under his hairline. It reminds me of a time when me and Malrik were playing swords with tree branches, and I accidentally cut him.

God, I need to get that thought out of my head. Li, it is not him, I'm just missing them and projecting that feeling onto a total stranger, there is no way they could be here anyway. I moved six states away and left them back in Texas. Mom made sure I could never see them again, trust me with no phone or computer, I have no way to even stalk their lives and see how they are doing.

I tried to-get a part-time job outside of school. But no one would hire me because I don't have a phone. The one time someone called the house phone, my mom cussed them out. I was punished for random people calling the house and disturbing her peace. Of course, I made the mistake of standing up for myself and yelling at her, only making punishment worse. If she would just let me get a damn phone she wouldn't be disturbed.

I could barely drag my body up the stairs to my room after that beating, and I missed 3 days of school because of it. CPS came knocking due to my absence from school, and my mom told them I came down with the flu and had forgotten to take the doctor's note to school. They did not push to make sure that is what was actually going on because the CPS workers here are shit.

I shake my head to get rid of the painful memory playing out like it was yesterday and not months ago. Although I guess it could have been yesterday since mom was drinking when I got home again and demanding money from me like I had any to help her pay for her liquor.

What was I doing again?

Oh, right, making my argument that just because you are small does not mean you cannot be dangerous and terrifying.

A couple of my mom's douche boytoys learned that I fight back and so did the creeps at school. Some of them even call me a psycho because I stab first and ask questions later.

Although no one at that school cares, people are trading drugs and sexual favors to get them out of sticky situations or out of debt. As if that keeps the creeps away, just because they are bigger than others and have slightly more money. It was almost like watching an old lifetime movie sometimes.

Oi!

Li, head out of the gutters, you spiraled again. Maybe I am a psycho over here talking to myself.

I look at the douche again as my vision focuses and notice him looking at me in concern? Nope, I want answers, not concern. "Why am I outside in the street at whatever godforsaken time it is?" I demand of whatever his name is.

As he opens his mouth to answer me, red and blue light up the night sky, and sirens are heard. I turn around at the sound and notice that they are all pulling up to my house: police cars, firetrucks, and ambulances.

"What the fuck?" I exclaim aloud.

I start to walk that way to figure out what is going on and stop remembering doucheface.

Turning around, he is gone, no trace of him ever being there.

Did I imagine the whole encounter?

Am I really going crazy?

Maybe too many hits in the head and the loneliness of not having any friends is making me conjure up invisible people.

Oof, a therapist would have a field day with my damaged ass.

Shrugging my shoulders, I continue my walk back to the house to figure out what shitshow my life is now. Getting closer, I ask the closest fireman what is going on and say I live there and thrust my hand at our little abode.

He stops and looks at me like he's trying to figure out if I am lying or not.

Like dude, I know I look a little crazy but I dunno what to tell him because I don't even know how I ended up out here.

They don't let me in the house, stating that they had an anonymous tip called in of abuse, and a fire from this address, and they have some questions I will need to answer.

I stand there dumbfounded because no one has ever cared about the abuse I have endured or bothered to try and help.

I knew there was no way out because I had no family besides my mother, and my father's side disowned me after he died, so I've been left to fend for myself.

I'm still standing there staring off into the distance because I'm not sure what to do or where I'm supposed to go. I'll be 18 soon, but not soon enough, and I have no money, and my clothes are rags.

I think the fireman can tell I'm starting to panic because he calls over an EMS, and they try to get me to take deep, calming breaths.

Slowly but surely, I don't feel like I'm going to pass out, and when they deem me safe, they lead me over to a squad car and tell me to wait there, and someone will take me to the station soon.

As I'm sitting in the back of the squad car, I can see neighbors coming out onto the street, staring and whispering while pointing at our house.

We by no means live in a good neighborhood, but a roof overhead to stop from getting rained on was better than nothing.

When mom remembered to pay the heat and water bill, it was a somewhat nicer place to live, but she mostly spent all the money on booze and drugs.

I'm not sure how long I had been sitting in the car when I watch them bring out 2 black bags on what looked like gurneys. Now I have watched enough movies to know those were dead bodies, but who did they belong to?

Mom normally goes out after giving me a beating because she doesn't like the way the boy-toys look at me.

As if that is my fault.

The rags I'm allowed to wear are too big, probably from the men's section, and it's almost like she grabs the worst possible selection she can conjure up.

So that begs the question... Who is in the bags?

Oh my god, what if it is my mom???

Am I suspect number one?

What should I do?

I don't even know how I got outside, and I don't know who that mystery guy was. Do I tell them I saw some dude over by the lamppost? I'm still not sure my mind didn't conjure up an imaginary person.

Oh man oh man I am so screwed.

I start breathing heavily and getting sweaty. My skin feels hot and itchy all over, and I feel like my heart is about to burst out of my chest. My head's pounding in my skull like there's a jackhammer going to town, and I'm not sure how to get out of the car, but I can't breathe.

The walls are closing in, am I going to die?

I mean logically I know it's a panic attack but I'm a dramatic bitch especially in this state.

No one is around the police cruiser I'm sitting in, so I start banging on the window.

I need out!

I need air!

I can't breathe.

It hurts to breathe

Little black dots start to appear in my vision as I slowly come to the realization that no one's coming.

Why did you think this time was any different? That's my last thought before everything goes black.

Liora

"Ugh, where am I?" I say croakily.

I look around and notice I'm in a white room, and a monitor is beeping next to me.

Am I in the hospital?

What the hell happened?

My head is pounding, and my skin feels itchy.

The last thing I remember was sitting in the police car waiting to be taken to the station to answer questions and watching them bring out 2 black bags.

Did I have a panic attack?

I immediately get up and look for my shoes, grateful to find them by my bed. After getting my shoes on and now sounding winded, I look around trying to decide my next move.

I'm hooked up to an IV, although I'm not sure what they are pumping into me, so I go ahead and rip it out. I can just say I accidentally did it if anyone gets suspicious.

I don't even get a chance to attempt to slip out unnoticed because my door opens, and a nurse comes through it. She looks kind, but I learned the hard way that looks can be deceiving. She looks up from her clipboard at me, then the IV on the bed next to me, and back to me with what looks like pity.

"I'm sorry, sweetie, you had a panic attack, and they brought you to the hospital. I was sitting with you so you wouldn't wake alone and confused, but I had to go help a patient," she explained.

I just stared at her warily. I don't trust anyone, nurse or not, they could have done anything to me while I was unconscious. I think she knew I wasn't going to say anything, so she continued, "Sweetie, when they brought you in, you were dehydrated and malnourished, that's what the IV was, fluids. There are also signs of abuse on your body, both self-inflicted and not. Would you care to explain what happened?"

Internally I'm freaking out.

It's been about a week since I cut. I never cut too deep so as not to draw too much attention to myself, but the other abuse???

I never wanted to open the lid on that bucket.

On the outside, I kept a blank look and asked, "Where is my mom?" She walks over and sits next to me, grabbing my hands and sadly says, "Oh, honey, I'm so sorry they found your mom last night along with another male in your house, both deceased."

What am I supposed to do now?

We had no money, and we had no family.

"What happens now? I'm still a minor and have nowhere to go."

She looked at me with so much pity, like she couldn't believe this was happening, and stated, "The detectives will be able to answer all that, but they thought talking to me would be easier in case you had a panic attack again." I just nodded, and she got up and walked to the door, I'm assuming to let said detectives in.

In walked a man and a woman, probably thinking I would feel more comfortable answering questions if a woman were there, but I didn't trust anyone.

"Hi, I'm Detective Stevens, he points to himself, and this is Detective Reyes. We just want to ask a couple of questions, and we will send you on your way, "he states.

Joke's on him, I have nowhere to go but ok, so I just nodded that I understood him.

"Are you aware that your mother and another male were found deceased in your residence at approximately 2:17 am this morning?"

"The nurse informed me before you guys came into the room that it was my mother and another male, I'm assuming her boyfriend, she was seeing at the moment. I remember seeing 2 black bags being brought out on a gurney, looking things, when I was sitting in the police car and then waking up here." I told him.

They nod their heads; he jots things down in his notepad. He clears his throat and says, "And where exactly were you, miss? Witnesses say you walked up to the scene after personnel had arrived, stating you lived there. Were you at a friend's house?"

I scoffed. As if I had any friends who would want to be friends with someone broken like me?

He quirked an eyebrow. "Something wrong with what I said?"

I just shook my head and said I don't have any friends; I wasn't allowed, and we moved too much to ever bother trying. He just looked at me, almost like he was searching for a lie, and it made me anxious.

I wasn't a fan of the feeling I was getting.

I think his partner sensed it because she asked the next question, "We are just trying to figure out what happened and where you were, so if you would please answer the question of why you weren't in the residence?"

I told them the truth.

I wasn't sure how I ended up outside. I just happened to wake up out there with a pounding head and no recollection of what happened, and that's when I saw the red and blue lights and heard the sirens, so I came rushing home to figure out what happened.

They exchanged looks, then looked at me before Detective Reyes continued, "We believe they were targeted by some dangerous people. Your mom or her boyfriend probably owed money for drugs or something, and a hit was taken out on them. Her boyfriend has known ties to a gang that runs drugs and has been arrested for distribution before, so it's very possible." Drugs, gangs, what the hell.

This was a lot to take in at the moment, and I'm not even sure where to start. I mean I knew she did drugs but getting involved in gangs is something I never expected. Although I guess anything is possible.

For all I knew, she whored herself out to pay for them, just like she tried to do to me when she didn't have the money for the tab at the motorcycle bar a couple months ago before we moved here.

Nope, don't go down that path. We don't need those memories surfacing right now before I start dissociating and need an outlet for the pain. When it gets bad, I would rather feel the numbness of nothing than the pain of reliving those memories.

The detective took a breath and continued, "We aren't sure how you ended up outside, maybe a guardian angel was looking out for you, there's no telling, and since no one saw you go outside we aren't sure what happened and were hoping you could fill in the blanks. That doesn't seem to be the case. Our condolences are with your family at this time, and if you remember anything, we'd really appreciate you telling us."

"Family? I don't have any family, it's just mom and me, or I guess just me now." I told the detectives.

They shared another look before finally speaking up, "We found your father's will, and since your mother didn't have one, his will is the only one we have to go off. It was stated that he had family in Texas? A sister and his parents. We contacted both, and your aunt is who you will be going to stay with, as she is more suited to take in a teenager and help with the aftermath of everything that has happened in your life."

"They disowned me a long time ago. I'm not sure they want me, no one's wanted me not since my dad died. Wait, why didn't my grandparents take me in?"

They shared a look again before looking at the nurse, who was observing us and looking at me sadly. She spoke up, "Sweetness, everyone has someone who wants and loves them, you just may not know it or have been shielded from it, and I'm so terribly sorry you don't know what that feels like."

I didn't know what to say, so I just looked down at my lap and tried to blink back tears because I wasn't sure what to do with the kind words, she said to me.

Detective Reyes spoke up once again, telling me that my grandparents travel a lot, so it is not ideal for me to stay with them, but my aunt is an artist/baker, so she has more permanent roots, which are more suited for me. All I could think was whether they were telling the truth or my "grandparents" just didn't want me, and they didn't know how to tell me.

"Your aunt Delilah should be here soon to help you get your things and take you to your new home. If we have any more questions, we know how to reach you, and if you remember anything else, please call and let us know so we have all the details. Do you think you can do that, Miss Liora? We will let your aunt know to be cautious of the surroundings until y'all are safely out of town." Detective Stevens informed me before they both exited, leaving me with the kind nurse.

A silence hung between us and as she was going to open her mouth to say something, I'm sure more of that kindness than what I am used to in the last couple years of my life than I am used to and I won't know how to respond to her, when all of a sudden, a knock rang out that had me tensing.

Liora

The nurse asked me if I was ready for her to open the door and see my aunt.

I took a deep breath and nodded my head for her to go ahead and open it while I fidgeted with my hospital gown shirt, looking thing.

Partially because I was nervous and partially because I wasn't sure what was about to walk in, I mean obviously I know Aunt Delilah is, but how is she going to react?

All I hear after the door opens is a gasp and pattering of feet, and a body is slammed against me as I get squeezed.

I go stiff as a board because touch means pain, and I'm waiting for the pain to start, and with the way I'm being squeezed, I can't raise my hands to protect my head.

Eventually, I begin to understand I'm receiving a hug as Aunt Delilah is sniffing and rubbing circles on my back. I'm assuming, in a way, she thinks is soothing to me, but I am more horrified than anything, so I just sit there, hands limp at my sides, waiting for her to let go, and thankfully, the nurse takes pity on me.

"Why don't we give your niece some space? It has been a lot on her these last 24 hours, ma'am," the nurse tells my aunt.

"Oh, my goodness. I am so sorry, Violet, I didn't even think. I was just so happy to see you that I got carried away and wasn't even thinking about everything that happened, sweetie," my aunt exclaimed as she jumped away from me.

I just nod my head at her, trying to convey that it's ok.

I was used to people not taking me or my feelings into consideration.

"Alright, well, once you are discharged, we will go back to your house and get your stuff, and then we can head to the airport and go back to Texas. Does that sound like an okay plan to you?" My aunt asked me like she genuinely cared about what I wanted.

I just nodded my head suspiciously.

Is this all an act?

Is she only acting like this because that nurse is here?

Have I been thrust into an alternate universe?

What the hell is going on?

I have no idea what to believe or trust anymore, and it's making my fight-or-flight panic worse because my poor nervous system doesn't know what to expect, so I don't know how to prepare. My poor body can't take it, and all I want to do is run away.

Luckily, she had turned away from me to ask the nurse how soon I would be discharged from the hospital, so she didn't see me having a near panic attack.

Come on, Li, you got this you're a bad bitch and bad bitches don't have panic attacks over a hug. I finish my little pump-up rant with a nod. I take a deep breath while I wait for the nurse to reply to my aunt.

"I would like her to finish her IV fluids before she leaves, since she was dehydrated when she got here, but then I see no reason she can't leave once that's done. However, I'm sure the doctor will have some instructions on things he would like you to do to make sure she does after she leaves. So, sweetie, if I can put the IV back in and get it going again, you will be free to leave soon. The sooner we do this, the sooner you leave," the nurse informed us.

I just sighed dejectedly and held out my arm because I obviously had no choice.

What happened to our body, our choice?

Okay, that was dramatic even for me.

I know I need the iv fluids but damn.

The nurse was swift with getting the IV in and then had my aunt follow her out of the room to fill out my release forms and talk to the doctor about my care and what condition I came in, I'm sure.

Whoopdeedoo. I mentally twirl my finger in the air because I love that, essentially, a stranger is going to know those things about my life. I mean, mom didn't exactly hide the abuse, but I did my best not to let it show.

Or at least I thought I did.

I wonder if my aunt will even care about it all, or will she think I deserved it. I had a social worker assigned to me once because I stupidly blabbed to a teacher, I thought I could trust, and they called child protective services.

Boy, was I a stupid kid.

Mom convinced the CPS worker that I was just a badly behaved kid and was being disciplined, and that I would make up stories to generate favor with everyone and make her look like a bad mom. Maybe some kids do it to seek attention, but I would never do something like that.

Anyways, the worker believed my mom over me and told me to start behaving and to lay off my mom because parents are entitled to discipline their children. She even told me she felt sorry for my mom for having to put up with a daughter like me, and what a saint my mother must be.

Oh yeah, what a joy she was.

I shook my head, hoping to etch-a-sketch that out of my brain.

Ugh, I am so bored.

No phone, no books, no TV, nothing to do.

I look around the room for something to do and spot the TV and almost palm five myself.

Remote, remote, remote, I chant in my head as I search around for it. Think, Vi, where do hospitals normally have the remote for the TVs? I think hard about it, and if I remember anything, a memory of me visiting dad in the hospital before he passed away pops into my head.

I'm around 7 years old, skipping along the hospital hallway holding Auntie Delilah's hand while holding the card I made for Daddy in the other. I know he is sick, and I'm hoping my card will help him feel better, even though I know it probably won't. When we get to his door, Auntie Delilah kneels and reminds me to make sure I don't climb all over him and to be mindful of all his wires. I nod my head. "I promise, Auntie Delilah," I tell her. She ruffles my hair as she stands back up and proceeds to open the door to Dad's room. He's laid up in bed sleeping but wakes up when he hears the door open.

"Princess!" he exclaims.

"I made you a card to help you feel better, Daddy!" I told him.

"Oh yeah, come here and show me, I would love to see what my princess made me," he tells me. I sit next to him on the bed, and he reads the card I made with a soft smile on his face, as he does. He places it on the little table next to him and tells me he already feels a little bit better, thanks to me. Little me can't help but smile so big at the fact that I was able to do something to help.

*"Want to watch some TV with your dad?"
He asked.*

*"Sure! Cartoons!" I exclaimed. He
grabbed the remote attached to the hospital bed
and pushed the button with a TV picture on it,
and bam, the TV turned on.*

I shake the memory away and take a
breath to compose myself. I try not to dwell on
memories of my father, if I can stop it.

"Whatever," I sigh.

I turn around and look around for the
remote on the bed so I can figure out how to
get the TV going.

Eventually, I found it tucked under the
pillow but inside the pillowcase. Because that
makes total sense, but at the same time is
totally my luck but whatever because ya girl
found le remote.

It takes a couple of tries, and I totally
have to smack it a couple of times against my
hand before it works, but I just about scream
in joy when the TV powers on.

Ok, please, oh please, oh please let
there be something good on the TV. I will even
beg if I have to. I'm not sure who I will beg to,
but it would be someone.

I push the guide button to make it
easier to see everything that's on and make it

easier to choose, when lo and behold, nothing happens.

Ughh!

Of course, this would happen to me because I have the world's worst luck ever!

Ok, Li, chill chill, try pushing a different button and see if that helps.

I try just pushing the channel button, and HALLELUJAH, it changes channels to a Hallmark movie. Love like that will never find me, so I try to change it again, and boom nothing the remote stops working. UGH! Of course! Guess, beggars can't be choosers. So, I settled in for a love story I'll envy but never be a part of.

Despite the beeping from the IV machine being done, I had managed to start dozing when my door burst open again.

Even though my heart skipped a beat due to the mini heart attack I just suffered, I showed no sign and sat up to let them know I was still there and waiting for them to come back.

In came the nurse, my aunt, and who I assume is the doctor.

My aunt looked like she may have been crying?

But why?

What would be making her cry?

Is it because she actually cares about me, and this isn't all an act?

No, that can't be it, she doesn't know me and disowned me years ago. I don't know what to do with anything going on anymore. Shaking my head to clear the racing thoughts running through it, I turn my attention to my aunt and the doctor. Holding my breath to see what is about to be spilled.

"Ok, Miss Morgan, after speaking with your aunt and seeing that you finished the bag of fluids, I see no reason as to why you cannot be discharged. I have briefed your aunt on the care you will need going forward, but if you have any questions, please feel free to call, "the doctor tells me.

I sit there numbly as my aunt fills out my discharge paperwork, as I try to distract myself from what my life has become and for what is still in store for me.

What about school?

Does she still live in the same town?

Do the boys still live in that town?

Why didn't my grandparents want to come see me?

All these questions and no bravado to ask them, maybe my mom was right. I am worthless and stupid. I get up and follow my aunt out of the door to my room and down the hallway to the elevator.

"Ready to go? She asks me once we get into the elevator.

I just nod my head because what else am I supposed to say? I have learned my lesson not to speak unless I have something intelligent to input, which, according to my mother, was never, so I kept having to be taught a lesson. Over and over and over again.

She frowns at me but quickly wipes the frown and smiles, then tells me," I am so glad you'll be coming to live with me, Liora. I have missed you so much."

I just look at the floor, unsure of what to say because, honestly, I don't know what to say. Is it rude not to answer her? Probably, but what else do I say?

She sighs and says, "I'm not sure what happened since I last saw you, but you are safe now. I know it is going to take time for you to understand that, and that is ok. I will be there every step of the way. You are not alone anymore."

My eyes fill with tears because that is the nicest thing I have heard since my dad was alive. I shuffle back and forth on my feet and clear my throat, willing myself not to break down bawling like a baby.

Jesus, someone shows me a little bit of human decency and I'm a big ass baby ready to become a puddle of tears.

Kill me now.

I decided to make my life easier and let her know we don't have to go back to my house because there isn't anything there for me to get.

My latest punishment in humiliation, my mom burned my extra pair of clothes for "rolling my eyes" at her, so now all I owned was what I was currently wearing.

My aunt stared at me incredulously like I had grown an extra head as we walked to her car. "It isn't any problem we can swing by on our way to the airport," she says.

I just shake my head and finally speak up, "What I'm wearing is all I own." Embarrassed, I quickly turn and look away.

I can hear sniffles, but don't turn to look at my aunt because I can't see anyone else crying. The feeling makes me want to freak out.

I'm definitely the one who would use a broom to pat someone's back to comfort them. You know, stand in the doorway and use the broom in a "there, there" type of way.

We eventually make it to the airport and board the plane without any more awkward questions.

Thank god.

As the plane takes off, my eyes drift close, and my last thought is... Will I finally start to be happy?

Chapter 1
Liora
3 years later....

I'm so nervous about starting my first semester at Rosepin University that I already have the jitters from how much anxiety there was coursing through my body.

Ok, Li, you've got this! I nod my head and get ready to head downstairs to put my duffel bag in my car before I say goodbye to Aunt Delilah.

I double-check that I look presentable in the mirror. My boring brunette hair is in my natural waves down my back from me wearing it in a messy bun after my shower this morning. I've got my war paint on, aka liquid eyeliner and mascara around my hazel eyes, and a lip stain to make my lips look a little darker than they normally are, but not too dark to look like I am trying too hard on move-in day. My outfit consists of a pair of skinny jeans and a t-shirt with the saying *"when I said I like it rough; I didn't mean my whole life.*" I thought it was funny and fitting and paired with my black Chucks.

Deciding I look decent enough plus it's only move-in day, so I doubt there's a lot going on today, I head downstairs. I find Aunt Delilah in the kitchen drinking coffee and trying to appear like she's not worried out of her mind.

I walk over to the fridge and get an energy drink out of it and pop it open. The first drink is like heaven. Aunt Delilah shakes her head at me over my drink choices, but it's no different than coffee, so she has no room to argue plus I only drink one a day if that.

"Are you all packed and ready to go?" Aunt Delilah asks me.

"Yep, even gassed up the car last night so I don't have to worry about doing that," I told her.

"Are you sure you don't want to just take online classes and stay here? You can help me in the shop, you know I don't mind, and the customers love you." She tries to reason.

"I'm sure, Aunt Delilah, it's time for me to stop using you to hide from the world, and it's time for me to step out on my own and make friends, maybe fall in love if I find someone to interest me enough. I can't hide in the apartment or the shop forever, you know that. Even my therapist said it was time for me to be out in the world again. I can't let my fears keep me from living my life, or I'll end up back in that dark place and none of us wants that. Plus, I'm ready to take on the world and show them the new Violet is not someone to be messed with." I explain.

She stares at me while having an internal battle. I know she's scared for me, but it's time. I have to face the world and stand on my own. Hiding behind my aunt isn't something I can do forever.

Finally, she heaves a sigh like it will help dispel all her worries and gives me a huge, squeeze-of-a-hug. She hugs me so hard I have to start tapping her because I'm losing my breath.

"Oh, sorry, sweetie, I didn't mean to squeeze so hard. I'm just worried and am going to miss you," she tells me.

"I'll be fine, I promise. I'll text if I stop for any reason, and I will send a text when I make it to campus. Plus, we can call and talk whenever you want. I'm not leaving forever Aunt Delilah." I assured her, hoping to ease her fears and partly mine as well, because honestly, let's face it, I have become dependent on her.

"I am going to hold that to you, young lady," she exclaims.

I hug her and we trade our goodbyes. I grab my energy drink and breakfast bar for the road because it is a couple of hours' drive. Aunt Delilah follows me to the door to see me out.

I climb into my black 4runner with teal accents, tossing my bag into the passenger side and sticking my drink in the cup holder. Slipping my shades on over my glasses I start backing out of the drive and wave at my aunt, who is animatedly waving back making me laugh a little.

As I put the car in drive, I give the place that has been my home for the last 3 years one last glance and see my aunt with tears streaming down her face.

That breaks my heart but if I turn around now, I'll never leave, and I need to get to the college so I can get my welcome packet along with figuring out where my dorm will be.

Chapter 2

Liora

I turn on my Apple Play as I hit the road. Picking my road trip playlist, I start jamming out to get in the right mindset for school before my mind starts wandering.

So much has changed since Aunt Delilah came and got me from the hospital 3 years ago.

While I am grateful for her saving me, it has been a big adjustment having someone who genuinely cares for me and my well-being. At first, I thought it was all a big ploy for the doctors, and she would be just like mom once we left, but NOPE.

She was the motherly figure I should have had all those years ago after my dad died. But of course not, I was stuck with the devil of all mothers, who hated my guts and blamed me for everything wrong in her life.

When we made it back to Texas, Aunt Delilah wanted me to do therapy and at first, I resisted but eventually gave in. My emotions and inner turmoil were wreaking havoc on my Aunt Delilah's empath powers. Sometimes she'll get so overwhelmed by all the emotions around that she'll pass out. She normally has pretty good shields up but overwhelming emotions, especially big ones can knock her shields down.

Where was I?

Oh right! My emotions after my mother's death and then coming back to Texas were a lot for me to handle, and my mental health suffered severely with all of it. I had my aunt really worried, especially after she caught me cutting too deep on my arm and having to be admitted to the hospital.

The doctors said it was a suicide attempt, but that wasn't my end goal. I was just trying to drown out the voices everywhere, and my depression was an added factor that didn't help.

I've always heard voices and just thought my mother was right and I was crazy. My aunt is who finally told me the truth and opened my eyes to the paranormal world. She said the voices I always hear are what others around me are thinking and it is a part of my powers.

My dad was a telepathic and that's probably where I got it from. It sucks he isn't here to help me train or learn anything about it. But *c'est la vie*. What can I do about it?

I'm not the best at shields, but thanks to Aunt Delilah, I did finally learn about how to do it. As long as I don't focus too hard on it, I can block it all out. But it comes in handy when I'm trying to find out someone's intentions.

Next thing I know, I'm pulling into the parking lot outside of the admin building at Rosepin University, and its late afternoon. Wow, Liora, how scary is it that you zoned out and somehow made it to your destination.

How freaky.

What if I ran red lights or stop signs? Bejesus, at least I didn't get into a wreck or run anyone over. Shake it off, Li, you made it, and that's all that matters.

Okay. I take a deep breath and open the car door to start getting out. I step onto the asphalt and go to shut my door. Shit I need my bag! Oof, I hope no one can see how nervous I am.

Closing my car door and getting ready to walk into the building I do a mental check to make sure I'm good.

Pits... Check.

No food in teeth... Check.

ID... Check.

Phone... Check.

Okay, Li, you got this. You are a bad bitch who has overcome a lot. College won't be the death of us. We fear nothing. A mantra my therapist had me learn for when I get too anxious or panicky. Does it always help? No, but false confidence is better than nothing.

Taking a calm, steadying breath I force myself to move from the safety of the parking lot and start heading to the admin building. As I walk up to the doors, I read the title and smile.

The Nexus: Rosepin Administration

Before I can even open the door, it opens, startling me, and I don't even have time to move or react before a body is barreling out of it and slamming into my short frame.

The force of it knocks me to the ground but my body is still tingling from the contact of the asshole who can't watch where he is walking.

"Oof my ass," I gripe.

I glare up at the bulldozing asshole who still has yet to even say anything to me. No apology. No offering a hand to help me up. Jeez, what a jerkwad.

He is staring at me with a look of horror.

What the fuck?

He quickly shakes out of his stupor and glares at me like I am the bane of his existence and not in a sexy way. More in the way that he would treat dirt on his shoe better.

Ouch....

"The fuck are you doing standing in front of a door like some bumbling idiot? Are you dumb?" Mystery asshole growls.

Blink. Blink.

I just blink at him in shock because, WTF. Shaking out of it, I jump back onto my feet and go to give him a piece of my mind.

"Excuse the fuck outta me! I didn't realize this was your private door asshole. Last I checked, this is a public space, and I am the one standing outside where it is bright and not running poor unsuspecting people over like some kind of animal. You're the asswipe who stormed out of the doors without looking at where he was going." I glare back and go to start poking his chest to make my point.

He grabs my hand before I can make contact with his chest. Squeezing my hand in anger? There are those weird tingling sensations again.

He drops my hand like it burned him and glares at me again while I'm still staring in shock.

"I won't fall for trickery from a bitch again. And if you ever pull this shit with me again, I won't hesitate to burn you down like the treacherous bitch you are." He bites out before knocking into me as he storms away, almost taking me down to the ground again.

"YOU'RE A CRAZY ASSHOLE!" I shouted at him.

Of course, he ignores me and carries on storming down the pathway making others scatter out of the way of the glowering asshole. My shouting doesn't do anything other than get ignored by what's his face and looked at like I'm crazy but the surrounding people.

I quickly look down and turn on my heel to go into the admin building with what I'm sure is a tomato red face. I can feel my anxiety amping up from the stares and whispers I'm hearing around me.

As I look around to figure out where to go, I notice the chaotic buzz of people milling around, already knowing where they are going or meeting up with friends.

"You look lost. Do you need some help?" I hear from beside me.

At first, I don't answer because I thought my shields had dropped but after a quick check I look over and see an older student standing and staring at me.

"Oh yes, I'm new, I'm looking for where I need to go to pick up my packet with everything I need," I reply sheepishly.

She nods like it's common, and maybe it is. That's when I notice the badge on a lanyard around her neck. **Student council**.

"I'm part of the welcoming committee. Student council is spread out throughout the campus to help any lost souls find their way to whatever their destination may be," she breezily explains.

"Oh ok, that makes sense." I nod at her.

"Where you need to go is right over there at the table that has a line of students, just get in your grade line and they will hand you your welcome packet." she explains while pointing over towards the right where I now see the banners with Freshman, Sophomores, Juniors and Seniors.

"Thank you!" I profess and scurry to the line I need.

I don't bother looking back or around me, I just stand there nervously before pulling out my phone to fidget with a game on it.

After maybe 30 minutes, I finally made it up to the table and they asked for my class power and my name.

"Liora Morgan and I have telepathic tendencies." I nervously state.

The girl nods and flips through the packets in front of her before pulling mine out and handing me my packet.

"Here's your packet. Your name and dorm building plus number are on the front, and here's your school-issued tablet, where any and all information regarding assemblies, class cancellations, mentor meetings, and any events going on will all come through this. Make sure you get it set up once you have a chance, so you don't miss any information. We hope you have an amazing school year," she parrots at me with a rehearsed speech.

I nod and whisper a thank you before walking away and looking at my packet. Ok, Liora, see that wasn't so hard. Easy peasy lemon squeezy, if I ignore the encounter with asswipe.

Walking out of The Nexus, I look at my dorm assignment.

Liora Morgan's dorm assignment. Grandiflora girls' dorm room 215. Roommate Trixie Beams.

Huh, my roommate has a cool name. Hopefully, she's as nice and cool as her name suggests. OK, Li, get back on track and go find your dorm room. I'll get my bags from my car after I find my dorm, so that way I'm not aimlessly wandering with bags.

I grab my student map to figure out where *Grandiflora Dorm* is and see that it's across from The Nexus. I start heading that way down the footpath that the school has.

On my way to the dorm, I look around the campus. It's so beautiful, I love how at ease I feel here. Halfway across the campus, I notice a rose garden. I stop walking and look over at the sign, and read *Venus' Rose Garden*, how amazing. I start walking towards it, almost like something is pulling me that way.

Smack!

I walk right into a wall? No, not a wall. A person. OMG! I ran into someone because I was distracted. I slowly look up at the person ready to apologize when I see it's the same asshat from earlier.

Great, just my luck. I have the worst luck in the universe.

"Are you fucking following me? Wow, so not just a treacherous bitch but also a crazy stalker who thinks it's okay to follow people." He grounds out before shooting me a glare that makes me want to wither into the ground and die. He stalks away before I even get a chance to say anything.

Great, not even a full day, and I have an enemy.

Whatever. Shaking my head, I continue towards my dorm completely ignoring the rose garden since I was knocked out of my trance, quite literally out of it.

I finally made it to Grandiflora Dorm without any more accidents. I bypass the elevator and walk up the stairs to find room 215. According to my packet, my door will register my magic and open up for me.

I'm skeptical about it, but here goes nothing. I walk up to the door and twist the handle before pushing it open, and lo and behold, it actually opens up to show my dorm.

The door opens to a main area furnished with a couch and a basic coffee table. The kitchen is to the right of the main area, then you can see 3 doors. 2 doors are open, which show bedrooms, one is decorated and obviously already claimed, the other is barren with no decorations. Assuming that one is mine, I walk into it and set my packet and tablet onto the school-issued desk.

Spinning in a circle with a shaky smile I take in everything. Holy shit, my own dorm in college. I've got this. With a nod I open the first door I see in my room. My closet is huge, and I don't have that many clothing items, but I fill maybe half. Opening the other door, I see a bathroom with another door on the other side. A jack and jill style bathroom, how cool! I've only read about those in books.

Closing the bathroom door, I leave my room to go open the other door I saw when I walked in. I know it isn't another bedroom because these are duo suites. I wonder what's in there? Opening the door with a little bit of fear, it opens into a laundry room.

Well, at least I don't have to worry about someone stealing my laundry from a community laundromat. Seeing multiple shelves, I already feel giddy about the organization that can be done.

Hopefully, my roommate won't mind my OCD tendencies when it comes to certain things.

"Oh! Hello, I didn't hear you come in. I guess I got distracted setting up, so I didn't get to greet you," a voice speaks behind me.

Jumping out of my skin because she startled me, I slowly turn around to say hello and meet my roomie.

"Sorry, I didn't mean to scare you. Sometimes I get ahead of myself."

"It's ok. I was in my own head, my name's Liora, although I guess you know that already, seeing how they put that info on the welcome packet." I ramble.

Sticking my hand out while trying to show some bravado, she shakes my hand back and declares us roomies.

Chapter 3

Malrik

What the hell is she doing here? How is she here? We've searched everywhere for her. After using my stealth skills, thanks to my dragon, to get her out of her house of horrors, I was sure she would recognize me on that street, but somehow, she didn't. I know I've changed a lot, and maybe that's why, or maybe she doesn't remember our childhood.

Why does that thought make my stomach clench uncomfortably?

Shaking out of my stupor, I go to storm out of The Nexus and hopefully bypass talking to her or seeing each other, but of course, fate has other plans.

In my haste to storm out, I slam right into her short, curvy figure. My body is still tingling, and my dragon is trying to come out. I just stare at my hand and try to ignore the growling in my head.

I know the tingling is supposed to be a blessing by the fates for a mate bond and my dragon wants me to wrap her up in a hug and claim her, but I'm frozen in horror.

No! Absolutely not. I will not be tricked again. Fuck that shit! Been there, done that, would rather not go through it again.

Shaking out of my shock, I glare down at her like she's the bane of my existence, which in a way, she is. Before she ever puts the pieces together and people find out I was there the night her bitch of a birth giver died. I'm in a world of hurt.

The guys would beat me for not bringing them along and letting her slip through my fingers. But she was underage and acted as if she had no idea who I was. Which, maybe she didn't know? No! Women are traitorous bitches.

My dragon rumbles under my skin, clearly upset with my mind and what I was thinking. Great, now I'll have to deal with a pissy dragon because I am ignoring his wants.

My anger over past events with the she devils who shall not be named, I spout out vitriol at Liora before storming away. Not before seeing the gut wrenching hurt look on her face that makes me feel like the shittiest asshole ever. So, at least her yelling at me fuels my anger enough to keep walking away. I know I'm sporting a don't come near me face because people are skirting out of my way.

Aimlessly wandering around the campus to cool off before heading to the house I share with the guys, because I don't feel like evading questioning from them. I'm trying not to be such a dick to them anymore after everything that happened with the she devil. It wasn't their fault that it happened, but I lash out at everyone around me because of it.

Trying to clear my thoughts and calm down, I go to walk into the rose garden to sit and just chillax when a body slams into me, shocking me because I'm not a small guy, so whoever slammed into me was obviously not paying attention.

I notice the mate bond tingles before she ever lifts her head because, of fucking course this shit happens again. Dammit! Can I not get a fucking moment away from her?

My anger gets the best of me again, and I call her a stalker and some other unfavorable words before stalking off. I'm so amped up that my dragon almost comes forth. Cracking my neck and stalking towards our house, I'm breathing hard enough that smoke is just about coming out of my mouth and nose.

Slamming the front door open and stalking through the house to the backdoor to bypass my nosey ass friends. But, with the day I'm having, of course, Jasper sees me and goes to make a joke before taking in my expression and changing course to go upstairs.

I feel bad that my friends are avoiding me when I have such a thunderous expression. I miss laughing and joking around with them, but I just can't ignore and get over what happened. Treating Jasper and Ryder the way I have, I am surprised they have stuck with me, especially since I haven't been pleasant company.

I storm into the backyard, and my dragon takes over easily because I was distracted. Shifting into my black dragon form, some of the tension eases away. Flying up into the clouds and calling upon my ability to hide in the shadows of the clouds, I let my mind wander.

Of course, it wonders to my **mami**, Liora. She looks healthier than the last time I saw her, which, thank god. Not that she wasn't pretty that night I saved her, but you could tell how skinny she was, although she still had some curves. But now? She's a sexy vixen and those curves... Ugh! I just want to take a bite out of them and mark her skin all up. My dragon rumbles at the notion.

Wait, no, no! We don't like her like that, and we won't be crossing that line and ever letting someone get that close to us again. Shaking my head, I decide flying helped a little and head home to eat and go to bed, hopefully putting the craziness behind me.

Shifting back before landing in the backyard of the house, I land silently and begin my walk to the screen doors. Sliding them open without slamming them takes some extra focus before walking into the house.

"Hey, how did flying go? Did it help calm you down a little? Jasper told me you came in with a thunderous expression." Ryder inquires but also leaves it up to me if I want to answer him or not.

I decided to be semi-honest with one of my oldest friends.

"Just a shitty first day the same girl bumped into me twice! She had to be stalking me because how fucking weird." I growl out, still peeved from the encounters.

"Sorry, man. Want us to send a message? We haven't gotten to intimidate anyone recently," he asks while sliding a plate of chicken alfredo over to me.

I just shake my head because I don't want them finding out she is on campus before digging into my food. It is a pretty decent-sized campus, so I'm hoping they won't run into her or even recognize her. But that may be wishful thinking.

"Alright man but if you change your mind let me know. I'm gonna hit the sack," he tells me before walking away and up the stairs.

I'm sure Jasper is in his room listening to music and messing around on his computers. The nerd, I'll have to make sure I check on him before heading to bed myself because if one of us doesn't he will get hyper focused on what he is doing and not sleep which just causes him to show his loose screw.

Finishing up my food I get up and round the counter to rinse it off in the sink before loading it into the dishwasher and pressing start before heading upstairs myself. Turning lights off as I go, I reach the top of the stairs and stop at the first door on the right, knocking. I wait for an answer before walking in.

Peeking into Jasper's room I glance around before seeing the computer chair empty and the bed empty? Where is he? Using my shifter hearing I hear the shower going behind the bathroom door and decide he will be good tonight. He normally showers before bed, something about no dirty body in the bed?

He has his own quirks, but then again, we all do; that is why we work so well. Deciding to leave him to his devices now that I know he isn't still hyper-focused on the computer, I continue down the hall to my room.

Entering my room, I shut the door behind me and just stand there for a moment before ambling my way across the room to my king size bed. Kicking off my shoes and pants so that I'm in my boxers I pull my shirt off and climb into bed.

Sleep comes quickly, and as I am drifting off. I just hope not to have any dreams of the she devil and what she did to me. I should've known I wouldn't be so lucky.

Right as I succumb to my subconscious, I get a preview of who will haunt my dreams tonight and wouldn't you know it's a certain curvy brunette girl stars in my dream and I can't decide if it's a blessing in disguise or some witchy magic at play again.

My last coherent thought is that I wish she hadn't come to this university.

Chapter 4
Liora

After our introductions, I told her I had to go grab the rest of my things from my car. She offered to come and help, but I need a minute to decompress from today's event and tell her it's all good, I have it covered. Heading out the door and down the stairs. I have to stop, step off to the side, and out of the way of a girl barking orders at some moving people.

"If you drop my stuff, I will put a curse on you for daring to drop any of my things and ruining my junior year," the girl screeches.

She is actually beautiful and alluring, but I can already tell she is not a nice person. Dropping my mental shields to get a read on the girl, she is thinking of some horrible things about the people moving her belongings.

I shake my head to forget about the horrible girl. I travel outside and start my walk to my car. Those bags aren't going to magically appear in my room, although that would be so neat if they did.

Too bad I can't do anything like that. I can barely keep a handle on my shields, not to become overwhelmed by everyone's thoughts and desires. Hopefully, they will train me well here, and I can learn more about these powers, plus anything that kinda goes along with it.

Finally, making it to my baby, aka my car, I unlock the hatchback and grab my suitcase and box of books. Can't leave those behind because you never know when you will want to read. Plus, it'll give me something to do when I'm bored and have nothing to do or anyone to hang out with.

Placing my suitcase on the ground and pulling the handle for easy access, I place the box of books on top so it will easily roll with it, and I don't have to worry about carrying them. I may act like a strong independent woman, but I will always find an easier way to do things, because I am not that strong.

As I start my trudge across campus back to the dorms, I can't help but admire everything again. I don't think the campus will ever not amaze me. It's just so ethereal, like something out of a book or a movie.

As I pass the rose garden, I make a mental note to go explore it when I get a chance because it looks so inviting and relaxing. Plus, I spy a waterfall towards what looks like the center, and I bet it makes an amazing place to read or study.

Wistfully sighing at the chance to do that, I continue making my way to my dorm while rolling my suitcase as I go. Making it back to the dorm, I'm lucky someone holds the door for me so I can get in with no problems. Muttering a quick thanks, I make my way to the stairs and look at them with apprehension.

Come on, Li, you aren't a quitter. It's either carry them up the stairs or take the elevator. Glancing between the 2, I decide I'm not that brave. Maybe one day I will take the elevator, but that day is not today.

Squaring my shoulders, I turn around to go up the stairs backwards. A quick look over my shoulder to make sure no one is coming down, I start slowly but steadily climbing.

I'm huffing and puffing by the time I make it to the second floor. Right as I get my suitcase over the last step, of course, the wheel breaks. I barely have time to catch it before my stuff goes tumbling over. Of course, thanks to my position, my body tilts and I'm going to tumble down the stairs with my stuff.

Right before doom, someone grabs me around my torso just below my breasts and pulls me back from certain doom.

"Careful there, roomie, wouldn't want such an amazing body to go splat at the bottom of the stairs on move-in day. Can you imagine the spectacle? Good thing I was coming out to look for you to see if you needed help. Hey, wait, why did you take the stairs in the first place? There is a perfectly good elevator right there," a chirpy voice says behind me.

She releases me and I just stare at her in shock. My mind is reeling at the rapid way she spoke to me. When I finally get my bearings, my mind processes that she asked me about the elevator.

"A load of someone's stuff and some movers were in it, and they were headed to a higher floor than us, so I didn't want to inconvenience them, but it's all good. I made it up here with almost no problems. Thanks for saving me from certain doom." I try to laugh the question off.

At first, she looks at me questioningly and opens her mouth to say something before deciding against it. Clapping her hands together, she grabs the box of books and nods her head at our door for me to follow.

Following her into the dorm, she sets my books in my room before sitting on the bed and looking at me expectantly.

"Ok, roomie, how about we play an icebreaker to get to know each other while you unpack?" Trixie suggests while getting comfy on my bed.

I nod at her and say in a somewhat confident voice, "That sounds nice and a good way to be on our way to good standing roomies."

WTF, Li, why would you word it like that? Now she is totally gonna know what a weirdo we are. I'm way out of practice when it comes to socializing and making friends. But at the same time, I am so desperate for a ride or die friendship. Hopefully, I didn't scare her away with my weirdness.

Trixie laughs before telling me she likes my weirdness. It's a pleasant change from the stuck-up personas of the people here.

"Ok, we know each other's names, so how about we start with simple things, and we can work up to something more personal?" Trixie suggests.

I nod and agree before setting my suitcase on the bed and opening it up.

"Well, you already know that my name is Trixie. I'm a chaos witch, and I know some can be triggered and flip to the dark side, but I'm a boss bitch and won't let that happen, I hope. I take it as my sign to say something.

"My name's Liora, I'm a telepath with some basic telekinetic tendencies, um, this is my first time in the world after 3 years," I tell her before quickly turning away and putting some shirts in the closet.

"Wow, so I'll get to be like your fun mentor?" she exclaims.

I shrug my shoulders noncommittally while being ecstatic on the inside because of the possibility of a friend.

"My favorite color is electric purple because it looks so badass when my magic comes out. That may be condescending of me, but my magic is amazing to look at," she gushes.

"That sounds so cool! I don't have any cool magic when my magical abilities come out, but I guess my favorite color has to be a tealish color, but where it looks bright." I voiced with excitement.

"Oooo, I love that! I can totally see that for you. Ok favorite TV show? Mine has to be One Tree Hill for TV with people and Demon Slayer for anime if I have to pick just one," she gushes at me.

"Those are both so, so good! For a show with people, I think I would have to pick Degrassi because of all the angst, and Fairy Tail for my favorite anime. What I love most is the feeling of family and all the great friendships," I gushed back, excitedly. I have finally found someone to chatter excitedly about my favorite things.

"YES! Finally, someone who understands the good stuff. Most of the girls around here watch trashy reality TV. Which don't get me wrong, some are good, but it just isn't that good to only watch such dramatic stuff," she explains haughtily.

"Agreeable in my opinion, and then you have to pay way too much attention to what you are watching, or you will miss vital bits. It is honestly tiring to me." I reply.

"Right, they are doing too much on there. Ugh, I can already tell we are going to be besties for the resties," she tells me before yawning.

"I have an extra blanket and pillow you can use tonight, and tomorrow we can go shopping for stuff to furnish our dorm," she says before getting up to leave and heading to her room.

She pops back through the Jack and Jill bathroom with the pillow and blanket for me before explaining kindly, "I noticed you didn't have one and the school doesn't supply them, so we have to bring our own from home or buy one once we are here. We could have gone earlier, but we got caught up talking and getting to know each other."

I mutter a thank you as she goes back to her room, shutting my side of the bathroom door. Setting the supplies on my bed, I quickly grab some comfy sleep shorts and an old baggy tee to sleep in.

I choose comfy vibes over sexy vibes because let's be honest, who do I have to impress in here? Before I can spiral internally over my PJ choices, I grab my bathroom bag and head in to brush my teeth and wash my face, plus do my business.

Opening the door slowly to make sure I am not interrupting Trixie. I step in once I realize it's empty and go about my business. About 10 minutes later, I feel somewhat refreshed and ready for bed. Plugging my phone in before climbing into the queen-sized bed, I get comfy and ready for a long night of insomnia because my mind never slows down or stops.

I should have known tonight would be a little different because of how strenuous today has been mentally because before I can attempt to fight it, a nightmare pulls me in of my horrible bitch of a mother and times I wish I could forget.

Chapter 5
Liora

Another day of hell. No friends to provide any escape, and now I have to walk over a mile home from school. Maybe I should just disappear. It would certainly make my mother happy. Mother isn't a good word for her because moms are supposed to love and care for their children, and that's not the case for me. Birth giver or even spawn point is a better way to describe her. As I turn into my shitty neighborhood of run-down houses, ours being in the worst shape because it's just a spot for her to lie around and do fuck all.

Dreading going in that door, especially with no idea what will greet me. Will she be asleep and leave me alone? Is she out being the whore she is with whatever fuckboy she is seeing at the moment? The fates must laugh at me or hate me for all the crap I put up with.

Walking up to the door, my whole being fills with dread at what lies beyond here. I sigh and open the door before walking into our very bare house. A quick glance around the living room. I see it's empty and let out a sigh of relief.

Possibly some reprieve from her. Walking to the kitchen to see if maybe there's something to eat or even drink, I see very barren shelves.

Opening the fridge, I find an apple on the verge of going bad and grab it before grabbing a glass from the cabinet and filling it with sink water. Once I have my boring dinner, I head to my room to hopefully study and sleep in peace.

Sitting on my old mattress on the floor, I take out my homework and get it all laid out to work on. Taking a sip of barely drinkable water, I grab my shitty pencil I stole from a teacher's stash, I get to work. Slowly, I relax a little as I settle into the routine of homework and nibbling on my apple.

Eventually, I fall into a restless sleep on my bare mattress. Just as I am going into a deep-ish sleep, I'm woken up by my birth giver.

Kicking me awake, she snarls at me over the apple I ate and how I must think I am so much better than her for taking what is hers. She continuously kicks and punches me over the damn apple. She threatens to send me to work on my back for her to pay for more drinks and fun. As I was dissociating from my awful reality, she yanked my head back and pulled my hair so hard I screamed. My screams become gasps as my shitty mother breaks a rib. Searing pain shoots through my body as I succumb to the darkness at *the edges of my vision. Thank god, a release from this is my last thought.*

I gasp as I slam up into a sitting position. Before I can full-blown panic, I get my bearings and see that I'm in my new dorm room. Settling down before I wake Trixie and cause her to worry and inquire about more of my life than I'm ready to answer.

Tossing my blanket off myself, I decide I might as well get my day started. Grabbing my phone, I see it's 6:28 am. At least it isn't too early, I think to myself.

Heading to the bathroom to do my morning routine before getting ready for the day. I strip down and step into the shower to wash the bleh feeling from traveling yesterday and unpacking everything to decompress.

After my shower, I feel more human and not so much like a gremlin. I stop in front of the sink to brush my teeth and wash my face. Once I'm done with that, I head back into my room and shut the door to the bathroom.

I toss my wet hair up into a messy bun, so it's out of the way as I head into the closet to pick out my outfit for the day. Grabbing a grey oversized crop top that says *"At-least life wants to fuck me"* and a pair of ripped skinny jeans. I head out of the closet and back into my bedroom to get dressed.

Once dressed, I grab my makeup bag and look at the mirror in the bathroom to do my everyday makeup, which is also the extent of my makeup knowledge. Once my winged eyeliner and mascara are on, I pop on some tinted lip oil and call it good with a quick nod of my head.

Back in my room, I decide to open my bedroom door so that Trixie knows I'm awake and ready whenever she is. I decide to grab a book to pass the time as I wait. Reading is such a good way to distract yourself from the real world and everything going on in it, plus it's an excellent distraction from a wandering mind.

Around 8 or so, I hear the shower kick on in the bathroom to alert me that my roomie is up and getting ready. I set my book aside and grabbed my phone to look more casual as I wait for her. Opening the games tab on my phone I pick out a matching tiles type game to help time pass as I wait.

Not long after that, I hear a knock on the bathroom door before it opens, and Trixie pops her head through with her eyes closed.

"Are you decent?" she asks.

"Yes, I'm ready whenever you are," I reply breezily, like I haven't been waiting.

Uncovering her eyes as she looks at me and lets out a little laugh after reading my shirt, she shouts to give her 5 more minutes as she heads back to her room. Getting up to leave my room, I pull my scrunchie out of my hair and let it drop in easy waves down my back before heading into the main area to wait.

Before I can even drop onto the couch, Trixie pops out of her room almost breathless and declares us ready to go.

"Let's head to Target and then maybe HomeGoods and see if we can't get the place livelier and spruce it up a bit. Ooo, and we can stop and get something to eat after," she excitedly chirps before heading out of the dorm and holding the door open as she waits for me to follow.

Heading towards the stairs, she links arms with me as we leave the dorm building. As we start our trek to the parking lot, she offers to drive since she knows the area better, and I still don't know my way around yet. Once we get to the parking lot, I follow her to her car, which, funnily is across from mine. Looking at my car and then back at her purple

GT mustang, I decide to offer something I never thought I would.

"Hey Trixie, how about we take my car since it is bigger and has more space for the things we need, so we hopefully don't have to make multiple trips? You can even drive, since, like you said, you know where we are going and it will be easier if you drive and I just pay attention." I offered her while pushing the fob to unlock my 4Runner.

"DAYUM, this is your car?? It's so badass looking. You just got so much hotter to me. Let's go shop til we drop bitch," she explains while fanning her face.

We climb in, with her in the driver's seat and me in the passenger seat. She starts the car and slips on my shades before we start our ride.

My phone automatically syncs up to my CarPlay, and my shuffle for my songs continues. As Falling in Reverse's **Bad Girls Club** starts up, Trixie cheers and turns it up as we hit the main road leading us away from the university. We're both singing along to the song as it blares from my speakers. This is something I have always wanted to do with someone. Something so little to others is such a huge thing for me and brings such overwhelming joy to my soul.

The shuffle of songs helps pass time with Trixie, knowing most of them, which gives us something in common. Is this what everyone gets to experience? I thought this was only something I would only read in books or see in movies, so to experience it firsthand is so spiritually fulfilling.

I'm so lost in my thoughts of a world I never thought would happen that I don't notice the car has stopped and Trixie has muted the music, staring questioningly at me. When she notices I'm not stuck in my head anymore, she says, "You okay? I tried to get your attention a couple of times, but you were deep in your mind, so I waited it out."

"Yeah, I'm fine, just thinking about things I had only seen or read. Sorry to worry you." I answer.

"All is good, girl. You're not the only one who can get lost in thought. You can talk to me anytime about anything, even if you think it's dumb or small. We're 4lifers," she expresses to me.

Nodding at her and giving a small, uneasy smile, I open my door to get out of the car. Shutting the door and walking to the front of my car, I meet up with Trixie, not even hearing her get out.

"Let's get shit done, bitch." She exclaims excitedly while linking our arms and pulling me towards Target.

Chuckling softly, I let her pull me along and basically hand over the reins since I don't know what all we need.

Chapter 6
Liora

Stepping through the doors, it's a little overwhelming how bright and loud it is in here. She leads me over to something called Starbucks. I can smell coffee and sugar, so I am assuming it's a coffee shop. I feel a bit better because it reminds me of Aunt Delilah's shop and all the yummy drinks she had. Walking up to the counter to order, I look up at the menu and start panicking because I have no idea what any of those things are. It's almost like reading another language.

I think Trixie can sense my unease because she leans over and says, "I never know what I want, so I always try something new. I can order for you if you would like. Do you like sweeter things, coffee, tea, or prefer bitter coffee?"

"I'm not really a coffee drinker, but I have a sweet tooth. I'll trust you to order something good for me, since I don't know what to order," voicing my gratitude.

"We'll take a grande strawberry acai lemonade and a grande vanilla bean frappuccino with frap chips and caramel drizzle." Trixie orders for us before paying for both of us, before I can offer. Once paid, she leads us off to the side while we wait.

"You didn't have to pay for me. I'll pay you back." I let her know.

"Girl, don't even worry about it, plus my treat, since it was my idea," she expresses.

Our drinks are ready pretty quickly. Once we get our drinks, we head over to grab a cart before starting our journey through the store.

"Okay, so we definitely need to get decorative stuff for the bathroom, living room, laundry room, and we can't forget your room. Oh, and groceries, because we need to be able to eat something," Trixie lists out as we walk towards the home section of the store.

"What if we do a theme for each thing to make it easier on us?" I question tentatively.

"Yes! I love that idea. How about we say what colors are a no-go?" she suggests.

"Yellow is something I'm not a fan of, just like pink. I don't mind a little bit, but I don't want to feel like Barbie threw up in the space, if that makes sense." I respond to her.

"No, absolutely, I agree with you on that. Some pink is ok, but not a lot. How about we do a colorful mix with funny sayings for the bathroom? We can even try to find some art to go with it for the bathroom," she tosses back at me.

We look up ideas and decide to do some blue and watercolor swirls, and some signs we like that hopefully we can find today.

"How do you feel about organization in the dorm?" I question.

"I love watching those videos on Paravine. They're so soothing to watch, but I don't know what I'm doing when it comes to stuff like that, but I would love to do it," she gushes.

"I love organization and being organized but have never had my own space to do it. My aunt thought it was a waste of money in her apartment because certain things had to be organized the right way in her cafe." I explain back to her.

"How awesome! Then I will leave that up to you, if that's okay with you," she ponders.

Nodding, we continue our trek into the bathroom section. I grab some glass containers with bamboo lids, a glass soap dispenser that's a really pretty blue shade, a glass container for by the sink, some stackable clear containers with slide out drawers, a white trash can with a lid for the bathroom, and some black floating shelves.

"Ok, you were quick with that, but I'm going to be totally honest with you... I don't know how you plan to use any of this," she chuckles while gesturing at what I have organized in the cart.

"Oh, I'm so sorry. I just started getting what I envisioned and didn't even think to stop and explain what I was grabbing and why." I reply sheepishly.

"The glass containers with the bamboo lids I was thinking would be great for Q-Tips and cotton rounds, the soap dispenser for hand soap, the glass container is for toothbrushes and toothpaste, the stackable drawers for organizing hair ties, extra supplies, feminine products and bathroom cleaning supplies, the white trashcan I was thinking we could DIY paint some swirls to match our theme and the floating shelves for a decorative plant, shower steamers and air fresheners," I explain while also pointing at each thing.

Taking a sip of my drink while Trixie just looks at me, shell-shocked. I can't help the small moan I let out over the drink. It tastes just like cookies and cream ice cream.

"First off, dayum, girl, your moan is such a sexy sound. And second, I am so glad you are in charge of the organization because I never would have thought of doing half of those things," she says cheekily.

Blushing, I mumble out a shy thanks because no one has ever said such nice things to me. We head to the home section to see what else we can get here before grabbing groceries.

First, we stop at pillows for the couch. It's a greyish color, so at least we will have many options for it, plus it's interchangeable for holidays. We grab purple and teal pillows to show our favorite colors in our shared space. It was actually Trixie's idea. She has such good design ideas, so we make a perfect pair.

We then get a purple, teal, and grey ombre soft rug to put in there under the coffee table. Next, we pick out bookcases and an entertainment center, and an employee takes them to the front for us, thankfully. Trixie says this way I can bring my books out and show them off, and I'll have room for any others, and we have room for any knick-knacks we find that we love.

When she said I could bring my books into the shared space, it made me feel all warm and fuzzy on the inside that she even wants my stuff out there and not just in my room. So, she doesn't see me cheesing, I turn away and head towards the bedding aisle to pick out things for my bed, plus get some pillows.

I pick out a beautiful flowery bedding with a burgundy background and wildflowers. I can't wait to see it on my bed. I have a feeling I'm going to love it. Next up I grab 2 pillows that have a cooling effect. That way if I have a nightmare I don't sweat everywhere.

"I love that and can totally see that in your room. Okay, I think that takes care of some basic room and bathroom. Now, let's go to the kitchen area and get some basics," Trix states.

We make our way over to the kitchen area. Grabbing a toaster, an air-fryer, a countertop ice maker, and a blender. Thankfully, the rooms come with a microwave, a basic fridge, and a stove/oven, so we don't have to worry about that.

Next up, we grab knives, silverware, and a holder for them, plates, cups, bowls, cooking utensils, a basic pots and pans set, mixing bowls, Tupperware, and a pitcher.

Our cart is just about overflowing already, so we decide to head to the front to pay and come get groceries later or tomorrow. On our way up to the registers, I veer off towards the big calendars because I would love a big one to help keep everything organized. Not realizing Trixie followed me, she perks up when she sees what I am looking at.

"Ooo, I have always dreamed of doing a shared calendar with my roommate, but my last couple of roomies hated the idea," she says sullenly.

"I have to have a visual representation of my schedule to help keep me organized, and I don't mind doing a shared one with you. We can put our class schedule on it in different colors, plus keep track of holidays and extracurriculars." I admit to her.

"How about we do a chalkboard one? We can get two. One for what you suggested and one for a cleaning schedule. Plus, I think the chalkboard ones are so pretty when all the colors are on it," she suggests.

"Yes, I love that idea, but we'll have to get the chalkboard markers somewhere else so we can get a big pack with lots of colors and maybe some skinny ones for more organized writing.

Grabbing two chalkboard calendars and adding them to the cart, we finish making our way to the registers because we have a cart full. We get in line at one and start loading the conveyor belt. We end up with a great system. She hands things to me, and I organize them onto the belt. We split the cost evenly.

Trixie pays first, and then before I pay, I remember to tell the cashier we have some furniture waiting up here for us and get it paid for. Trixie offers to push the cart with the furniture while I push the Target cart. I am glad she offered to push that one because I don't know how I could push it out to the car. Lol.

Getting to the car, we eventually get it all loaded into it just barely. We may be slightly out of breath, but we did that damn thing with no help.

"Whew, I wasn't sure we were going to get it all to fit, honestly. And now that it is all in, we're going to make multiple trips. How about we take this stuff to the dorm and then head back into town?" She suggests.

Agreeing with her, we climb back into the car and start the journey to our current home while jamming out again.

Chapter 7
Liora

Making it back to the campus, we both just stare and all the things in the car, almost in apprehension at the fact that we have to carry them across campus. As I let out a sigh and go to grab things, I notice Trixie starts walking towards a group of people in the parking lot. Stopping what I'm doing, I just watch her, wondering what the hell she's doing.

I can't hear what she's saying, but she turns and points at me before continuing whatever she's saying to them. The group looks at me before smiling at Trixie and nodding their heads. Letting down my shields so I can try to figure out what is going on, I hear....

Oooh, how hot are these girls?
I guess helping them can't be too bad if
we can get something out of it
Man. Easy pussy for grabbing.

How stupid can boys be? Flutter your eyelashes and comment on how strong they are, and they become gullible.

The last one was from Trixie. Wonder what she had to promise them to get them to help? As long as it isn't sex, I guess it doesn't matter because now we can move things along more easily. I throw my shields back up as they all walk over, Trixie skipping along with a gleam in her eye.

Once at the car, Trixie explains in a sugary voice, "These nice, strong boys agreed to help us out, isn't that so nice, Liora?"

"Um, yes, thank you for this," I mumble shyly.

Opening the hatchback, two of the guys balance the boxes of furniture between them while the other stacks a couple of things on top for them. Then the rest of us load up on bags and pillows from our trip to Target. We then begin our trek across the campus.

As we walk, the guys are joking amongst each other while also acting like it is all light and trying to flex about it all.

As we near our building, I'm already annoyed with the pissing contest the guys have been having. I sigh in relief at the fact that we're finally at the doors. We go in and they push the button for the elevator. As I turn towards the stairs, the elevator opens and a fine as hell looking man steps out. He has a swagger-type walk like he is better than everyone. He nods at the guys helping us and at Trixie before noticing me.

He starts to nod at me before stopping and staring in shock with his mouth open. He shakes himself out of it as I turn to continue up the stairs and he calls out, "Li? Is that really you? What the hell are you doing here?"

I freeze in fear because I don't recognize this man, but he sure as hell knows me. My fight-or-flight kicks in so badly my shields have dropped from my concentration being broken, and I don't know what to do. Thankfully, Trixie notices I'm freaked out and comes to my rescue, basically knocking the weird dude over.

"The hell is your problem? She obviously doesn't know who you are, so tell me how you know her before I kick you in the nuts," Trixie grinds out.

"Oh, sugar, you may not know this version of me, but you will. Wait until the others find out I found you," he says back, like this whole thing is funny to him.

"Don't come near her, asshole," Trixie calls out as she leads me away from him and up the stairs. I can feel his eyes burning into my head as we walk away. Rounding the corner on our floor, I turn and see him still looking at us with a cat got the cream smile. I shake my head before breaking eye contact with him. I'm still disoriented from the overload of voices, so I can't figure out who is who or who is saying what.

Making it to our door, we see the guys standing outside the door impatiently. They shift around like they are agitated, but also apprehensive. Focusing hard to distinguish their voices from the overload of all the others on the floor, I hear…

How the hell did this Liora chick already catch his attention?

Dammit, we'll have to put on the moves before he lays claim

Jesus, that guy scares the hell outta me.

Hmm, why are they scared of that guy? Who is that guy? Why did he know who I was, but I'm not sure who he is? Is he from the same group that killed Mom? Or is he from the group that I would like to never see again?

Shaking my head and coming back into reality, I realize we're in the living room of our dorm, and Trixie is just telling the guys to set it all off to the side for us. Once they do that, Trixie tells them thank you and herds them out the door. Get it, herd, like she is herding cattle? I crack myself up, too bad no one else can hear into my mind.

"Thank you for helping us again. Just text me when y'all want to meet up to cash in your reward for helping us," Trixie says to the guys as she shuts the door in their face.

"Whew, I'm glad we had the help, but not again. They were insufferable, like maybe for a hit-it-and-quit-it. One of them wouldn't be so bad, but not as a long-term boyfriend," she shudders out.

Snickering at her, I nod and say, "No, but for real, that was horrible 0/10. Do not recommend, but it was funny to see their faces as you herded them out like cattle."

"I love that! I think for now they will be called the cattle dogs. You're a genius. I'm so using that," she cackles.

"Alright, roomie, let's go finish our shopping and then we can work on setting up tonight/tomorrow since we only have the weekend before classes start." She suggests.

Nodding in agreement, we set back out of the door and across campus again. I can't help but sing in my head, making my way downtown, talking fast, faces past, and I'm homebound, or however that song goes. In my head, I'll sing how I want. Getting back to the car, Trixie hops in the driver's seat like it's natural, and we start our trek into town again.

It doesn't take long before we're pulling up to HomeGoods and getting out of the car. Trixie grabs the cart, and we mosey through the store, taking our time because why not? We get some flavored syrups for, and I quote "girls' night cocktails or whatever". I find fridge organization, and I can't help but smile. Grabbing a clear egg container and some fruit containers, I add them to the cart, and Trixie perks up, "I know exactly what those are for!"

I chuckle at her antics. Next, we end up looking at more cooking utensils and cups because why not? I grab cutting boards and cookie sheet pans while Trixie comes running up with matching wine glasses that say bad bitches with a glitter bottom and insulated tumblers that say besties for the resties #rideordie. She's smiling so big I can't help but get excited with her about it.

"I absolutely love these. I've never had anyone who wanted to do matching things or even someone who I could see as a bestie," I tell her excitedly.

"Right! Like, how amazing, and the fact that there aren't any others means it was fate for us to get them. You are the first person I genuinely can see a connection with." Trixie shares.

Smiling at each other, we continue while chattering about anything and everything. We continue throughout the store, getting things from each section. A wooden organizer for the toilet says "nice butt" had us giggling at it, and I told her we could put extra toilet paper there. Next, we get rugs for both our rooms and the laundry room. We each picked out two soft blankets they had for movie nights and a wicker basket for them to go in.

As we head to the registers, we grab some pretty hair ties, claw clips, headbands, bows, and even some candles they have as you wait in line. Once we finally make it to the bend, I see all the big reusable bags, so I grab a couple. Making it back to Trixie, she is looking at me expectantly, so I explain, "We can use these when we get groceries so that it's fewer trips for us, plus we won't have to ask anyone for help."

"That's such a smart idea! I never would've thought to use it like that," she says in amazement.

We check out and head back out to the car to load it all up. We put it all in the backseat so we can leave the hatchback empty for groceries. Once we're back in the car, we decide to stop and get drinks before heading towards a Walmart.

Pulling up at Walmart, we grab our drinks before heading in. Once in, we start by grabbing all the hygiene essentials, basic medicine, feminine products, and cotton rounds. As we're in that section, Trixie finds me in the hair dye aisle.

"Wanting a change?" she asks.

"I've always wanted to dye it but have always been too scared to actually do it," I reply.

"You know what? Why don't we get ours done tomorrow before classes start? Kick this school year off with a bang," she wonders.

"Sure, that would be nice," I whispered.

Before long, we make it to the actual grocery section and grab necessities. Milk, eggs, juice, butter, bread, soups, meat, chicken, soda, water, etc., we make it to the produce sections and divide and conquer. I get fruits and salad fixings while Trix gets bakery goods. We also get laundry goods.

Checking out, we head out to the car and start loading it all up into the hatchback. We climb into the car exhaustedly and decide to just grab a pizza for dinner tonight before heading home. As night is falling, we pull back up to the campus and basically have to hype ourselves up.

Getting out, we round the car to the hatchback, opening it up. We load our arms up before I sigh, "Too bad there isn't a spell that can make everything itty bitty and easier to carry."

Smacking her face, Trixie exclaims, "Omg, how could I forget about that spell? My mom made sure I knew it just in case I ever needed it."

Laughing softly, I reassure her it's okay because I would've probably done the same. Trixie says one word while staying steady as a wall, "Minimizer!"

I stare in awe as the bags all shrink to where they fit perfectly in the three reusable bags that I had been holding. How cool is magic! I wonder if she would teach me because that would come in handy. I grab two bags while Trix grabs the last bag and the pizza.

We make our way across campus talking about all the things we're gonna do once we're back inside. This has been the best day ever. I hope we have many more days like this.

I'm so glad I got a roommate as awesome as her. I don't know what I would do if I got stuck with some mean girl who hates me on sight. In the many cities my mother moved us to, I dealt with an excessive amount of those. This kind of kinship is something I have only ever dreamed of.

Finally, making it back inside the dorm, we drop the bags haphazardly onto the floor before sitting on the couch to eat. As we figure out what to watch, it dawns on us that we never bought a TV. Trixie quickly pulls up her phone and orders one with delivery and pays extra for it to be delivered within the hour.

"Thank god they accepted my extra on the delivery fee. We need a TV. How are we supposed to get this place ready without something in the background for us to listen to?" Trix exclaims.

"Lol true, but we could've just listened to music and gotten the TV tomorrow, so you didn't have to pay extra," I explain softly.

"Oh, true. Good thing money isn't a problem. My parents each gave me a good lump of money for anything I needed to get the dorm ready. Guess it's a perk to having divorced parents."

Nodding like I understand, we grab the pizza and open it up to start grubbing when there's a knock at the door. Glancing at each other because we don't know who could be here for us, we both creep towards the door. Trix slowly opens the door and peeks through the crack before opening it with a relieved exhale.

"Did y'all order a TV? I know it's here earlier than expected, but my shift was over, and I had to come this way anyway, so I let them know I could drop it off," a low baritone voice announces.

"Oh yes, that's us. Thank you! Y'all were very speedy with the delivery of it." Trixie mutters out.

"I can set it up for y'all if you need me to. It won't take long at all, like five minutes max," he replies.

"Um, sure, that would be great. Can you set it up on the floor for now? We won't have an entertainment center to set it on yet." I reply softly.

Nodding, the guy walks into the dorm with the TV and gets to work while Trix and I continue eating. A little over five minutes later, the TV is out of the box and on the floor, powering up for us. We thank the guy as Trix leads him to the door and out of it.

Trix sits down and continues eating while she logs into apps so we can start watching something. After two slices, I'm too full to eat anymore, so I decide to put things away. As I put away groceries, Trix finishes eating and comes over to ask what I needs her to do.

"Can you find the organization bins and get the plastic off on them, and I'll organize as I go?" I ask.

"Sure thing, babe," she replies cheekily.

We work in harmony for about thirty minutes, and we get all the groceries put up and organized before we look at the rest of the stuff we have to do.

"Crap, I need to get my new bed set put into the washer before it gets any later," I exclaim.

Grabbing it and the laundry soap, I take it into the laundry area and get started. Once the load is started, I decide to organize the laundry soaps into the containers I got for them at the store. Walking back into the living area, I see Trix putting all the bathroom bins and bathroom things on the table for me to mess with.

"Hey, I tried to organize everything you need to do that, and I will start hanging up decor and getting the rugs set up for us," Trix suggests.

"That sounds like a good idea," I tell her before we go to our individual piles and get started.

First, I head into the Jack and Jill bathroom so I can already put things into the areas I want. Then I organize the cotton rounds and Q-tips into the container with the bamboo lids I picked out for them. Next up, I put the shower organizer onto the wall with the basket attached. Then I organize our shampoos, conditioners, body washes, shave creams, and razors. Once that's done, I grab the soap dispenser and add soap to it before organizing our toothbrushes, toothpaste, and mouthwash. Lastly, I get the under-sink organized and put away neatly. Pretty proud of myself for getting it all done, and it only took a little under an hour to do.

Just as that thought leaves my mind, the washer beeps that it's done, so I rush to put my things into the dryer. Getting that started, I head back out to check on Trixie's progress. Heading into the living room, I don't see her there, so I head to her room, and it's empty. I find her in the bathroom putting the bathmat down.

"We forgot to get a shower curtain! How the hell did we manage to forget that?" Trix mumbles.

"It is all good. We can order one," I suggest.

"Genius, lemme see what we have to work with," she says. She scrolls on something called Amazon before picking three options for me to pick from. To stay on theme with the other things we picked out, I picked the one that says Get Naked. Trix laughs and says, I hoped you would pick that one.

Once that's done, we head back into the living room and decide we have made good progress for one night and sit down to watch some TV until my bed stuff is done. We're two episodes into Fairy Tail when the dryer buzzes. Trix offers to help me set the bed, and I agree. Thankfully, between the two of us, it doesn't take long at all to get it done, and we decide to call it a night. I head into the bathroom to do my bedtime routine while Trixie goes and makes sure all the lights and TV are off.

As I finish up in the bathroom, Trix opens her door to make sure I'm done so she can get ready for bed. Heading into my room, I shut the bathroom door so I could change into some comfy clothes before bed. Sliding into my freshly made bed with bed sheets I absolutely love, I can't help the soft smile on my face as I drift off to sleep, more exhausted than I realized.

Chapter 8
Jasper

That was a sloppy ass blowjob what's her name gave me. I eventually had to just choke her out to get the job done, but I definitely won't be going back. Being the only one in the elevator, I get to drop the playboy act since no one is around. Honestly, I don't know why I still do it. Actually, I do, but how am I meant to continue in life when we still can't find her? Before I can get too worked up about it, the elevator doors ping, signaling the opening.

Pasting my persona back on, I see three guys and that weird witchy chick with a bunch of items between them. Ah, they must've fallen for the witch's tricks and are helping her move in. As I move out of the elevator, I give a nod to them. I overhear douche 1 saying how they can't wait to cash in their favor with the hot new chick that was with the witch.

That's when I notice someone else in the lobby looking like they are on their way towards the stairs. Hmm, must be the new chick the douchebags were talking about. Deciding to give her a nod and leave, she glances at me, making me freeze in shock.

I shake out of it when she turns to continue up the stairs, causing me to call out desperately, "Li? Is that really you? What the hell are you doing here?"

Wow dude, way to sound like a weirdo. What if that isn't her? Am I just imagining everything? It wouldn't be the first time something like this has happened, but I swear that's my sugar, Liora. Before I can say anything else, that witchy girl just about bowls me over and glares while saying, "The hell is your problem? She obviously doesn't know who you are, so tell me how you know her before I kick you in the nuts."

As the witchy girl whose name starts with an A or a T, I have no idea, is threatening me, which makes me want to laugh, I get a whiff of sugary candy, almost like a fresh bag being opened, mixed with the scent of earthy chaos. I know the Earth Chaos is the witch girl, but that sugary smell smells just like my Liora. She used to love eating Skittles and always carried the scent of sugar because of it.

"Oh, sugar, you may not know this version of me, but you will. Wait until the others find out I found you." I drawl like this is the best thing to happen to me. Which, to be fair, it is.

"Don't come near her, asshole." Trollie, Trelli, whatever it is, leads her away from me.

I can't help but continue to stare at her as they walk away from me. I probably have the dirtiest smile on my face when she looks back before continuing around the bend onto the second floor. Tapping into my enhanced hearing thanks to the snack I had, I can just barely make out the chatter of those guys wondering what was taking the girls so long.

Hmm, as long as they don't touch Liora, they can keep their limbs, but once someone crosses that line, it's game over. I may be the one with golden retriever energy out of the three of us, but I can still scare the hell out of people when needed. I wait outside the doors for those guys to come out just to make sure none of them get any ideas.

I don't have to wait too long before they are coming out of the doors complaining about missing out on easy pussy, but at least they got one of their numbers. I see red. Using enhanced speed, I grab one of them and throw him into the side of the building.

"Never come near her again. If I catch you near her, I will rip out your throat and hang you from the flagpole as an example. Do you understand me?" I growl out at them, my eyes flashing red to make sure my point gets across.

"Y-Yes, sir, I mean Jasper, sir. We meant nothing by it. We didn't even know the witch was taken. Our apologies," they mumble out as they scurry away like the hyenas from The Lion King.

By the time I registered, they said witch when they ran away, it's too late because they are long gone. Dammit. Whatever, hopefully they stay away from Liora too. Shit. I need to tell the guys I found her. Using our mental link, I say,

"Emergency house meeting!"
"What's going on?"
"Is everything okay?"
"I'll explain at the house. I'm on my way."

Putting up my mental shields, I head towards our place over by the other student houses. I roll my eyes at the push against my shields. No doubt it's that asshole dragon I call one of my closest friends. Walking up the stairs to our door, I walk in, already finding the guys in the living room. Ryder is sitting on the couch tensely, and Malrik is pacing back and forth.

"You'll never guess who I just found." I sing out.

"No way you found that weasel, Brad?" Malrik rumbles out.

"What? No, I didn't find Brad. If I had, I would've killed him, not called an emergency meeting." I shoot back like that's the dumbest idea ever.

"Well then, who did you find and I swear to all that's metal I will lock you up in the basement if you just called us here to talk about whoever you fucked recently," Ryder growls out in irritation.

"First off, hurtful. That has only happened once, and secondly, no, I found something we've been searching for. I found Liora today, all grown up right here on this very campus." I tell them excitedly.

"Liora? No. There's no way she's here. We have looked everywhere for her. Her mom kept her on the run." Ryder says in disbelief.

"I swear, dude, it's her. The same sugary sweet smell she had growing up. But she didn't recognize me and seemed different." I tell him honestly.

Malrik is still staring at me while he ranges from different emotions, but guilt is high up there. Ryder catches on as well as we stare at Malrik in disbelief.

"Did you know she was here?" I question.

"So, what if she is? I don't care about her anymore," he grinds out.

"HOW COULD YOU!" Ryder shouts out.

"You had no right to keep this from us. You should have told us when you found out," he argues before launching himself at the dragon.

I'm silently watching my closest friends have an all-out battle that I never thought would happen like this. Thinking back on yesterday and how angry Malrik was, I realize he must have run into her.

"You ran into her yesterday, didn't you? Is that why you were so upset because she didn't recognize you?" I question him.

My question successfully pauses their fight before they stare at me. Ryder gets off Malrik and backs away while looking at him with a slight amount of pity.

"Sorry man. I'm sure it wasn't easy seeing her again and her not recognizing you. That must've been gut wrenching no wonder you were so upset yesterday." Ryder says apologetically.

Looking taken aback, Malrik just mumbles out a half-assed yeah before storming out the back and taking flight.

"Well, shit. I didn't mean to lose my chill like that. He is going to be horrible to be around." Ryder mutters.

"Yes, but he'll get over it. He had a tough year last year." I reassure him.

"That's true. Even so, I worry about him. Well, I'm going to go take a shower and head to bed. Hopefully, I have a class with her, so I might get her to trust me," Ryder mutters, unsure of himself before heading up the stairs to his room.

Standing with my hands on my hip I say to myself, "Well damn, I didn't know I would cause all that over my revelation." Shaking my head, I decide to grab water before going to my room and sit down on my bed, drifting to sleep thinking of my sugar.

Chapter 9
Malrik

Damnit! This is a fucking disaster. Ryder hasn't gone after me like that in a while. The last time that happened, we were sixteen, and my dragon had taken over from feeding on my anger, and I broke his game console. I sported a broken nose until my shifter healing kicked in and healed it. It still took almost a full day because of how young I was.

I continue flying around to ease my anger a little. I know I should've been honest with the guys, but I'm still convinced the mating tingles are all a sham. Fuck, she only knows me as the asshole who was rude to her on move-in day, but I know she doesn't know who I am. At least she didn't recognize me from that night.

By the time I make it back to the house, it's dark outside. Hopefully, the guys are sleeping because I don't want another confrontation tonight. As it is, they're going to kill me if they ever find out about the mate bond. Liora didn't seem to know what it meant, which is weird. But I guess growing up with the horrid bitch of a mother that she had, she probably doesn't know about anything in our world. If she ever puts the pieces together and tells anyone before I have a chance to deal with it, I'm going to be in big trouble.

Shifting back, I head inside and stop in the kitchen to grab something to eat. I normally do the cooking because it's something that my dragon rides me about, making sure everyone is cared for. I have slacked this past year thanks to what that bitch Lilthe put me through.

My dragon really should have known the difference, but her pheromones were too strong. Well, that's what I'm sticking with. Her and the way she acted and treated the guys always irritated my dragon.

I thought it was just because of the way she treated everyone, and even the way she would boss me around or get irritated easily with me. But it was like I had wool over my eyes about everything because I thought she was my mate. I should've known something was fishy when it manifested last year, especially since I thought Liora would be my mate. And the way she stood up to me that night, I knew she was a firecracker.

Too bad I'm not someone who finds joy in getting her fired up or even wanting to see her. And the mate bond just complicates things further for me. Maybe I should just stick to a hit it and quit it situation, that's all I can handle right now, and even then, very seldom do I go looking for it.

I decide to just make some ramen, which irritates my dragon, but whatever, the overgrown lizard can get over it. I want to go to bed and hopefully sleep the day away. Ignoring my dragon rumbling in my head, I head up to my room, managing to bypass the guys for the night.

New plan for school, just avoid Liora and focus on getting through the year with hopefully nothing bad happening. Especially no touching, so the bond doesn't grow any stronger than it already is.

Chapter 10
Liora

Waking up Sunday morning, everything is already feeling homey and like it's my own space. Trixie and I have breakfast together before heading into town this time in her car. Pulling up to the salon, I'm suddenly nervous and unsure. What I want to do to my hair may not even look good. As we walk up to the doors, the need to flee hits like a wrecking ball.

I walk up and grab the door before turning away and walking back to the car. Come on, Li, don't be a scaredy cat. It's just a hair dye. If I hate it, I can always shave my head or wear a hat. Not realizing I had been muttering to myself out loud, Trixie walks up and lays a reassuring hand on me while saying, "If you aren't comfortable doing this, you don't have to. You can just watch me get mine done, and we can leave, but shaving your head is so not an option, okay."

"Yeah sure. What are you doing?" I ask.

"I'm thinking of doing pink ends," she says while twirling her hair.

Nodding, I follow her into the salon and take a seat in the waiting area while she goes and gets into a salon chair. As she starts the process, one of the other stylists comes over, "Hi, are you Liora?" I nod at her, and she then asks, "Are you ready? Just follow me over here, and we will get started."

My feet don't move at first. I'm frozen in fear. Come on, don't wimp out now, Li. Trixie isn't scared, so this is obviously a safe spot. Take the plunge and do the hair you have been wanting to do for years. Nodding at myself, I follow the stylist to the chair next to Trixie and take a seat. Trixie sends me a smile, which helps me relax a little bit.

"Alright, hun, what are we thinking about doing?" the stylist asks.

"Um, well I have always wanted to do like a pastel rainbow look but am not sure it would look ok." I reply unsurely.

"Omg, that would look amazing on you!" Trixie exclaims.

"I agree. You have the facial features to pull that off, and if you hate it, I will fix it free of charge," the stylist suggests.

Nodding, we get started on the process. She gets all the bowls of color mixed and then uses magic to start the process altogether. I'm so in awe at the way the brushes are all working in tandem while she parts my hair for it all. Once the color is on, she tells me I have to wait 30 minutes for the dye to set in, so I look over at Trix and see she's already being rinsed out.

Guess that makes sense since her hair is shorter than mine and she was only getting the ends done. I'm glad she came with me since I don't think I could've done this on my own. I've been sitting for maybe 10 minutes when Trix comes bounding back to her chair with a towel around her head.

"I love the head scratches the salons give when you get your hair done," she sighs happily.

Before I can reply, her stylist is back and plugging in a hair dryer before undoing the towel around Trixie's head and going to work on drying it. I watch mesmerized as she moves with such ease. I'm so lost in a trance watching the show, I don't notice my stylist heading back to me before it's too late. She has to gently touch my shoulder to get my attention. Looking at her sheepishly, she tells me it's time to go wash me out.

Heading to the bowls with a chair attached she helps me get into the seat and settled in. Once settled she turns the water on and starts the process of washing the dye. I can't help but let a small moan out when she starts scrubbing my hair before blushing like crazy in embarrassment.

"Don't even worry about it, it happens often." She reassures me.

Nodding, I close my eyes and just enjoy the feeling of someone else washes my hair for me. It doesn't take long before I relax enough to start dozing off. Before I can fully fall asleep, I hear the water cut off and a towel being wrapped around my head. Telling me to go sit back in my chair and wait for her, I do as I'm told and see that Trixie is already done.

"I love your hair! It looks amazing." I gush.

"Thank you so much. I love it as well. I know pink isn't my favorite color, but it looks amazing with the blonde," she admits.

"I think it came out amazingly," I tell her.

"Hey, how would you feel about not seeing your new hair until it is done? Like, let it be a surprise for you." She asks soothingly.

I don't say anything at first and just kind of mull it over. Surprises aren't my thing just because of the bad history I have with them. But on the other hand, I trust Trixie, and I know she wouldn't let anything happen to me. It is the first time I have felt safe with someone other than my dad and my boys. It's a strange feeling trusting someone again.

"Sure, I guess that could be fun as long as you're honest with me about how it looks," I say shyly.

"Totally, I wouldn't lie to you about something like this," she voices honestly.

Smiling at her in thanks I get settled as the stylist turns me towards the covered-up mirror. I hadn't even noticed her covering it up but thankful she did. At least the mirror can be covered, and I don't have to wear a blindfold.

She gets started on blow drying my knotted-up hair. I don't flinch while she does any of it. I learned my lesson as a child: stay still and don't complain so I don't get beat. I sit as still as I can. Once she's done blow drying, she asks if I would like a cut too.

"Um... sure I would like to keep some of the length I have, and I'm not sure what else," I mutter.

"Oooh, girl, you have to get some bangs! You could do longer ones that way you can easily style them into your hair." Trixie exclaims.

Nodding in agreement I tell the stylist to do something like that. She grins and gets to work cutting my hair. Once she is done with that, she curls it with a wand looking curling iron.

"Are you ready for the final reveal?" the stylist asks.

"It looks amazing!" Trixie gushes.

Nodding at them that I'm ready, the stylist walks to the mirror and grabs the sheet covering it before pulling it off to show me the results. I stare at the mirror in awe. Is that really me? I never thought I would look like this. I look like a whole new person.

"Is that really me?" I mutter unsurely.

"Yeah, bestie, that smokin' hot person staring back at you is you. That color looks amazeballs on you." Trix voices.

Looking at the stylist, I tell her she must be magic because I have never felt like this before. She laughs at me telling me no magic involved other than when it helped paint the colors onto my hair. Nodding at her we head up to go pay for our hair. Before we leave, we tell the stylists thanks and then head to the car.

"I took a video of the reveal. I think you'll love it. Plus, I took a couple of pictures for you." Trixie tells me.

Thanking her, we start heading back to campus, but before getting there, we stop for flavored teas.

Making it back to the dorms we put on Fairy Tail again and decide to divide and conquer with building everything. Trix takes the entertainment center while I take the bookcases.

It takes us longer than we originally thought to get it done because we kept getting distracted by watching tv. But we eventually get it done and high five each other in victory. Getting it all set up the way we want is like our whole project coming together beautifully.

"That looks amazing. We did a great job, if I do say so myself." Trixie says while giving herself a pat on the back.

"Right! We did the damn thing." I exclaim.

"Okay, now to gather up the trash and go haul it out," she says, clapping her hands together.

Nodding at her we start gathering it all up. Luckily it only takes us one trip to do. When we get back to the door there's a package in front of the door. Reaching down to get it I see it's addressed to Trixie and hand it to her.

"I bet this is the shower curtain we ordered for the bathroom," she says in excitement.

She opens the package in a rush before pulling out the curtain with a big ass smile on her face.

"Come on! Let's go put this up now!" she shouts, rushing away from me.

Following along while shaking my head, she already has it hung up while staring at it like it's the final piece of the puzzle.

"It looks great. It puts the bathroom together amazingly." I tell her.

"Isn't it!" she gushes.

We head back to the living room and sit on the couch with our leftover pizza and continue watching tv. Sometime later Trixie dozes off. I take that as my cue to wake her up and head to my room to start getting ready for bed.

Chapter 11
Liora

Another day of hell. Will this ever end? Why does she hate me so much? What did I ever do to her? I miss my dad. And I'm so hungry. She keeps forgetting to buy food for the house. When was the last time I was able to shower? Broken ribs and a broken arm are so not a good combo. Mom wailed on me when I asked if she could bring home something to eat. I think back on the way she wouldn't stop hitting and kicking me, no matter how hard I cried. When I felt my ribs snap, I couldn't help the gasp of pain I let out. But when she broke my arm, I couldn't stop the scream of pain I let out. Thankfully, my brain and body were overloaded with pain, and I got to fall into a dreamless sleep.

Gasping as I sit up in bed, covering my head in preparation for a blow that never comes. Slowly relaxing, I take a deep breath and uncover my head before just lying there in silence. These dreams are going to be the death of me. I need to start completely exhausting my brain and body so I can sleep without the nightmares. I wonder if Trixie knows of any potions that could help me sleep through them.

Deciding to go ahead and get a start on my day, I head into the bathroom. My curls still look good, so I leave them before brushing my teeth and doing my daily makeup. Since it is the first day of school, I figure I need an extra barrier of confidence, so I put on some burgundy lipstick and call it good.

Going back into my room I go look at my closet and figure out what to wear. Picking out ripped jeans and a v neck t-shirt that says *"sarcasm because hitting people is frowned upon"* then grab black knit cardigan to wear over it. Grabbing my lifted chucks, I call my outfit good and head into the living room to get an energy drink.

As I pop open the tab on my drink, Trixie comes out of her room for her morning drink. She's dressed in jeans and a distressed tee with a pair of Vans. Her hair still has a slight wave to it from yesterday.

"You ready for your first day?" she asks me.

"As ready as I'll ever be," I reply, trying to sound confident.

As we go to head out, she grabs a journal and her school tablet. I turn and run into my room, grabbing my tablet and my phone that I had left in here.

"Shit I forgot to buy any supplies for school!" I say exasperatedly.

"It's all good, girl. I haven't bought any of mine either. I'm waiting to see what I need for my classes. Here I have an extra journal you can use today. It's a leftover from last year." She reassures me.

I sigh in relief while smiling at her in gratitude. We head out with drinks in hand, along with our journal and tablet. She even takes the stairs with me, saying that we have extra time. We both head towards **Blooming Rose: Academic Building** for our first class.

We both have Potions 101 with Professor Tritus, Spell Casting Safety Course with Professor Dragor, Stamina Booster with Professor Latman, and Magical Combat with Professor Pyran. Then I'm on my own for a beginner med class with Doctor Prism, and Trixie has Magical control with Professor Embers, then back together for Herbology with Professor Lyra.

Anything medical or even holistic healing has always been so intriguing to me. The way you can help heal people is such an amazing concept. Plus, Healers are so incredibly rare and coveted. We have one on campus who is in charge of the med bay building. I hope to meet him and maybe even learn from him.

We head inside our Potion class together and luckily find seats together towards the front, but also somewhat in the middle. Sitting down, I open my journal, and Trixie hands me an extra pen that she just magicked out of thin air. Smiling in thanks, I write today's date and Potions 101 on the first page.

Turning towards Trixie to ask what she thinks this class is going to be about, she is already looking at me with a look like she wants to say something.

"I heard this is supposed to be a fun class!" she says.

"Really? I hope so." I reply.

Before we can say anything else, the Professor strides in and sets a drink onto the desk at the front of the classroom.

"Welcome to Potions 101, my name is Professor Tritus. No, you may not shorten it. You get one chance in this class; there are no do-overs on work. There will be some partner work, and no, you may not pick when the time comes. Today, we will just go over the syllabus and my class expectations." The professor's voice carries with such authority.

As he was introducing himself, he passed around the syllabus to everyone. As he walks back to the front of the class Trixie leans over to whisper, "Damn he is one fine looking specimen."

Nodding at her, I continue taking notes as he talks about the expectations of the year. Fingers crossed, I get paired up with Trixie or someone else who is nice. Before the hour is even up, he dismisses class, saying, "Don't get used to getting out early, it won't happen often."

Trixie links are arms, and we follow the throng of students to go down the stairs when I feel eyes burning into the back of my head. Turning to look, I don't see anyone staring right out at me.

"Hey, you okay, girl?" Trixie asks in concern.

"Um yea I just felt like someone was staring at me but when I turned to look, I didn't see anyone." I say shrugging.

"Hmm, who knows, girl? Maybe you have caught the attention of someone. Anyways, let's get going before we're late," she says, tugging me along and out of the almost empty classroom.

Chapter 12
Unknown

Wow, she is stunning, that's all I can think of. Her rainbow hair looked beautiful on her and those lips? Can't wait to feel them. She looks innocent and unsure of everything but there is also an air of insecurity around her. I just want to corrupt her. There is something about her that appeals to me. And this class has given me the perfect opportunity to approach her.

As I get up, I notice I'm not the only one entranced by her beauty. There's a couple that have definitely taken notice of her and are nudging each other while pointing at her. My anger is rising and I'm thinking of all the ways I can rid the trash. Most aren't that important to the community or school, but the metal mage may be a problem.

Not that he is strong but his brothers on the other hand? A hassle I don't want to deal with at the moment. But the moment he tries to take her, or I see him getting chummy it's game over for him regardless of his family and their reputations.

If anyone's dangerous, it's me. She turns her head, possibly finally feeling me staring, but instead of revealing myself, I decide to blend into the other students and make my way out of the class. I'm going to think of her until she is mine.

What would be even better is if we formed a mate-bond. Then she would have no choice but to follow my every order. Just thinking about it is making me rock hard. I need to go find that slimy succubus and figure out how she tricked someone as strong as him last year.

Chapter 13
Liora

Heading to our next class, I just try to take it all in with all the students running around. It's a little surreal getting to experience all of this with a friend. I'm glad Aunt Delilah let me have those years to hide from the world and get therapy, but I also felt like she didn't want me to go anywhere other than the bakery. It was almost like going from one cage to another, but I know that's not how she meant it. After my mom had us on the run for so long, and Aunt Delilah not being able to find me, I can see why she held on kinda tight.

I'm so lost in my head that I don't even realize that we have made it to our next class. Spell Casting Safety Course with Professor Dragor. We're one of the last ones to enter the room, but luckily, there are two seats together in the front row. Not bothering to look around anymore than that, we sit down as the Professor strolls in.

He doesn't have anything with him besides a cup of some kind of spicy liquid. I say spicy because it almost smells like fire, and when he takes a sip, his eyes roll back like it's the best thing ever. He has a very demanding and powerful energy. Plus, he looks like he could crack my head open like a walnut.

"Welcome. My name is Professor Dragor, and I will be in charge of Spell Casting Safety. I'm sure you all may think you don't need this course, but you do. All it takes is one wrong word or pronunciation and your spell is completely different than what you were originally casting. And that can be fatal. So today will be a discussion of the syllabus and a quick icebreaker to get to know your peers, and then you will be released early today," his voice booms through the classroom.

He drones on about the syllabus, and it seems to be pretty similar to our potions class, just for spell safety. If this is how every class is going to go today, I might have to gouge myself just to stay awake. I'm jostled out of my mind suddenly when he claps his hands loudly together to get everyone's attention again.

"Alright, the way the icebreaker will go is you will say your name, a fact about yourself, and if you're comfortable with it, what you are. I will start us off, My name is Professor Dragor and I'm a fire dragon, and something about me is that my mate also works here at Rosepin she will be some of y'all's Magic control Professor and if I find out any have been disrespectful towards her you will have me to answer to." His voice bellows while ending on a growl.

He then nods at the next person to start going. I zone out as everyone goes around until Trixie stands up next to me while brushing my side to get my attention.

"Hi! My name is Trixie Beam, I'm a chaos witch, my favorite color is purple, and I like hanging out with friends," she says excitedly.

Then it's my turn, I stand shakily and look down in nervousness because now everyone is staring at me. O hate when all the attention is on me. Sighing quietly to prepare myself I open my mouth, "My name is Liora Morgan, my favorite color is Teal blue, I like watching tv and I'm a telepath with telekinetic tendencies." I mutter quietly before sitting down and hiding my flaming face.

"You did a good job," Trix whispers, leaning over to me.

I smile in thanks and try to pay attention to what is going on around me. It is not until the 3rd person after us speaks that I'm locked in.

"Name's Ryder, I'm a metal mage," I hear before the next person goes, but I am still stuck on that Ryder's name. His voice was so silky and smooth. It feels like my nerve endings have been stuck in an electrical outlet. I can feel goosebumps on my arms. Hmm what a coincidence that his name is Ryder? No, Liora you're just projecting again. I wonder what he looks like. I bet he looks like the most delicious snow cone on a hot day that you just can't wait to lick.

Great, now I'm hungry. Did I eat this morning? I remember my energy drink, but I don't think I ate. Gosh Li, we told Aunt Delilah we would take care of ourselves. It's fine, all is fine. It was one meal. As long as I try not to miss too many, I'll be okay. Wait, did I eat dinner last night? You did; you're just stressing yourself out.

I come back out of my mind to Trix snapping in my face. Shaking myself to reorient my surroundings, I blink up at Trix while smiling sheepishly. "Sorry I completely zoned out there." I say to her.

"All good girliepop, but the class is almost empty, and the professor is staring at us for taking so long to get out." she whispers.

Nodding at her I gather my things, and we make our way-out mumbling apologies to the professor while he just stares at us expectantly. Aw damn I completely missed out on seeing who the hottie with the panty dampening voice looked like. That's what you get Li, zone out and miss out on some eye candy. I wonder what his magic looks like when he is wielding it? He said metal mage, right? I wonder what a metal mage does? Does he eat metal like Gajeel from Fairytail? Damn now I wanna see him in action, I have so many questions. I'll have to get a better eye of him next time we're in class.

We managed to get out semi-early. We decided to go ahead and head to our next class because thanks to my space out it ate up some time. Stamina Booster inside the **Rumbling Rose: Athletics/Pool** is where our next class which in human terms is supposed to be like a P.E class. Yay so excited! NOT! I know it is important to be in shape because the more stamina the longer we can use our magical essence and some more complex spells. But ugh working out what a drag.

Taking a step towards the bleachers, I notice a trio with an intimidating aura around them. One with an easy going smile, one with a faux laid-back persona and the last one is looking down and almost a bored stance.

When he lifts his head after being nudged by the blonde one, I recognize him immediately. It's the same asshole from my first day here.

He scowls at me like I am an inconvenience he wished he hadn't met. I roll my eyes at him as me and Trix take a seat down the bleachers from him. He opens his mouth like he is about to retort at my dismissal of him when the Professor strolls in. Saved by the class starting.

"Good morning my pupils, I am Professor Latman and I will be in charge of this stamina booster class. This class will be workouts both individual and in groups and every now and then a challenge for your group to complete. And sometimes me and Professor Pyran will combine our classes for the challenges. If you have Magical Combat next you may as well stay since this is the same room, you'll start in." the professor says.

He reminds me of an energizer bunny. I smile at the imagery of it in my head. I wonder if he drinks coffee or something to be this energized or if it is just how he is. He also looks lean but fit at the same time. Honestly the more I think about it he's not too bad on the eyes.

"How lucky are we that we get to ogle that fine ass specimen every weekday?" Trixie whispers to me.

Nodding at her in agreement we both smile at each other, while bumping fist together. It's so nice to have someone to joke like this with.

Feeling eyes on me I look around and notice the trio is all glaring at me. What the hell did I do? I don't even know these guys. Flipping them the finger and turn away but not before seeing the shocked expression on them. Whatever, let them be assholes.

"Alright, today will be an easy day. We're going to play a friendly game of blobball, with absolutely no powers. Go ahead and split into 2 teams. And no, you are not dressing out today we're just playing one round." he exclaims while clapping his hands together.

Trixie grabs me and leads me to the right side to be on their team while saying something about how the more powerful people are on this side. Whatever I would rather be with the underdogs but sure I will be on the winning team today. Once teams are split up we gather on separate sides of our court, glancing around by outward appearances it looks pretty even on both sides.

That's when I notice a group of people. Oh god dammit I'm on the same team as the trio of asswipes with captain asshat close by.

Trying not to get too close I hope this will be a fun game. When the whistle blows everyone rushes forward to grab the balls to start lobbing them at the other team. I stay towards the back in hopes of not being ran the fuck over but of course captain asshat barrels right into me knocking me right on my ass.

"Get the fuck off the court if you don't know what you're doing. Jeez you are always in the way." he snarls at me.

Trixie runs over to help me off the floor because I am in shock at what just happened.

Fuck I think he broke my ass.

Can you break an ass? What is his deal? There wasn't even a ball near me.

"God you are such an asshole Malrik, she is not that short that you couldn't see her standing here. You purposely ran her over.

What is your problem with her?" Trixie shouts at him.

Malrik? What are the coincidences of both a Ryder and a Malrik being at this campus? Nope I'm just being ridiculous.

"Don't worry about it Trix I'm okay it's not the first time I've been knocked over and I'm sure it won't be last." I whisper to her before trying to walk off the court.

I don't even make it one full step before a sharp pain race down my legs. Hissing in pain, I just keep going. I will not be weak in front of him.

He definitely doesn't need any more ammunition to use against me. C'mon Li, you got this. It's not the first time you've been in pain. Sitting down with the help of Trixie on the side of the bleachers with the people who are out on our team and try to ignore the stares. Jesus, that guy really needs an attitude adjustment.

Just as I think that I watch Trixie just barely touch Malrik with the tip of her finger. Did I just see a purple light? I watch the purple zap Malrik gets before shouting and buzzing like he stuck a fork in an outlet.

She was sneaky with it because Professor Latman didn't see her. I smile to myself at his discomfort and in his buzzed out state a ball smacks him in the face. Now that makes me chortle.

The glare he sends me could crush me to bones of dust. Luckily before anything else is said a whistle shoots through the air.

"Alright, good job everyone. We definitely need to discuss court etiquette before next time but overall, it went well. If you have magical combat next stay seated everyone else, see you tomorrow." Latman speaks loudly.

Trixie takes a seat next to me while glaring at the trio like the assholes they are. I decide to try and ignore them while willing the pain in my legs away. I get warm and tingly, but the pain goes away. Huh thanks Trixie. Was it Trixie? I didn't know she knew any spells like that. Oh well who cares at least I'm not in pain anymore.

Only a couple people leave class while the rest of us stay sitting in the stands waiting. Some are talking to friends and others are sitting quietly. I'm just observing everything and everyone. A trick I picked up thanks to always having to watch my back growing up. Plus, I'm trying really hard not to acknowledge the eyes burning into my head.

I'm not sure how long I sit trying not to move, it's long enough my body feels stiff when the Professor finally walks in, the gym doors banging shut behind him.

Everyone shuts up and just stares awaiting whatever he will have to say. He looks at each of us before clapping his hands and bellowing, "Welcome to Magical Combat, my name is Professor Pyran. This class will focus on sparring and getting you ready for anything. And I'm sure Professor Latman already told you but there will be combined classes for the challenges, now go into the changing rooms and find your dress out gear and then we are going to do some warmups so I can see where each of you is."

Oh, shit we have to work out on the first day. Could this day get any worse? Please whoever is listening let it be an easy day.

Following Trixie into the girls changing rooms I find the locker with my name on it and inside there is a t-shirt, sports bra, spandex like shorts along with a pair of tennis shoes and weirdly enough it's all in my size. Taking my clothes, I decide to go change in the stalls for some privacy.

As I'm about to pull my shirt off to change I hear a knock on the wall, "It's just me Li, if you get done before me wait for me please and I'll do the same." Trixie says.

"Sure, sounds good." I replied.

Quickly changing into my dress out clothes I see it shows a lot of skin and my poor boobs are being squished in this bra. It shows the circle scars from when my mom would put her cigarettes out on me sometimes, I was awake, sometimes I was passed out from whatever torture she inflicted beforehand.

Sighing I step out of the stall intending to go look at the mirror to see how bad it really looks. I don't see Trixie, so I walk over to the big mirror noting there aren't many girls left in here. Looking in the mirror, I can see it doesn't look overly bad and as long as my shorts don't roll up too much the scars on my thighs from me won't show. I wish the shirt was looser. This one is tight on me and shows off all the curves I have been too scared to show off, sigh.

Trixie comes up next to me before I have a chance to try and find a jacket to cover up. She looks great in the outfit and I'm envious of her confidence and don't give a fuck attitude.

"Well holy damn Li you look Hot as hell. You've been holding out on me, I wish I had those curves. Gah, let's get out there so I can find something to do to get that out of my mind." she says while pulling me out of the changing rooms grumbling under her breath.

Giggling at her but her words make me feel a little better about everything. My mom and kids at all my old school have knocked my confidence way down. So, to hear Trixie say that did boost my confidence up a little bit helped me.

"Oh, stop Trix. I'm chubby and I don't look that good but thank you for saying that." I say blushing.

As we walk out everyone is standing around talking and luckily, we aren't the last ones out. Thank god, it would be just my luck to be one of the last ones out. Blending into the crowd as we wait for instruction, it doesn't take long for him to start.

"Alright now that everyone is out here, we can get started. First things first, everyone take 2 laps around the gym. GO" he shouts.

Me and Trixie stay pretty even with each other not full out sprinting but at a fast-paced jog. I'm glad I have someone to do this with. We stay towards the center of the gym so as to not get trampled by the shifters who are racing each other for the top spot. Of course, douche canoe and his 2 friends finish first.

When we finish, I have to lean my hands on my knees trying to catch my breath because I am trying really hard not to flop onto the floor like a fish. Wtf was that, Jesus

Christ, I need to work out more. At least we weren't last, thank god. Everyone staring at you while you try to finish, no thanks I am so good.

Once the last person is done, we are told to get a drink and then head to the mats. Trixie sticks close to me as we take a seat towards the side of the professor. It isn't until I look around that I realize we are right in front of the douche posse. Ugh dammit just our luck.

Chapter 14
Liora

Whatever, just ignore them and focus on the professor Li. Maybe they won't say or do anything. Of course, I'm not that lucky because I can hear captain douche spouting off about how weaklings shouldn't even be in this class because his dragon will just roast everyone. Rolling my eyes because how obnoxious of him.

"Alright I want everyone to split up and spar. First to the mat is out and will need to sit on the sidelines while the winner will continue on. This is a spar only so no magic and those who do will be out." Professor Pryan barks out.

Everyone gets up and finds a partner.

"Hey wanna make a challenge out of this?" Trixie asks.

"What do you mean?" I ask.

"Like a race in a way. We split up and see how far we each make it or if we will make it to the point we face one another." she explains.

"Ok. So, let me make sure I understand. This would be like a friendly race?" I ask.

"Exactly. So, are you game?" she asks me.

"You are so on. I'm gonna win." I say excitedly.

Me and Trix split up to see how far the other will go before meeting up if we do. I haven't felt this pumped in a while. I can feel the competitiveness running rampant through me. I want to win.

I pair up with a girl a little taller than me but not by much. She's bouncing around like she has too much energy and doesn't know what to do with it.

Maybe I can win this. I've had to fight for my life on some occasions, so I feel like I'm pretty scrappy when needed. As long as I'm not up against someone using magic, I should be ok. Ok you got this Li, you can do this, you've faced so much worse.

She charges me first by throwing out her right fist barely giving me a chance to duck underneath it. Jesus, she really tried to hit me in the face. How rude charging before making sure I was ready.

Guess that's why they say never take your eyes off of your opponent. Lost in my head earns me a punch to my stomach. I let out an oomph because Jesus, what the hell is this girl's problem?

I don't know what I ever did to her. She goes to swing at me, and I swat her hand away, but she just keeps coming and I keep ducking and trying to dodge her.

"I'm going to take you down. You can't have him." she grunts out when I land a hit on her shoulder.

Huh? Have who? I haven't caught the interest of anyone. This girl is obviously off her rocker. She grabs onto my ponytail and starts yanking while attempting to hit me in the face. What a bitchy move to pull and the fastest way to piss me off. My hair is the one thing I can't stand someone grabbing in a way to get me on the floor.

Seeing red it's almost as though I'm having an out of body experience. I start attacking her, hitting her in the boob she lets out a shout of pain but effectively letting my hair go thank god. Now that I'm out of such a vulnerable position my hands go up in a semi defensive move. As she goes to charge me again, I kick my foot out effectively knocking her down to the mat. She gets up and goes to charge me in anger when a large body steps in front of her, halting her.

"You're out, the rule was first one to the mat and that was you so now go sit down. You can try again another day." Professor Pyran rumbles out, eyes flashing at her.

She huffs but does as she is told thank god because she looked ready to smite me. I wonder what her power is?

"Good job on getting out of that vulnerable position even if it was a dirty hit." he tells me before moving on.

Grinning slightly at the somewhat praise I got from him. Me hitting her in the boob may have been a dirty hit but what about her pulling my hair?

I go to look around for my next opponent. I don't get much of a chance to pick someone when there's a presence on my mat. I wish I could've picked my opponent and not my opponent pick me.

Ah dammit really this guy? He looks like he is about to kill me. Shooting a quick glance around for Trixie or another opponent, I see that Trixie is already sitting off to the side, shit and there isn't anyone else by themselves double shit.

Fuck my life man.

"Well, well if it isn't the weak bitch all on her own. It wasn't all that impressive taking down Sarah, she's just one of the weak followers." he grumbles.

"If I'm so weak you could've picked someone else to pair up with, you know. I don't know what your fascination with me is." I ground out.

His eyes flash in anger before he darts forward intending to land a punch. I barely dodge it and had he been going all out I don't think I could've. Fuck he is totally going to kill me, isn't he? His fists are darting out faster than I really have time to comprehend landing hit after hit. It packs a punch, but I can tell he is holding himself back. I get my hand up and hit him in the face.

I think I catch him off guard because it causes him to still before his eyes snap back to me, his eyes flashing between his blueish green eyes and black. Oh, shit I fucked up. I don't even see him move before I'm flying through the air.

Huh?

Why am I in the air?

I land hard as hell on the ground off the mat. My head smacking off the court with an audible smack. My teeth clatter together biting my tongue in the process. A coppery taste feels my mouth. Shit and why is everything ringing? Fuck I have taken some damage before but holy fuck what happened.

"Open your eyes Liora! Come up, wake up." I hear a voice shout.

Trixie? Huh when did I close my eyes? Slowly attempting to blink my eyes back open I see I'm surrounded by people. Trixie, the Professor and the trio of douches.

"Oh, fuck oh fuck. I'm so sorry I didn't mean to lose control like that. Fuck my dragon just lost it." captain douche says.

Oh, yea he lost it. I hit him and he lost control. Shouldn't he have better control of his dragon?

My eyes start drifting closed again

Fuck I'm tired.

Everything hurts.

"She needs to get to the healer now. You hurt her, so you can take her while you cool down." Professor Pyran shouts.

I hear a grunt in approval before my body is picked up gently. Gasping in pain my eyes fly open. I look up at captain douche. So, he can be nice to me. He isn't too bad on the eyes.

What is this tingling I feel?

It is warmth almost like coming home to a warm fire and safety. This feeling it gives me has my eyes feeling up with tears.

"No, don't cry *mami*, please it's killing me that I did this." he pleads.

Mami? Why does him saying that sound familiar? I'm slowly losing consciousness being in his warm embrace with the tingles surrounding me in a soft embrace. Just as I slip to oblivion I remember the night my mom died.

Chapter 15
Malrik

Stepping up to her mat after glaring and scaring away anyone else before they have a chance. I see her heart drop at the sight of me before she starts glancing around. My stomach drops at the obvious dread in her eyes at seeing me. Fuck I know I've been a jerk but seeing her almost scared of me kills me.

No, she's just messing with me with that stupid mate bond so, I get mad and lash out saying, "Well well if it isn't the weak bitch all on her own. It wasn't all that impressive taking down Sarah, she's just one of the weak followers."

"If I'm so weak you could've picked someone else to pair up with, you know. I don't know what your fascination with me is." she snaps back.

I can't help but admire her tenacity, she may be shy, but she has no problem confronting me. I charge her and start swinging, holding back as to not do too much damage but also so she sees me as an opponent. She tries to dodge all of my hits. She's actually holding her own pretty well considering this is our first combat class.

She manages to hit me in the face stunning me. I can feel my anger rising and I have fight off the urge to transform into my dragon.

I know my eyes are flashing as I try to wrangle my dragon back under control. He doesn't like that. Fuck she actually hit me what the hell. A momentary lapse in my control over him and I see through my eyes but not in complete control of my body as I uppercut her in the stomach. Oh, fuck there was quite a bit of power behind it and her body is airborne.

Oh shit, what the fuck did I just do? I stare stunned at first before Jasper and Ryder almost flatten me in their haste to go check on her. I see the witch run over and the professor before getting my ass in gear and hustling over.

As I get to her, I see the witch shake her and yell at her to open her eyes. Oh, shit did I kill her? The guys are hovering almost in a panic but still not touching her. She slowly opens her eyes almost like she is in a daze before trying to doze off.

I see her somewhat look around at us but not fully as I kneel by her, I rush out, "Oh fuck oh fuck. I'm so sorry I didn't mean to lose control like that. Fuck my dragon just lost it."

Wow, very eloquent. I don't get to stew for long because the professor points at me and barks out, "She needs to get to the healer now. You hurt her, so you can take her while you cool down."

Fuck! I try not to snarl at him. The more I touch her the worse the bond will get. This was my fault the least I can do is take her to the healer then I can just do a drop and go. Grunting at him I lean down to pick her up trying to be as gentle as I can.

I don't think it works very well because as I lift her, her eyes fly open as she gasps in pain. Dammit I really am an ass. I didn't mean to hurt her like this. Fuck I feel terrible and when I see her eyes fill with tears just rip my heart out now.

"No, don't cry *mami*, please it's killing me that I did this." I plead.

I didn't mean to call her that, but I don't think she knows who I am yet so small mercies, I guess. The tingles still make my skin crawl, but it also feels right to have her in my arms. Just as I think that her eyes close and she goes limp in my arms.

Fuck I start running to the healer because now my dragon is roaring in my head over our mate being unconscious. It takes everything in me not to snarl at him that she wouldn't be hurt if he hadn't lost control.

I probably look crazy, my tall ass running with this petite thing in my arms limp. It probably looks like I'm kidnapping her.

Banging the doors open to the **Whispering Bloom Medical building** I shout out, "I need a healer now!" one comes rushing up asking what happened and I quickly explain how it was an accident, and she went limp. As they take her and set her on a gurney, they let me know they'll take care of her.

Mentally fighting with my dragon over what to do I eventually just take a seat in one of the chairs and wait. My dragon won't let me leave the building. I feel nudging on my mental shields, so I drop them and as soon as I do, I'm bombarded by the guys.

Is she okay?

You better stay with her.

I can't believe you sent her flying like that. I think it will be in my nightmares.

What is her condition?

They shoot off their questions one after another in my head.

She is with the healers now.
We're on our way don't you dare leave!

Quickly answering them and slamming my shields up but not before Ryder's message comes through.

Fuck they are going to kill me. At least the healers should be able to do a little bit to help. They aren't true healers but the closest thing we have to the real thing. Healers are rare now because the demons hunted them down in hopes they could use their powers to boost the new aged demons, but it never worked the way they had hoped so they started killing healers off.

Healers have the power to bring back demons, supernatural's, and humans from going mindlessly berserk. The healers we have are essentially witches and not very strong supes and demons who have learned some magic from either the last healer or the book of healing. Either way as long as nothing is too bad, she should be in good hands. At least I hope she is, or I may as well have Jasper drain me of all my blood.

The guy's rush in not long after all of that. I stand abruptly awaiting the punch in the face I know I deserve. When it doesn't come, I look at the guys questioningly.

"Anything yet?" Jasper asks hopefully.

Shaking my head no at him before saying, "No, none of the healers have come out yet. They told me they had her, so I don't know if they thought I left or not."

"What the fuck were you thinking hitting her like that." Ryder growls out.

"Man, I didn't mean to, she hit me in the face, and my dragon took over before I really registered what happened. I would have never hit her like that had I been in complete control. Have I been raging because she was back in our lives? Yes, but I would never intentionally hurt her like that." I explain hoping they will believe me.

Mates aren't supposed to be able to hurt each other physically, emotionally maybe because I know I've hurt her with my words.

It's probably because I didn't have ill intent towards her or the fact that our bond isn't complete or hell that I won't acknowledge her as my mate who knows.

"Dude, you totally hit her like you were hoping to turn her to mush. It was not a pretty sound hearing her smack onto the ground like that." Jasper says grimacing.

Sighing before plopping into a seat I rub my hands down my face and open my mouth to talk to the guys. I truly didn't mean to harm her like that, and I know my dragon feels the same because he feels horrible.

Before I really get a chance to say anything a healer walks by us and Jasper is in her face demanding to know the condition of Liora. She looks at us skeptically like she doesn't want to answer when Ryder pipes up and telling her that we are courting her for a chosen mate. That seems to loosen her lips while I feel a little sick.

"She had a concussion and some internal bleeding, she also had bruising on her tongue, likely where she bit down as she fell. She isn't as strong as a supernatural should be, so it's concerning because she seems malnourished. We are keeping her here until she wakes up and we can assess her status better, but you boys are welcome to go and see her. She's in the door on the left." she explains while pointing."

Quickly thanking her, the guys take off while I follow at a leisurely pace. Ryder is going to kill me when he finds out there was some truth to what he told the nurse.

Walking in behind the guys I see Liora laid out like a sleeping angel and force myself to lean on the wall so as to not touch her. I've done that enough already. As it is when if I try to force my dragon out, he will probably have a tantrum. The guys take seats and just stare at her until she wakes up as if that isn't creepy at all.

We don't have to wait long before she sits up mid scream. She clamps down on the scream before it really starts but the panic and terror in which she woke up has my dragon pacing and grumbling in my mind. But the thing that has me storming out partly in anger and partly in some fear is when she looks at me and says, "I remember you. Are you the one that saved me?"

Chapter 16
Liora

Shooting into a sitting position mid scream. I clamp down on it quickly when I see I'm not in a place I recognize with the trio around me. Eyes focusing on captain douche I point and say, "I remember you. Are you the one that saved me?"

I don't think I have seen someone flee a room like that in years. He reminded me of a cartoon character the way he spun on his heel and fled. Jeez I could be mistaken but the way he fled has me thinking I remember him exactly from that night. Although he looks different. More jaded and like he's aged 10 years. Plus let's be honest, I have a shit memory.

"Wow I didn't know remembering something would make him flee like his ass was on fire." I state snarkily.

"Hmm what did you mean you remember him?" shaved head asks.

Well shaved head is an exaggeration. The sides are shaved but it longer on the top almost a messy look like he's run his hands through it.

Tilting my head I study the expression on his face. Is he mad? Was it what I said or something else? He is staring at me in a tense position. When he notices me not answering him, he leans forward with his arms on his knees.

Before he or I say anything the blonde one with a hyper chaotic energy around him pipes up, "Ignore him. How are you feeling? You took a pretty nasty fall."

Staring at him I just give a thumbs up because um what the fuck else am I supposed to say? I don't know them enough to answer things like that. My enemies don't need to know how vulnerable I feel or how much pain I'm really in. Pain is like a toxic friend that I can't seem to run from.

I do feel a little bad when his face falls at my lack of response but come on I don't know them. The last thing I need is for these Greek god looking men to see how weak I really am.

"Oh, I know how about we introduce ourselves you know our names? Would that help the weirdness and help you feel a little better about everything?" the blonde one says.

Nodding my head slowly at him I wait for them to go first because like hell am I giving mine up first and then they go back.

"Alright Sugar well my name is Jasper and the brooding asshole analyzing you is Ryder." Jasper says cheekily.

His energy is infectious, and I can't help smiling softly at him.

"My name's Liora, um thank you for checking on me, but I think I'm just going to go and finish my classes for the day then go to bed." I say softly.

"Are you sure you shouldn't just go lay down?" Jasper says.

Shaking my head I tell him, "I'm fine this isn't my first dosie doe with getting hurt."

I hop off against my own better judgement and immediately the room spins, and black dots dot my vision. I feel my body go to fall forward when suddenly two pairs of hands on my body holding me upright and making my whole-body light up in those tingles that I don't understand. Now I have the worried gazes of the guys on me.

"You are most definitely not okay, how about you lay back down." Jasper tries coaxing gently.

Ignoring him and shaking my head no, I close my eyes and will the lightheaded feeling away. Once I feel a little steadier, I open my eyes and step away from the warmth of the guy's hands and turn around to tell them I'm fine.

But as I get a good look at their faces, I close my mouth at the way they're staring at their hands before eyes flick back up to me. They just keep staring with a glazed overlook in their eyes that is kinda freaking me out. When I see that they are frozen after almost 2 minutes I decided to take it as my cue to just leave.

"Alright well I am just gonna go." I mutter before slowly walking out of the door.

Closing it softly and still not hearing any movement I shrug my shoulders and start my walk out of the building. Looking at the time I see that if I hustle, I can make my med class just barely.

What is it with those tingles I feel when those 3 touch me? Maybe their magic? Maybe they're zapping me somehow? No, Malrik is a dragon so he can't be zapping me, right?

Damn I missed lunch, so I'm really going to have to be careful going forward. Not eating is going to catch up with me if I'm not careful. I will easily fall back into bad habits of not eating or taking care of myself. Don't put yourself in that mindset Li you have been doing better.

Barely making it into the classroom and taking the last seat which is unfortunately at the front of the class. The professor eyes all of us before grabbing a stack of papers and starting to pass them out still not saying anything to us. It isn't until he is back at the front that he opens his mouth to say anything.

"Welcome to Beginner Med, my name is Professor Prism. In this class we will learn about the history of healers and how most supes or demons can learn basic healing with the help of salves and potions. Now it's not near the potency of a true healer, but we make do. Exams are 25% of your grades and no I don't allow make-up work because there isn't any reason for your work not getting turned in. For the final exam I want everyone to try and come up with a new healing solution whether that be a potion, salve or spell. You can choose to complete it as a solo or as a group whatever you are more comfortable with, however if you do it as a group you need to register it with me so I know who is doing what." he speaks loudly to everyone letting his eyes roam over all of us.

As I skim over the page in front of me I see it's a syllabus and as I am reading over it I see that it says we should get the number of someone else in the class so that if for whatever reason we miss a class we can message our buddy for notes or whatever.

Glancing around I don't see anyone I know in here which to be fair I don't really know anyone at the campus other than Trixie and the trio. Can I really count them as knowing them though? Of course, you can Li, they gave you their names and you gave them yours that puts you at acquaintance status.

Nodding to myself like that all made sense. I realize people are greeting each other and exchanging numbers while I was off in my own world. Great Li now you look like a weirdo, get up and find someone to talk to.

Standing up I look around for someone who seems like a safe bet but quickly lose my confidence at how everyone seems to already know each other for the most part.

Where do I fit in?

As I'm trying to psyche myself up to walk up to someone, a guy walks up to me. He walks like he is oozing self-confidence. He isn't too bad on the eyes either, not as good looking as my guys though.

My guys?

What the hell?

They aren't my anything other than douches.

"Hey, I saw you off by yourself and thought I would introduce myself. My name's Daemous. Have you managed to find a buddy for this class? If not, we could be buddies?" he says introducing himself while sticking a handout towards me.

"Um sure my name is Liora. Wouldn't you prefer someone else? I'm sure I wasn't your first option but thank you for considering me." I reply shaking his hand.

Hmm I don't get the same warmth that the guys give but this is more of a spicy type of warmth or like when your foot falls asleep. The pins and needles feeling. That totally makes sense to me and if others don't get it that is on them.

"Nah I know some of the people in here and they would rather not do the work or half ass it, plus between you and me many people are stuck up and assume because of their status it grants them things and they don't have to work for it." he whispers towards me like it is a secret between us. He gives me a smile when he notices my expression.

I smile softly and thank him. Grabbing my phone, I hand it to him, and he does the same so we can put in our contact info. I see he already has a name for mine that says rainbow cutie.

I look up at him questioningly which has him putting up his hands up placatingly and saying with a cocky grin, "Hey it's true you have rainbow hair, and I do think you are cute. You can change it if you would like though just know I will change it back."

I roll my eyes at him and add my phone before giving him his phone back and he grins big when he sees that I didn't change the name.

"Well thank you pretty girl. I look forward to some study sessions together, I'll text you 'kay?" he says before sauntering out off and joining the throng of students leaving class.

Hmm okay I guess class is over I think to myself before I start gathering my things back up and leaving class too.

As I head to my last class of the day, I can't help but think about the guys and how different each one is. I wonder what Jasper and Ryder are status wise.

Lost in my own thoughts again as I round the corner and crash right into Trixie. We giggle before apologizing to each other.

"Hey! I was just coming to find you. We got out early so I thought we could walk together to the next class." Trixie explains.

"Sure, I'm so down for that, but can we hit a bathroom on our way? I really need to pee." I tell her.

"Same girlie. Let's go." she says, linking our arms up again and leading me to a bathroom.

We go in and do our business. As we are washing our hands she asks in a kind voice, "Are you sure you are really, okay? The sound your body made when it connected with the floor was scary."

"I'm okay I promise it wasn't my first rodeo having something like this happen and I'm sure it'll be my last." I explain to her while nodding and smiling showing her I'm okay.

"Okay if you are sure but if you start feeling off or weird just let me know and we will go get checked out again. I wasn't there when you woke up because the nurse said you already had people in your room and would be fine." she says

"Yeah Jasper, Ryder and Malrik were there when I woke up so it is all good although it was surprising to see them in there, I still don't know how they convinced the nurse to let them in. I guess because Malrik was the one that brought me." I say shrugging my shoulders.

"Uh Haha yeah I guess." she says, letting out a suspicious laugh.

Ignoring it because it isn't really my business why she got like that. We head out of the bathroom and go towards our last class of the day thankfully.

As we walk into our last class of the day, I see that we are among the last one to make it in. We walk towards the middle of the room and take a seat not even bothering to see who is around. Sitting down I pull out my notebook and write the class at the top.

As I turn to talk to Trixie about class I feel a kick on the back of the chair. Turning to ask what the fuck is their problem when I see that it is the trio and look at that captain douche is back and glaring at me.

Jasper smiles cheekily at me and waves hi. I reluctantly wave back and turn around towards the front and get ready to take notes. Right before the professor closes the door to get started one last person hurries through the door.

What was his name?
Dimon?
David?

Dosan?

Eh whatever something with a D. He saunters right over to the only empty chair which just so happens to be right next to me. Well at least it gives me another familiar face.

As I was busy trying to remember whatever his name is, the professor had already started talking and passing out papers. Dropping them off at the end of the aisle and people just passing them down.

When whatever his name is hands me the stack, his hand lingers on mine before he pulls away. Weird, but not saying anything I continue on the assembly line of passing down the stack after grabbing my own. His chair jostles a little bit before he sends a glare over his shoulder at the trio of douches.

"Oh, sorry I guess I stretched too far." Ryder deadpans.

Choosing to ignore whatever animosity they have against each other I focus on my paper. Ugh another buddy system. Wow, more phone numbers. Well do I really have to give out my number if Trixie and what's his face are in here?

"Alright I want everyone to find a buddy to swap numbers with, and I want everyone to converse and introduce yourselves." Professor Lyra says in a sweet voice.

Heaving a sigh, I start to stand up and move away from my chair when of course clumsy me trips and if it weren't for what's his face, I would've been the talk of the class.

"Um thanks...." I trail off.

"Wow pretty girl we just met last class, and you already forgot my name? It's Daemous like demon and famous smashed together." he faux a hurt expression before sending me a smile still keeping me in his arms.

I hear the rumble and feel the waves of anger washing over us that has my hackles raising up because wtf is that, but it's gone before I can pinpoint. Still holding me Daemous sends a smirk over my head at someone I can't see.

Stepping out of his weird spicy embrace I mutter a thanks before going over towards Trixie when I'm intercepted. Jesus what is with today? Looking up at the body in front of me I see that it is Jasper.

Tilting my head at the red hue of his eyes I think back on earlier I don't think he had red eyes. No, definitely not. Hmm maybe he's a vampire? I arch a brow at him and await whatever caused him to stop in front of me.

"Hey sugar, wanna trade numbers and be buddies for class?" he says, trying to sound cheerful.

"Um sure but why not trade with your friends?" I ask.

"We live together and for the most part would rather get other buddy numbers from classmates. Well..... Maybe not Malrik, he's not really a people person." he states with a small chuckle.

Giving him a smile at the way he said it. I glance around and see Trixie and Ryder trading phones, so I go ahead and hand Jasper my phone and he gives me his. Seeing the blank contact, I decide to just type my first name and number because I don't think there are any other Liora's on campus.

"Well thanks sugar I'll be seeing you and if you ever need anything just give me a text or a ring, okay?" he says before walking back to Malrik and Ryder who I guess is done with Trixie.

Glancing at his contact's name I can't help the smile when I see he put sexiest man ever. I roll my eyes but change it back to Jasper because I like to give nicknames in my phone and he hasn't earned that one. Plus, I don't know him well enough to know who is texting me if I don't change it to his name.

Trixie walks back to me before asking if I'm ready to get out of here. Nodding at her we grab our things and head out.

As we leave the academic building Trix asks, "Wanna go ahead and go to the store and get everything we need for classes? Or grab coffee or whatever and get it another day?"

Thinking about which one sounded more appealing. Okay I barely thought about it, coffee sounds amazing, but I know if I don't go get what I need now I'll put it off until I am in trouble. Nodding my head in finality I say, "How about coffee as we go get what is needed because if I don't get everything today while I'm in a class mindset I will procrastinate that shit until it is too late?"

I pause because dang I really don't want to go deal with a bunch of students, but I know I can't put it off too long. I know myself and if I don't do it when I think of it it'll never get done.

"Yeah, store today. No procrastinating that stuff. Plus, I wanna get a printer so I don't have to use the library one." I tell her.

"Sounds like a plan lets go. A printer would be a great idea. It would be our luck to turn something in late because the libraries

printers are all being used." she says pulling
me towards the coffee shop.

Chapter 17
Malrik

God fucking dammit. I had hoped she would forget about that night; it has been years. I can already feel the guys nudging my shields but fuck I need a minute before I speak with them again because fuck. Leaving her room and walking down the hall I see her witch roommate stop one of the healers.

"Hi, my name is Trixie I'm looking for my roommate Liora. Could you point me towards her room?" she asks frantically.

"Um her potential mates are with her now and we can't let others back there after we hit room capacity." the healer explains.

Mates? FUCK! How the hell do they know? Did I drop my shields? No Ryder would beat my ass if he found out and Jasper would probably rip my neck out. Wait she said potential.

"Mates?" Trixie questions.

Before another thing can be said I grab her arm and drag her out before getting in her face.

"You will NOT say anything to her. You will NOT repeat what you heard in there to anyone. If I find out you blabbed to anyone, I will burn you to a crisp." I threaten in a dangerous voice before walking away at her stunned and slightly scared face.

Hopefully she got the message because I will kill anyone who starts blabbing about this.

The human side of me isn't ready to accept this bond and probably never will and after hurting her today my dragon is feeling protective of her and pushing to be close to her. He's still wary of her and the mate bond, but something feels different about it this time. Almost like it's meant to be? Fuck I sound all mushy now, nope time to go act like an asshole and warn people away.

Sitting in our last class of the day with that squarmy asshole Daemous keeps egging us on with the way he keeps smiling and finding excuses to touch Liora and I am having a hard time keeping my dragon under control. It doesn't look like the other two are handling it any better. I'm grateful when the professor tells us to find a buddy for class.

Although when she trips and almost falls,I think I just about crack a tooth at how hard I'm clenching my teeth at the way he's holding her. I swear if he doesn't let go, I will barbeque his ass right now Professor be damned.

It's like he knows what he is doing because he smirks over her head at me. Just as I'm about to barbeque his ass for the blatant audacity of him she walks away from him where Jasper intercepts her. Well thankfully it seems to chill my dragon out a little bit.

Jasper

OH SHIT! OH SHIT! MATE?! MY SUGAR IS MY MATE? WHAT THE FUCK?! I completely balk and zone out in awe. I can't believe I found my mate after all these years. It is the one girl I have always sought after.

Oh, shit Ryder and Malrik! We're a family. Will this break us apart or cause irreparable damage?

Feeling a nudge at my walls I let them down and am flooded with Ryder's voice.

Holy shit dude! Mate she is my mate! Liora is my mate!

Liora? Is your mate too?

Too? Like she's your mate?

Yes, tingles and everything plus when I touched her it just felt right in my soul

I felt the tingles as well so I guess we are sharing a mate, oh crap we should probably talk to Malrik about it

Yeah, probably but I think this is a tread lightly situation. One because of Malrik and what happened to him but two I don't think she understands everything, or she would've reacted different

Yeah, I agree. We will talk to Malrik tonight at the house

Yeah, sure man she left the room when we started talking

Yeah, I noticed that as well. We can talk more about it later at the house.

Taking that as my cue I put my walls back up before parting ways and heading to my next class.

Ryder

Well fuck I wasn't expecting to find my mate and I was especially not expecting it to be Liora. I can't believe I share a mate with Jasper.

At the same time, he is one of the few I would trust with my mate, and I know if either can help it, she will be very safe. Plus, an added bonus we knew her as kids and loved and protected her. Sure, we have lots of years to make up for and we need to learn who the woman she is now and what makes her tick.

I will start observing her and learning all her likes and dislikes because fuck Jasper if he thinks he will be the favorite. As we part ways, I start thinking about the best ways to subtly learn about her. Also figure out how to get her to our house without Malrik turning her into ash.

Hopefully after talking to him tonight things will smooth over and not be so weird between us. I miss the old Malrik that bitch Lilthe really did a number on him plus I still beat myself at the fact that I missed the signs and didn't help him the way he needed it.

Chapter 18
Liora

After grabbing our coffees, we decide to hit the campus store first before we head to town to grab the other things we need.

Walking into the campus store you can definitely tell we weren't the only slackers on getting our shit.

"Damn there are so many people here." Trixie says sighing

"No kidding, I'll have to be careful not to touch too many people or I'll be overloaded with thoughts and voices." I tell her warily.

"I gotchu girl. We will try and be quick in here." she tells me.

We each grab one of those cute metal basket things and start our journey through the store. We each get the books we need for class and I wander over towards the laptops and printers.

Yea we're getting a printer. I don't want to have to deal with the library if I can avoid it. I would much rather do everything from the safety of our dorm. I turn to ask Trixie which printer we should get when I immediately bounce off of a wall.

Wall? Did I seriously just walk into a wall in front of all these people? I mean it wouldn't be the first time I've walked into a wall but whatever. Before I fall, I'm grabbed by someone. Opening my eyes I see it was a wall but not your typical wall it was a wall of a person.

Trailing my eyes up, I see Daemous? Hmm weird that he is here, is he following me? No come on Li he is probably just getting what he needs as well. Yes, that has gotta be it.

"Hey, I didn't mean for you to bump into me. I just thought I would come and see if you needed help." he says scratching his head.

"Oh! No, I am okay. I was looking for my friend and not paying attention to my surroundings. But thank you though." I say stepping away from him.

I don't make it very far when he grabs my arm to stop me and asks, "I know we just met but would you maybe want to go out with me or get a coffee or something?"

I just stare at him at first because um one I have never been asked on a date and two we just met today. But at the same time, he isn't so bad on the eyes and seems nice enough. Although I don't feel as attracted to him as I am to the guys. Doubtful they would ever feel the same. Plus, Malrik seems to hate my existence, and Ryder is more indifferent like he couldn't care less, Jasper is the only one I could maybe see wanting me around.

It's those thoughts that has me saying, "Um... sure I guess that could be okay."

His face lights up, "Great I will text you about when the best time to meet up will be."

He walks away after that, but I can't help but feel weird about the whole interaction. Shaking my head I look for Trix and see her hunkered down with backpacks and books. I head her way since she is already standing in line.

"Hey, got everything you need?" I ask.

"I think for the most part I do, I got you a backpack and I have a matching purple one. I thought we could get stuff and personalize them if you are down for that." she suggests.

"Thank you! I love that idea, we can make a hangout out of it. How about we do it tonight. Also, which printer do you think we should get? I didn't want to just pick one because I don't really know much about what's good and what's not, so I figured you could pick." I ask.

"Um let me look really quick. We can get the canon one they are supposed to be good on ink I think." she replies.

Nodding my head at her and repeating canon in my head a couple times.

"Plus, I have something to tell you and talk about." I say after a few minutes of silence between us.

"Oh? Do tell my bestie. Is it good or bad?" she says, wiggling her eyebrows.

"Well, it's not bad I don't think." I reply warily.

She just lifts her eyebrow questioningly at me, so I sigh and say, "I was just asked to go on a date with that Daemous guy from our last class."

Before she can answer we hear a crash and turn to see what happened and Jasper stands there staring at us eyes flashing to red and back with an angry expression. He seems to get his anger under control because his face drops like he is hurt before walking off.

Feeling my stomach sink at his expression and the way he stalked away from us. I feel horrible now about everything. No, I shouldn't, it isn't like Daemous asked me to marry him. It's just one date. I haven't been on one before. If Jasper is that upset, he can talk to me about it.

Trying to put Jasper out of my mind we pay for our items and head towards our dorm room to drop things off and change. But I still have a weird ache in my chest from the encounter.

When we get to the dorm we split up and go into our respected rooms to change and whatnot. Closing my door, I go ahead and strip off what I wore today. Tossing it all in the basket I go ahead and toss on some yoga shorts and an oversized crop.

Throwing my hair up in a messy bun, I head back into the main area and see Trixie already standing there dressed similarly to me except instead of an oversized crop she's in a fitted crop top.

"Hey, great minds think alike lol." she says with a small chuckle.

"How about we make a quick run to target for school supplies and then hobby lobby for patches for our backpacks?" she asks.

"Yeah, sure that sounds great to me um I guess let me put some pants on and grab my shoes." I reply, turning to head back into my room.

"You had better not change, I will electrocute that ass! You look smokin' hot and if I knew you swung that way I would've put the moves on you already." she says pointedly at me.

I smile at her antics and say, "If I ever want to try that out, I will let you know but I firmly prefer guys." I tell her.

"I promise I won't change so you don't shock me and just put shoes on and we can go." I say putting shoes on.

Gathering my phone and bag we head out and make our way into town to get what we need.

Chapter 19

Jasper

Fuck did I really hear that right? Did she really just say that she is going on a date? And with that smarmy asshole Daemous? Oh, fuck I have to tell Ryder. Shit I know she is staring at me, but I can't even say anything, so I just stalk away. Fuck the shit I dropped someone else can pick it up.

Storming out of the campus store I march towards the house I share with the guys. They should be back by now from classes but if not, I will tell them to come home urgently.

I can feel my teeth pushing against my gums and the urge to rip out someone's neck is riding me hard. Fucking shit! That ballsy ass motherfucker is really trying to take our girl. Slamming my way into the house I can see that both of the guys are there already. They turn to look at me when I enter, already sensing how pissed off and out of control I am.

"What happened?" Ryder asks semi calmly while Malrik shouts, "God damn it what now?"

"I'm so glad when it is me upset it almost seems like an inconvenience for you but yet the smallest things set you off and we try to be there for you." I snap at Malrik.

Malrik pauses and looks at me in shock while Ryder just raises an eyebrow at me in confusion. Well damn now I feel a little bad but fuck he can be such an inconsiderate asshole sometimes. You know what no because I'm sure he will be just as pissed when I tell them what I heard.

"Damn man, are you okay? I didn't mean it in a bad way; I just mean it in a fuck we can't catch a break." Malrik explains.

"It's fine man. I'm just pissed, and I think you guys will be too when you hear what I just did." I explain.

Malrik goes back to cooking what looks like a chicken alfredo as I take a seat and try to calm down. Ryder is still looking at me questioningly and I know it won't take long for him to pipe up.

"I think we all need to have a serious talk about everything." Ryder starts as Malrik puts bowls of food in front of us. Called it.

"Okay yeah I agree there are things we need to talk about." Malrik says.

Me and Ryder share a look.

How are we going to tell him?

Do we just rip the band aid off?

As I'm still trying to get my thoughts together and figure out the best way to say this Ryder just blurts it out.

"I found my mate."

Well shit okay I guess that's how we are doing it.

"I found my mate as well." I say excitedly.

Malrik just stares at us almost in turmoil. I know he has a bad experience because of what happened and that is understandable, but I won't miss out on my mate because of it.

"I found my mate too." he says begrudgingly.

We stare at him in shock because what? What are the chances that we all find our mates this year? Wait, is it really his mate or are we having a repeat of that succubus and her spell?

"Are you sure? I don't mean to sound like a dick, but I want to be sure before we have a repeat." Ryder asks delicately.

Malrik does a slow nod before reluctantly saying, "My dragon is riding me hard to claim her, and he doesn't get irritated at her and the way I can feel a pull in my chest. And I feel like I'm coming home when we touch it sends such a warm feeling through my body and is almost calming."

Me and Ryder just stare at him for a little bit. Honestly, I'm so happy for him, and he deserves it. I just hope he doesn't ruin her.

"That's great man. Just try not to use your past against her." Ryder says.

Malrik just looks at him apprehensively like he doesn't know what to say or do. He almost looks scared of his new mate. I wonder who it could be? I hope it doesn't fracture our friendship.

Chapter 20
Malrik

As I look at the guys I can't help but be apprehensive about telling them who my mate is. Ryder will kick the shit out of me and Jasper may rip my throat out when he finds out. But at the same time, she doesn't seem to remember us or anything. Sure, she may remember me from the night her mom died but I can explain that away.

"I think we should all blurt out our mates' names on three. How does that sound to y'all?" Jasper says excitedly.

Nodding my head slowly compared to Ryder who isn't as apprehensive with it. Jasper stands up excitedly and rubs his hands together before sharing a look with Ryder. Hmm I wonder what that is about, I think.

"Okay 1,2,3 go!" Jasper shouts.

"Liora" Jasper shouts.

"Liora" Ryder says with a small smile.

"Liora" I mumble.

Silence. Oh, fuck we all said Liora. Oh, fuck we share a mate. Well at least our family won't split up. It would also make sense why we're closer than just like best friends, almost like we have a bond to keep us as a found family. We can also register our family as complete hopefully.

"Wow! So, our mates all have the same name, or we have the same mate. I don't mind sharing a mate with you guys. You guys are who I would trust with my mate if anything happened." Jasper says.

Ryder just sits there contemplating. Damn he is hard to get a read on of what he is thinking.

"Me and Jasper already knew we shared a mate and I was curious about whether or not you would as well. It makes a lot of sense on why we haven't been able to move on from her and why we all felt like we were missing a vital piece of our family when she disappeared." he says pausing.

I want to be mad that they didn't say anything but at the same time when they find out how long I have known they may smite me.

"However, how do you actually feel about it because I don't want you to feel pushed about it but also if you hurt her again I'm going to cuff you and let Jasper drain you to the brink of death." he says with a growl.

Swallowing slightly and glancing around. Ryder is definitely not one to mess with, but Jasper is the one most should actually be terrified with. Fuck I don't want to have this conversation.

Nodding I say, "I'm still not sure about it all. I know my dragon is this time, but I can't get over my anger over what happened with the succubus and how she manipulated me."

"I understand that but if you let that hold you back too long you could lose her forever." Jasper says gently.

Nodding in understanding I don't answer because what else can I say about this whole thing.

"So, when did y'all figure out she was your mate?" I ask.

They look at each other smiling before Jasper says, "So, we actually found out in the healer room. She went to stand denying any help from us. When her body went to fall forward because she was dizzy, we both reached out and that's when we felt the tingles."

"I don't think she knew what it all meant though. And I'm pretty sure we freaked her out over how we froze and started communicating telepathically." Ryder says while rubbing his chin quizzically.

Hmm no wonder she hasn't put two and two together. Is she really that ignorant to our world? I would've thought someone would've said something to her or explained it. But it may work out in our favor.

"Wait! How did you find out?" Jasper asks.

Well shit. I'm not sure how they will take this.

"I found out on the move in day. I crashed into her and then was a dick, but she met me toe to toe. She isn't scared to get in my face and tell me off. Although she never was when it came to me." I say scrubbing my hands across my face.

I see the guys clench their fists as Jasper goes to punch, but Ryder holds him back and looks at me.

Chapter 21
Ryder

Fucking shit. I know he has some shit to work through but to know for that long and not say something is maddening. When I see Jasper go to punch him, I stop him. This isn't the time to start brawling with each other.

Dammit. I need to calm down before I throttle him. I did that already when he revealed he knew Liora was on campus and didn't tell us anything. Finding out she's his mate makes more sense on why he has been such an ass to her.

That succubus Lilthe really fucked him up. I still can't believe how well she pulled it off. Using the spell to amplify a potion that will mimic a mate bond is a forbidden spell.

She got off easy with only having her powers stripped for 4 months as her punishment. The only reason it wasn't more severe was because she didn't make it herself and claimed to also be under the spell. Plus, it helps her dad is high enough up the demon council so, he influenced a lot.

I know Malrik struggles with everything now and only really fucks a girl if he can hit and quit it. Which is why I ask, "Are you going to reject her?"

"Fuck no you better not." Jasper exclaims.

"If that is his choice, we will respect it." I say sternly.

Jasper stalks over to the armchair and plops into it glowering at us for even considering it.

"No. I-I don't know. I'm conflicted about it all. It's great we share a mate, and my dragon does want her, but I don't know if I can get past old wounds." he reluctantly admits.

Nodding I say, "Would you be willing to try and just be her friend for now? No one is saying you have to mate her now. You could take it slow and maybe get to know who she is now. Then you can make your decision regarding her and the mate bond. But just know we aren't going to leave her if you do decide to reject her so she will be around regardless. But you need to get to know her without feeling forced so just take it slow" I offer.

He contemplates it for a while most likely waring with himself and his dragon, but this is something he has to decide for himself. No one else can make this kind of decision for him. He has to figure out what he wants in his life.

"I think that maybe I would like that. Start off trying to build a friendship because it will help me see that she isn't like Lilthe. Then I can worry about the mate bond and what I want to do with it." he finally says almost unsure of himself.

Nodding at him in understanding and I even see Jasper heave a breath of relief and nods his head at Malrik. We know we want her. He is the only one that is very standoffish.

"She doesn't seem to recognize the mate bond so that could work in our favor. We can build up that repertoire with her as friends without the pressure of the mate bond." I tell them.

"What if when she finds out we knew and she gets mad and hates us?" Jasper says fearfully.

"That is a risk we will have to take. Getting to know her as friends will help us get in our good graces and help show Malrik that Liora is nothing like Lilthe. Plus, the more time she spends with us the more the bond will push her to seek us out." I say.

"Ok so, the plan is to build a friendship with her and not act on the mate bond?" Jasper asks.

Nodding at him so he can see I agree now to wait on what Malrik thinks about it.

"I think that will work but I think if she figures it out or pushes for more then all three of us should be there for it to make the decision." Malrik states.

"Hopefully she won't be too mad at us when she finds out we've known all along." Jasper says.

We all agree on that and go to start making dinner and wind down for the night when Jasper suddenly exclaims, "Fuck I forgot to tell y'all what I overhead and why I was so upset when I came in."

"Oh yeah. Ok so what happened?" Malrik asks.

"We are going to have a to keep an eye on that asshole Daemous he is getting way too fucking ballsy." Jasper starts ranting.

"What did he say?" I ask cautiously.

"That motherfucker asked Liora out on a date! And she actually said yes and has his fucking phone number!" he shouts while pacing. His eyes are flashing as he wars with his monster.

"You have got to be kidding me!" Malrik erupts.

I am silent as I process everything and decide on our plan of action for the situation. I would think that she's already feeling some effects of the mate bond but maybe she is so confused on her feelings that she is going to give him a try?

Yeah, hopefully that's it and he's not like another mate because fuck we can't stand him. He's always got something brewing and he's constantly getting into shit with everyone.

Does he not have a mate? I mean I know not everyone finds theirs quickly or while they are young. The rich and desperate can go and get a bleeding heart rose and find a priest to use in an ancient ritual to find their missing mate if there is one. Or there is the option of courting a chosen mate of course.

"Ok we stick with the plan and just try to snub Daemous anytime we see him too friendly with her, okay?" I state with no room for arguments.

Chapter 22
Liora

We make it back to the dorm after our trip to town again. We unload everything on the coffee table and turn on tv to eat and veg before we start designing our backpacks. I am so excited to get to do something like this. I've never had anyone that wants to do matching things with me.

Trixie is definitely someone who will help me come out of my shell and be bolder about everything. Once we finish eating, Trixie starts separating out everything into piles. So, the things she picked to one side and what I picked on another side. Then in between us are what we mutually agreed on to match.

We got patches, pins, and even a chain to make a backpack charm bracelet which I love.

"Ok let me go find the iron that supposedly came with our dorms and then we can get started." Trixie says before getting up.

"Want me to make drinks?" I shout to her.

She shouts a yes please back to me. Getting up and grabbing the rum, orange juice, and grenadine I set to start making the drinks. Once I have ice added to the cup, I use my telekinesis to twirl the straw in both cups and take them back to the coffee table.

She comes bounding back iron in hand and says, "Let bad bitch bestie night commence!"

I chuckle at her antics before diving right in. Slurping down my drink because it's much needed after the day I had. I can't believe so much has happened today, it's a little shocking when I think back on it.

Grabbing my letters to spell out my name in blues and purples, I start the process of ironing them onto the backpack.

Once that is done, I start separating out the charms for each of us. We each have the first letter of our names, a bff charm, a book charm for me and a lightning bolt for her, then just some smiley faces and cookie charm. Putting that all on a charm bracelet we connect them to the small pocket of the backpack to make it like the zipper.

Once I'm done with my backpack, I start putting my supplies into it and organizing everything for tomorrow. I even put my gym clothes back into it so I can put them back in my locker.

I finish my drink while Trixie is finishing her backpack because she was being indecisive on how she wanted to set it up. I contemplate making another before deciding not to get so relaxed that my shields drop. I would rather not have a nightmare worse than my normal ones.

As I have been in my head Trixie has finished her drink and is finishing up her charm bracelet. I tell her I'm going to go get ready for bed, she nods and lets me know she will see me in the morning.

Doing my nightly routine, I lay down and decide to play on the tablet and finish getting everything set up. Seeing a message from an unknown number that says

Unknown
Stay away from Malrik!

Hmm. Weird, who would even send something like that to me? I barely even know the guy. Plus, I don't think he's even seeing anyone or atleast I don't think I've seen him with anyone. Whatever, I can ask Trix tomorrow about it because I just do not feel like getting up again. My body is drained from today and I desperately need rest, or I will fall into bad habits again.

Deciding to ignore my mystery messenger I fall asleep before I really even mean to.

I seem to be in some kind of woods. What the hell? What would I be doing in the woods? Hearing twigs start snapping around me, the sound making it echo out here.

"Hello? Is anyone there?" I ask tentatively.

Wow Li, because a killer is definitely going to introduce themselves before they kill you. I facepalm myself because how dumb can I be?

As I'm looking around, I see a figure in the trees. Tilting my head as I study them wondering who it is. I don't feel a friendly vibe from them but also not completely malicious either.

Whoever it is starts to walk closer towards me before they vanish before my eyes. What the heck I think as I look around.

All of a sudden, the person is in front of me with a deadly smile as they go for my neck. I feel white hot pain lace my body.

What is happening?

I don't understand.

Why is this happening to me?

Am I being punished for something?

Everything is starting to feel really heavy.

I can't even scream the pain is so bad and it feels like I'm choking on something.

I don't understand.

Am I going to die?

The guys. Where are they? I know I wandered a little too far while playing hide and seek but I didn't think it was that far.

Just as I think that I hear some shouts behind me.

"Liora!" Jasper shouts.

"STOP IT!" Ryder yells.

"Get your nasty teeth off of her bloodsucker!" Malrik growls.

The guy is shoved off causing me to let out a small scream. Next thing I know I am laying on the ground.

The sky looks pretty. Not too blue but not dark either. It's starting to change colors for sunset, and it looks so pretty.

Jasper is crying.

Why is he crying?

I try to smile but I don't think it has the desired effect. The pain is starting to fade and I'm not sure what that means. I try to lift my hand up to Jasper's face, but I can't really move.

"Don't cry. I'm okay." I say whispering.

He shakes his head and says something, but it feels like I am underwater, I can't really hear what he says. I think I hear growls.

It's cold

Why am I cold?

I want my bunny.

Where's my bunny?

I don't want them to be worried about me, I'll be okay.

I can feel myself shivering from the cold. Malrik picks me up and starts carrying me. It looks like he is crying too but I don't know why. He is really warm; I just want to snuggle up and go to sleep.

I think I drifted off because I feel him shake me. I attempt to smile at him and say sorry, but I think my body gives up because it all goes black.

Sitting up my dream still at the forefront of my mind. I wonder how the guys are doing? Are they happy? I wish I knew how to get a hold of them. Ah well whatever.

Getting up I go to start getting ready when I notice the sweat stain left in the bed.

Ew.

I take a shower and get ready. Walking out of my room I see that Trixie is already waiting.

"Hey, I thought I might have to wake you up." she says while tossing me an energy drink. "Thanks. Yea, no I just had a weird dream about people from my past." I say before taking a drink.

Nodding, she says, "I'm here if you want to talk about it."

I don't say anything at first because I'm thinking about it. She starts grabbing her backpack and drink.

"I dreamt about these 3 boys I knew from long ago. They were like my best friends, and I miss them. I just hope they're happy and doing okay wherever they may be." I tell her honestly.

"Ah I see. I'm sorry you haven't seen them. Have you tried looking for them?" she asks gently.

"No, I don't even know where I would start. Plus, what if they don't want to see me? Then I'll just feel silly for missing them and hoping to see them again." I say tentatively.

"We can look up their names on social media? What are their names?" she asks.

"Um, there was Malrik Rose, Ryder Jackson, and Jasper Evans." I say ticking the names off of my fingers.

She gapes at me in shock.

"What?" I ask.

"You do know we have 3 guys with the same first names as those you just said, right?" she says, staring at me.

"Yea? So, the names might be common." I say back as we leave the dorm. She shakes her head and says something under breath. Sounds a lot like unbelievable but I am going to choose to not know. Hmm what does she know?

Could we really be at the same campus? But this Malrik isn't the nicest to me in fact he's rude as hell anytime he sees me.

A memory tries to wriggle to the forefront of my mind, but it goes away before I can latch onto anything.

Chapter 23
Liora

It takes a couple days before I understand why she acted like that when I said their names. It happens during our magical combat class. I was in the dressing room changing when I overheard some girls gossiping about some of the guys in our combat class.

It's the pretty girl from move-in day who wasn't very nice to those movers. It looks like she is the leader of the others maybe? In novels they would call her queen bee.

I don't normally pay any attention to the other girls, but it was the conversation that made me stop and listen.

"Malrik would be stupid to not take you back and make you, his wife." a follower says.

"Of course, he'll forgive me soon and this will all seem like foreplay. The day I become Mrs. Rose will be glorious." That pretty succubus says haughtily.

Almost like the zing you see a cartoon character get when an idea comes to them, is what it feels like when it clicks.

Omg!

Omg!

Are they really the boys from my childhood?

Do they remember me?

How did I never put one and one together?

Do they know it's me? I mean I have changed quite a lot.

I think back to the day I technically met Jasper he said something about how he couldn't wait for the guys to find out I was here or something like that.

So, they knew all along?

I don't know why that makes me feel so sad. I guess they don't care about me anymore. Especially with the way they have acted lately. They were probably glad I was gone. Even if I wished for them to save me from my mother and the horrors I was forced into.

"Hey, are you okay? You look sad." Trix asks gently while grabbing my shoulder.

I nod and attempt a small smile, "I'm fine honestly just got stuck in my head."

She looks at me questioningly before pressing a little harder, so I finally answer honestly, "The Malrik, Ryder and Jasper here on campus are the boys from my past, aren't they?"

When she nods before saying, "It's a very big possibility. What are the odds that years later y'all ended up at the same university?"

I continue, "They have probably known this whole time and were still mean and dismissive of me. So, I'm just trying to come to terms with the fact that the guys I would dream about when life got bad have wrote me off and forgotten about me." I say sadly.

"Awe I'm sorry hun. I don't know why they have been acting like that, but we can give them the cold shoulder if you would like." she says.

"Yea, I guess I just don't want to let on that I know them because what if they just don't care. I don't know what will hurt more. Them acting like they don't care or them hating me for something I haven't even done. I think the way Malrik has been hurts the most because he was who I went to about all of my problems." I tell her sullenly as we leave the changing rooms.

I can't stop staring at them, now that I know who they really are. They had to have known. Mmhm Li forget about it, this is the combat class don't lose focus.

We're paired up again with the same rules as before. Ok no more nice girl it is time to start putting in more effort. I know the moves that have already been taught so I should be fine and powers not being used will help in the long run.

Oh yay, one of the followers is my first opponent. She knows some of the moves, but she is sloppy which gives me the chance to take her down to the mat.

My next opponent is one I know I can beat easily since I have faced her before. We battle and just like I knew I won.

Glancing around the room I see Trixie is fighting her opponent, so I glance around and of course my eyes stray towards the guys. They are glorious to behold. My heart hurts to stare at them but at the same time I can't help it.

Shaking my head I turn to see who it is that steps up onto my mat as my opponent. My eyes widen slightly when I see that it's the pretty lady that said she would be Mrs. Rose.

Great just what I need.

We start fighting dodging the others moves while still landing some hits. It's not until she whispers, "Stop staring at Malrik. He is mine."

I feel burning anger at her words, and it takes everything in me not to peek into her mind and dredge up some blackmail. Okay Li take a deep breath and calm down once I'm somewhat calmer I look back at her.

"You are crazy." I tell her.

I punch her when I say it. She slowly looks back at me before staring at me with disdain.

"You have done it now." she growls through a nosebleed.

I don't understand what she means at first. Until her eyes glow with a slight pink tint in them. Is she really about to use her powers? How do her powers even really work? I barely get to really think about it before I'm plowed into from behind.

"Ugh." I grunt out.

Who the hell just rammed into me in the middle of the fight? I push at the body holding me down trying to get them to get off.

Why aren't they moving?

I stop shoving when I realize we are being stared at.

"Wow, trying to get down and dirty in the middle of class is so slutty. Are you really that desperate for it?" the pretty girl says.

Laughter breaks out. I feel my face grow hot from embarrassment. Oh my god. Why won't this guy get off of me. Why does it seem like he is trying to get into my clothes?

Kill me now.

"Get off of me please." I try with the mysterious person.

When he goes to shove at my shirt it rips and I can't help my reaction. I scream in terror. Please no. I can't go through this. I don't think I will mentally survive it.

He's suddenly ripped off by Malrik? Malrik throws him away from me, but the guy gets up and goes to charge at me again. He ends up being held back by Malrik and Ryder against the wall.

Where did the handcuffs come from?

"Stop with your fucking pheromones!" Ryder yells at the pretty girl who I was fighting against.

Pheromones? Who is he yelling at?

"Oh, calm down Ryder, it was just a harmless joke." she says back.

"That is not a joke Lilthe. As soon as the professor is back, I will be reporting you." Jasper says coming over to cover me back up.

I'm still on the floor?

Why am I still on the floor?

Get up Li. don't let them see how bad this affected you. As soon as Jasper goes to touch me, I can't help how bad I flinch back.

"Hey, it is ok. I won't touch you if you don't want to, but I thought I would cover you back up." he says softly.

He is treating me like a skittish bunny.

Which I guess is fair after the way I just reacted. I know he is trying to help but I'm not seeing him all the way still clouded by what happened.

I quickly grab at my shirt and go to run from the room when I trip, causing more laughter. Now I can't stop the tears from coming. I'm so embarrassed that I just wish the ground would open up and swallow me whole.

Slamming into the changing rooms, I go into one of the stalls and can't keep the sobs in. It was supposed to be different here. I didn't think something like this would happen. What kind of prank even is that? Who would prank someone with a prank like that?

As I'm trying to calm myself down, I start hearing screams.

Huh?

What the hell?

Is someone attacking?

Before I can panic, I hear the changing room doors open before there is a slight knock on the stall doors. I'm trying to quell my breathing so they can't tell that I'm crying in here.

"Li? It's me, I brought you an extra shirt. Are you okay?" Trix asks.

"Y-Yea I-I'm f-f-fine." I sob out.

"There's no one else here hunny, you can come out. I just want to make sure you're okay." as she attempts to coax me out.

I open the door slowly checking it is just her in here before throwing myself at her part in relief, part to cry some more.

When I finally get calmed down, she helps me clean up my face and turns her back while I change. I toss my shredded shirt in the trash before squaring my shoulders.

"The professor came in before I came to check on you Lilthe is being reprimanded, and the professor says you can leave and go home for the day if you would like or you can come finish class." she tells me.

I think about it and honestly, I don't think I'm ready to face everyone yet. I would love nothing more than to drop out of this school and just get my degree online. But I really want to see this through, I'm just so tired of being everyone's punching bag.

No, I can't let some cunty bitch run me off. Mind made up I decide I'll take the professors generous offer to go home for the rest of the day and recuperate. So, I grab my bags and leave out of the back door, so I don't have to see anyone.

I go all the way to the dorm and break down again. Crying myself to sleep.

Chapter 24
Jasper

When she flinched away it felt like a stab to the heart. But seeing her trying to hold back her tears really gutted me. When that bitch Lilthe trips her when she goes to run, I know Liora was pushed too far.

When the doors to the changing rooms slam shut behind her all hell breaks loose. Liora's witchy friend rains down chaos magic against Lilthe.

Lilthe doesn't back down though, using her pheromones against the guys she has been with recently to take most of the damage. It's not until Trixie? I think is her name grounds her to the ground and goes to summon a fatal purple lightning looking ball of magic that the professor comes back.

"What the hell is going on in here?" he bellows.

"She just attacked me for no reason, she is crazy!" Lilthe tries to say while conjuring some tears up.

Wow what an actor no wonder she had all of us fooled when she mimicked a mate bond with Malrik. I have never liked her and today really just nailed that nail in the coffin.

"Bitch I will show you crazy if you EVER come after Liora like that again. That was a dirty ass trick you pulled, and you fucking know it." Trixie? Says while glaring and still having some purple sparks around her fingers.

The professor looks around seeing Malrik and Ryder standing near the slumped over dude that's till cuffed to the wall before landing back on Trixie.

"Explain what happened." he barks out.

"That bitch Lilthe used her magic when she was losing against Liora. She used her pheromones to amp up the guy Malrik and Ryder have handcuffed to the wall over there because she had him so worked up. When he tackled Violet to the ground it was almost like he was sex crazed he started pulling at Liora's clothes. She screamed because he wouldn't stop. When Malrik tossed him off of her and she went running towards the changing rooms Lilthe tripped her and then laughed at her." Trixie explains.

"Whatever TRACXIE it isn't my fault she can't take a damn joke I mean what a baby." Lilthe sneers.

Trixie goes to lunge at her again but the professor steps in between the girls as a way to diffuse the situation because no one wants to see a chaos witch lose control especially not in a closed in room. They don't have a bad rep for no reason, and I would hate for a repeat of freshman year.

"I have heard enough. Trixie, please let Liora know she can come back to class or leave for the day especially after something like this. I will let the dean and her mentor know what happened so they can inform her teachers. And as for you I will be taking you to the dean because that is not the kind of joke we should ever play. CLASS DISMISSED." he growls out while leading Lilthe out of the combat class.

I watch as everyone starts to disperse but before anyone can go into the girls changing room Trixie threatens them with a bolt of lightning to fuck up their hair.

It works because suddenly the girls have all the time in the world to stretch and gossip until Trixie comes back and tells them they can enter now.

When I don't see my sugar follow, I get worried and decide to approach the witch. As I get to her the guys have stepped up flanking me, "Hey is she okay?" I ask.

"Why the hell do y'all care huh? You didn't stop Lilthe from doing it and she only targeted Liora because she thinks she still has some stupid ass claim on you and your status." She states bluntly while looking at Malrik.

"I'm not with that nasty bitch Lilthe and I never want to be again. So, get it out of your head that it is my fault. I odn't control what she does." Malrik growls at her.

"Are you dumb? Liora was attacked today because of you! You need to set Lilthe straight because if not Liora may never forgive y'all." she grinds out.

"What do you mean she might not forgive us?" I ask.

"It wasn't hard to figure out. The fact that y'all kept up this ruse has cracked the memories she held onto." she says pointedly before leaving us staring behind.

Did Liora figure out we are mates?

Does she remember us now?

What happened to her to make her more skittish than she was as a child?

Why did she react the way she did when that all went down?

So many questions and not enough answers.

Chapter 25
Liora

Trixie allows me to wallow and hide out for the weekend. It took me a while to process what happened and the reaction not only, I had but Trixie and the guys. My professors emailed to let me know an email was sent by either the dean or my mentor to let them know I was excused from my classes for the day. It being Friday just helped give me a couple days to decompress.

When Trixie got home that night, she told me how she tried to kick Lilthe's ass and the professor stopped it and then how she ripped into the guys over it all.

I went through all the motions over the weekend. Sadness at how horrible it was that no one helped at first, panic at the way it brought up memories, and anger at the fact that I don't even know any of these people and that is how they want to treat me?

Plus, I'm angry at the fact the guys have acted like they don't particularly want me around. I did receive some texts from them all, even Daemous, which I'm still not sure about him.

Jasper
Friday...
Hey, just wanted to check on you and see how you are doing.

Ryder
Saturday...
Let us know if you need anything

Daemous

Friday...
Hey, I heard about what happened. Are you okay?

Sunday...
Hey, do you want to go to lunch together?

Me
Sure, I guess that is fine. What time?

Daemous
How about 1? We can go grab food from the diner by campus or the school cafeteria.

Trixie tells me what he says from where she is sitting on me, so that I wouldn't back out of it. In her words I need to get out of our dorm.

I think about my options. I still get a weird vibe from him so I don't know that I want to go off campus with him so the cafeteria may be my best option. But the idea of seeing everyone again is unsettling when I don't know what to expect.

I never answered Jasper and Ryder's texts either. Are they mad or do they just not care?

"Earth to Liora." Trixie says, snapping her fingers in my face.

"Huh?" I say.

"What do you want me to say to Daemous?" she asks.

"Tell him the cafeteria. I don't feel comfortable leaving campus with him. Don't say the last part to him." I say as I push her off of me so I can stand up.

Me
I would prefer the cafeteria.

Daemous
I will meet you there.

Closing out of the chat I decide I may as well take a shower to get ready seeing as it is already 11.

Once I'm done in the shower, I do my normal make up before peeking out of my door for Trixie.

"Hey Trix, what should I wear?" I ask.

She comes bounding into my room with an excited gleam on her face as she starts to rummage through my clothes.

"It's a little chilly for a dress, but you could always wear leggings underneath or just go with your usual, nice jeans and instead of a funny saying shirt we could dress it up?" she inquires.

"Um I think I would prefer my jeans, but I don't think I have any nice shirts." I tell her.

"Okay let me run to my room to look for a nice shirt while you start getting dressed." she says running off.

I shake my head at her antics before pulling on a pair of light wash skinny jeans that form my legs and ass well. Although they aren't near as tight as they used to be. Shrugging my shoulders I slip on my white lifted converse then as I am securing my bra Trixie comes barreling into my room out of breath.

"I *gulp of air* found the perfect shirt! Wow your tits are amazeballs. I knew you had a nice sized rack but dang. Girl you gotta start showing it off and this shirt will be perfect." she says with a gleam in her eyes.

I slid on the shirt which is nice and soft. It's a dark purple with a plunging neckline. It actually looks really nice, and my boobs help lift it up without looking indecent.

I smile at my reflection before deciding to wear some lipstick in the shade, *leave me be*, it isn't one I wear too often but I'm hoping it will keep Daemous from trying to kiss me.

Glancing at my phone I see that it is already 12:30 so I gather my wallet and head towards the door.

"If you need a scapegoat to get away quickly just text SOS and I will know you want to leave and will call about something 'kay?" Trix offers.

I smile in thanks before leaving the dorm and heading out of our dorm building. I don't rush but I also don't walk too slow. As the cafeteria building comes into view I see Daemous already waiting for me, so I walk up and greet him. Before I even make it all the way I see a girl walk up to him before glaring at him and stomping away from him. When she goes to walk past me, she slams into my shoulder huffing for me to get out of her way.

Well damn maybe she should watch where she is going, I don't even get a good look at her as she is moving too fast. Oh well.

Daemous spots me and does a small smile and wave which I return because that is the friendly thing to do right?

Chapter 26
Liora

After we say hello to each other he leads us into the doors of the cafeteria. His hand grazes my lower back as he leads me towards the line to pick something out.

As I'm looking at the options for today, I decide on some chicken alfredo because it is what sounds good. When I turn towards Daemous to see what he wants I see that he is already staring at me.

Weird.

I turn back towards the front as the line moves and when we get to the front to order what we want he gives me a weird look like he can't believe I ordered the chicken alfredo.

Whatever I think as I roll my eyes.

When we find a booth towards the side and take our seats he gives me a look. I can't figure out what he wants so I finally ask, "What?"

"Shouldn't you eat a salad instead? The girls I normally go out with all get salads, sometimes some grilled chicken." he says.

Oh hell no.

"I will eat whatever I want, and no one is ever going to tell me otherwise. If that is a problem for you then I think I should probably go." I state while starting to stand and leave.

His eyes get wide in what would be panic but there is something else there anger maybe?

"No, I didn't mean it like that. I guess I'm not used to girls who don't get a salad and take a couple nibbles before being full. That is all I swear I didn't mean to upset you." he says placatingly while grabbing my arm to get me to stay.

I slowly sit back down as I pull my arm out of his grasp. He sighs in relief before digging into his steak and scallops' potatoes.

I figure what the hell and eat my food. I have to bite back on a moan because holy hell. It is so delicious and creamy. When I finish, I really have to stop myself from grabbing the last breadstick and scrapping my plate clean with it because it's just that fucking good.

When we finish our food, we get up and get ready to leave. As we leave the cafeteria he offers to walk me back to my dorm. I shrug at him because why not it would be rude to decline.

As we walk past the entrance to student housing I hear growls. Huh what was that? When I go to turn, I see the guys standing there glaring at me and Daemous.

Why do they look so mad? I feel Daemous put his hand on the small of my back giving those weird spicy tingles again. Before I can move away from him or anything Malrik has grabbed my arm sending the warm tingles up my arm before handing me off to Ryder. They stand in front of me facing off with Daemous.

Are they jealous?

"Stay away from her, this will be your last warning!" Malrik growls out.

Daemous smirks mockingly and states, "Despite your beliefs lizard but she chose to go have lunch with me."

The guys turn to me in shock. I shrug at them and say, "It was just lunch in the cafeteria, I don't see what the big deal is."

"Him? That's who you choose to go on a date with? Do you even know how much of an asshole he is?" Jasper tries to warn me.

"It was just a lunch date. I don't know why y'all even care. It isn't like y'all have acted like you want me around anyway." I argue.

"You're ours!" Malrik snarls in my face.

"I'm not anyone's, you oversized asshole." I growl back at him.

"Ok let's all settle down. We didn't mean to come off like we have any say in who you interact with." Ryder tries to diffuse.

I cock my head and say saccharinely, "You most definitely have no say in who I date, kiss or fuck RyRy."

Jasper and Ryder have to hold the hothead back from coming at me again as I turn to walk back towards Daemous. He slings an arm around my shoulder as I get to him.

"See you later, Malice." Daemous says.

As we turn to walk away from the guys, I know he has done something else to the guys over my head that I don't see but it has someone shouting curses at him.

When we are out of sight of the guys I shrug Daemous' arm off. I was only allowing it to make a point to them. Although I probably just gave away that I remember them using Ryder's nickname, but I can't help it when they get on my damn nerves, and I'm mad at them right now.

He walks next to me, not seemingly upset that I shrugged his arm off. He walks me to the doors of my dorm before asking, "So does that mean I get a kiss for walking you back to your dorm, you know since you can kiss whoever you want?"

I think about it and decide that a peck wouldn't be bad, but I don't think I want to go any further than that. Leaning up to peck his cheek he turns just in time, and we end up kissing.

I freeze in shock because that is not where I was aiming for. Snap out of it Li. As I try to pull back, he follows and attempts to deepen the kiss. I have to shove him a little to get him to get off of me.

Stumbling back, he sends me a smile saying, "Sorry I didn't mean to get carried away."

"Um yeah, sure, thanks for lunch." I mutter before darting into the building, not bothering to invite him in or anything.

Chapter 27
Liora

Making it back into my dorm, Trixie is curled up on the couch watching a movie.

"Hey, how did it go? You never texted so I am assuming it was good." she asks when I come in.

"Honestly, I just don't like him like that. Something about him rubs me wrong. But it was okay I guess and then we ran into the guys, and they were being dicks." I reply.

"What did they do?" she asks.

"Just typical alpha male bullshit. They don't want me to see anyone else but yet they aren't putting in effort for me." I reply.

"Wow, what jerks." Trix says.

Nodding I tell her I'm going to go change into comfy clothes and wash away the events. After my shower I start to feel a little more relaxed and get dressed before heading into the living room to hang with Trixie.

She's still in the same place as before, but it looks like she finished her movie because the end credits are rolling.

"Hey wanna watch a movie together? We make it a whole night? Popcorn, drinks, and face masks?" she asks when I go to sit down on the couch next to her.

"Sure, that sounds fun." I reply.

"YAY! I will go grab the face masks, if you will make popcorn." she squeals as she runs away.

I get popcorn going and turn to ask if she wants me to make drinks when I see her giving me puppy dog eyes. I look at her questioningly because what is she wanting?

"Will you pretty pretty please make those lemonade drinks you made that one time?" she asks giving me her best puppy dog eyes.

I roll my eyes because I was gonna offer to make them anyway before I nod at her that I will. She pumps her fist and says yes. Chuckling at her antics I turn and start gathering everything else I need to make them.

Mixing rum, lemonade and some blue raspberry syrup, I add it all to a glass then put some ice and one of our colored bendy straws to make it fancy. And yes, the bendy straw makes it fancy I will die on that hill.

I put the popcorn into a giant bowl, grab our drinks and head into the living room where Trix has already started setting everything up for what looks like an ultimate girl's night in.

"What do you want to watch? Anime, action, rom-com, musical, or scary?" she asks, picking up the remote.

"Hmmm either anime or musical. I want something funny and light- hearted to help me get in a good mind frame for tomorrow." I tell her.

She nods before putting on Zombies 2. We watch that whole movie singing along as it goes. Once we finish the first movie and most of our popcorn. I get up to refill drinks, and we decide to go ahead and put on our face masks while we watch the next one.

About 20 minutes in we peel off the face masks, and each go and rinse our faces off. Wow my skin feels so smooth I wonder what kind of face mask that was.

"Hey Trix, what kind of face mask was that because my skin feels so smooth?" I ask her when I head back into the living room.

"It was a magical one. I found it in the store shop here on campus and thought what the hell. It's imbued with witchy magic or fae magic I always forget but it also has other things in it to help clear up your skin, make it soft, and relax you." she tells me.

"We will definitely have to do it again." I tell her.

"It's recommended to only do it once a month because of the magical properties." she informs me.

Nodding at her. We settle in and finish the movie, Zombies 3 before cleaning up. Once that is done, we head to our rooms for the night.

I get home later than usual because I had to walk through the rain and wind, so it slowed me down. Dreading going in because I know mom is home, her car is in the driveway. I push my ear up against the door to try and hear if there is any noise. Not hearing anything I slowly push the door open and close it behind me. I don't even bother stopping in the kitchen first as she caught me off guard last time so I just head to my room. As I make it to my door and go to open it mom comes out of her room yelling, "And just where the hell have you been?"

"Nowhere it's raining so it took me a little bit longer to get home." I reply while looking down at the ground.

"Did I ask you to speak? Insolent whore. It's very doubtful the rain slowed you down that much. You were probably off whoring around." she sneers.

You technically did ask me a question but whatever I think to myself. I shake my head at her and try to tell her that's not true but before I can even complete the sentence a slap rings out through the tiny hallway. I grab my stinging cheek and will myself not to cry because she gets off on it.

I try to just go to my room, but she grabs me by the arm and starts pulling me along while saying, "I need you as my payment for tonight."

"NO. No, I don't want to do that anymore. I don't like it." I argue trying to yank my arm away.

"Come on, it's not that bad. Your future husband will love that you can do that." she tells me.

"Well, that is if you can even get one after all the whoring around you do you slut." she says cackling.

She shoves me into the back of the car that I can't get back out on my own because of the stupid child locks. I don't even really remember the drive to the clubhouse trying to will this to all be a bad dream. Shocker it's not.

We pull up to her favorite place in this godforsaken town. The clubhouse to the local motorcycle gang, Shifters MC. They definitely don't have any morals, or they would know how wrong this all is.

"Now be a good slut and don't fight it because if they have to drug you to make you compliant then that's more payment they are owed and I will NOT be responsible for your payment do you understand?" she growls at me in a low tone when she pulls me from the car.

"Mom, I really don't want to do this. Please, I'm your daughter, why do you make me do this?" I plead with her hoping she has some type of motherly instinct to know this is wrong.

She just slaps me again and pulls me towards the clubhouse. I shuffle behind with my hair down. I really hate this. I just want to disappear. I wish the guys could come save me.

"Hey sugar! I brought her just like I promised you." She tells the captain? President? I don't know

"Follow me." a gruff voice says.

I peak from my peripherals and see that it's busy and wow people are going at it right here in the open. Nasty. We go into a room, and the door gets slammed behind us.

"If she doesn't comply it's your ass." he growls at my mom as she releases me.

"I talked to her and she understands. If she doesn't comply you can drug her and do as you like." my mom tells him.

"Look at me." the voice growls.

I don't look up praying that he is talking to someone else. My mom pulls my hair causing my head to snap back and my eyes to look up. I gulp because he is one big, scary looking dude. He could totally squash me like a bug.

"Can I have my party favor now?" Mom says in what she may think is a sultry voice but sounds all cracked from years of drugs and what not.

He tosses a baggie of something her way as she leaps for it like a dog for a treat.

"Get out of here I'm sure someone out there is willing to play with you." he snarls at her.

She scampers from the room. The door shutting to my impending doom. I know what is to come next but god I don't want to.

"Come here." he demands.

When I don't move at first, he takes his belt off and slaps it together before snarling, "Get your ass over here now."

His voice echoing in what makes me start to move my feet.

"Crawl to me like a bitch in heat." he states.

Gross, I don't want to. I reluctantly get to my knees and slowly crawl. I don't add any sway or anything I just try to get it over and done with the fastest. When I make it to him his eyes look hooded. Yuck.

"Undo my jeans." he demands.

I just looked at him at first. But when I don't move the belt comes down. It came down so fast I didn't even notice it swing until there was pain on my back. Crying out I go to scramble and undo his jeans when he grabs me by my hair and says, "The more you disobey the more lashes you get. All it does is turn me on and want to give a good hard fuck whether it's your mouth, cunt or ass do you understand?"

Nodding that I agree he releases my hair. I have to resist the urge to rub it. I continue undoing his jeans and free his ugly, smelly dick. It doesn't look right. Maybe all the drugs? If all guys look and smell like this, I don't want any part of anything sexual.

He tugs on it a couple times before telling me, "Turn around and take you punishment like a good girl."

I turn around because what else am I to do? The first slash on my back wasn't so bad but the next 2 had me screaming out in pain. The door opens before I get another one. He looks a lot nicer.

"Well, well what do we have here? Are you ok sweetie, do you need help?" the other guy asks.

Nodding at him I go to open my mouth and explain when he lets out an absolutely evil laugh.

"They always fall for that." he chuckles.

I'm confused and I think he can see that because he comes towards me and lifts my face up.

"Hmm they're so pretty when they cry." he says before licking my tears.

I jerk back in disgust because what the hell. I don't make it far before he grabs my shirt and yanks me back towards him.

"Oh, you wanna fight? Fine." he snarls.

RIIP. is the only sound I hear before I feel a breeze on my torso. He just ripped my shirt. What the hell? Oh my god.

"Oooo those are some nice-looking tits. I bet with some proper nutrition you would fill out beautifully." he whistles.

I try to hold my shirt together when another smack on my back takes my breath away. I drop my shirt, and it slides off my body.

"Don't forget about me." the president snarls.

"I think it's time to play, what do you say?" he says, coming to stand in front of me. I shake my head and try to scramble away when I am held in place. Crying I start begging them to leave me alone when smelly dick gets close to my face. My hands are held in place as his dick gets closer to my mouth. Squeezing my lips shut to prolong?

I hope they find a conscious something. The other guy bites down on my shoulder so hard I swear there is blood dripping down the front of me. My mouth opened on a scream and the smelly dick wasted no time shoving his dick towards me.

I slam into a sitting position screaming. I stop as soon as I realize and hope I didn't wake Trix. wishful thinking because I barely get time to calm down before she's bursting into my room lightning bolts adorning her hand already.

"WHAT? What happened? I'll zap their ass." she says crazily.

I just stare at her in shock because what the hell? Well at least now I know if we ever have an intruder, she will be ready to zap their asses into next year.

How many people has she zapped for that to be the first thing she says? Or is it just an automatic response to the unknown? She seems so badass even with her crazy pajamas on.

Shaking my head I attempt to tell her, "It's okay Trix. I just had a bad dream from my past, and I couldn't stop the scream before it started."

She heaves a sigh almost like she's disappointed she doesn't get to zap anyone. She seems almost zap happy. I'll have to watch her so that she doesn't get overzealous and zap the wrong person.

"Are you okay love?" she asks, sitting next to me on my bed.

I'm not expecting the question she asks. Do I tell her the truth? Would she judge me horribly if I do? Will she think I'm a slut or a whore. Even though I wasn't a willing participate in any of my mother's horrible actions. I just became her doll to use for payment when she got too far in over her head in debt.

"Yeah, it just wasn't a fun memory to relive." I tell her.

She nods in understanding and offers to make breakfast and then we can sit and chat since it's so early.

I mumble a thanks.

I'm so glad that she is so understanding about everything. On another note, I am so fucking glad that no other telepath has the power to breach past my mental shields. I would be horrified if anyone witnessed what I went through.

"Go ahead and take a shower and get to feeling better and I'll throw your sheets in the wash." she tells me gently.

I nod and head to the bathroom to take a nice, blistering hot shower hoping to hopefully wash away the phantom hands and mental scars. That was a memory that I hoped I would never have to relive again.

Chapter 28
Liora

Once I am out of the shower, I do feel better and decide this is definitely a day for comfort, so I pick out my worn ripped skinny jeans, favorite black converse and an oversized anime long sleeve.

I hack my hair into a messy bun and do my normal make up before heading out into the kitchen. Mmm it smells so good. I love a good creamy cinnamon roll.

"Hey, feel better?" Trix asks when I sit down on the counter next to her.

Nodding at her in response because what else can I do?

Cry?

Rage?

Breakdown?

"Do you want to talk about it? Or is this a forget it ever happened moment?" she asks and I know she wouldn't push if I chose not to answer her on the matter.

Do I?

Am I ready to share some of the darker things I went through with my birth giver?

Would she judge me?

Would she hate me?

Would she betray me and tell everyone?

No, I don't think she would really do that to me. Trixie hasn't betrayed me yet. It might be nice to finally tell someone everything. I haven't even told my old therapist all of the depraved things I went through.

"It's not a nice or short story. I went through some rough things and still have the mental scars and some physical ones as well. If I tell you then no one may ever know." I explain.

"We still have almost 2 hours until classes. Let's eat and then we can talk it all over. I swear I won't breathe a word of it." she tells me holding a hand up like a girl scout.

We eat some delicious cinnamon rolls and drink some orange juice at the little table. Once we're done, we wash our cups out in the sink and set them to dry.

I grab out some water before sitting on the couch and wait for Trixie. It doesn't take long before she ambles over and plops down next to me, so we are facing each other.

Taking a breath, I start telling her about the dream. Even though I'm awake and much older it still makes me feel like it just happened. My body shivers and I can't stop the steady flow of tears that start to run down my face.

When I get to where I woke up screaming, I have to pause and take a drink of water. Trixie hands me a tissue to blow my nose as she does the same. When I look at her, she is crying too.

I didn't mean to make her cry.

"I'm okay. Sorry, continue on if you want, if not that's okay too don't feel like you have to." she tells me shakily.

Nodding at her I take a breath. Should I tell her what happened next? Or spare her the details? I might feel better if I finally tell someone everything.

"I'm not going to go all in the way into detail. But I will try to explain everything that happened that night without breaking down." I attempt to explain.

"So, I'm sure you can guess what happened next. I wasn't raped by penal penetration, but they did grope and stick their fingers inside me. Before it could get to that part they were raided by the police. And no, they didn't care about what was happening they just had my mom take me and leave so they didn't have to file the paperwork." I whisper out the last part ashamed.

"I am so so sorry that happened to you. I know sorry doesn't mean much but it's all I've got right now. It does however make more sense on why you tread the way you do. Plus, what happened in class makes so much more sense." she states giving me a great big hug and petting my hair in a soothing manner.

"Thank you." I whisper into her shoulder trying not to break down again in sobs.

"If I ever get my hands on your attackers, I will zap their asses to hell and leave them there to be demon food." she says with small purple bolts flickering around her fingers.

I've never had someone who was so protective over me. Once dad died that was it, I was neglected and abused. It makes me wonder why my mom was even with my dad because the switch up when he died was crazy.

The rumors she spread about him and then going completely off her rocker with the drinking and other things.

I don't realize how long I was in my mind, but an alarm jostles me out and back into the present.

An alarm on her phone suddenly goes off while she scrambles to turn it off. Oh, shit is that the time?

"Damn it's already time for classes." Trixie sighs.

We gather our things, and I grab an energy drink to go because I need it since I didn't really sleep. Shit I hope nothing crazy happens today, I need a nice chill day.

Chapter 29
Liora

I can already tell it isn't going to be a fun day when we get to Professor Latman's class and see him talking and laughing with Professor Pyran. I wonder what is going on?

Everyone hustles to get changed while whispering to each other about theories on how it is all going to go. Fuck. I really hope it isn't anything bad, I mean come on I just want a fun day. Hopefully it is just a giant mix class for sparring.

"Oh god what kind of torture do you think they are going to put us through?" Trix asks after we change.

"Torture?! No one said anything about Torture Trixie!" I exclaim.
Oh my god.

We're going to die.

What the hell have I signed up for?

I haven't even gotten to have sex with any of the cute guys here.

What? No bad Liora.

Where is a bag to blow in? That's what people do right?

Goodbye to all of the things I haven't experienced yet.

I never even found out if the guys liked me.

RIP to my life, see you soon dad.

"LIORA!" Trixie shouts in my face gently shaking my shoulder to snap me out of my down spiral.

"Are you good now? Jeez girl it was a joke. Poor choice of words on my part after this morning. I'm sorry." she says when she sees my eyes have cleared and I'm back in this moment.

"Sorry, I didn't mean to spiral like that. My mind can be a dramatic bitch sometimes." I say sheepishly.

"Alls good girl. We've all had our moments. Now let's get out there before we get yelled at." she replies, pulling me by the arm.

Once we're all out in the gym Professor Latman claps his hands together to get everyone's attention. He has to clap a couple times before everyone shuts up and focuses on him before he talks and when he does i feel dread and relief.

"Alright everybody. You already know Professor Pyran but he's here so we can discuss y'all's first challenge. Yes, yes, I know already? Yep, it's time to see where everyone is and it won't even be one of the harder ones. We are going to start y'all on an easy one so that everyone has an idea of how it will all work once in there." he states.

"Yes. As Professor Latman stated, your first challenge is coming up. It will be this Friday. You will be in groups of 3 and spend the week training together and coming up with gameplans. And no, you do not get to pick your own groups. We will choose them so that there aren't any cliques ganging up on others." Professor Pyran says.

Grumbles are heard throughout the gym. Oh, damn I hope I'm not with anyone I don't know or don't like. Oh, shit what if I get paired up with one or more of the boys? Nah doubtful. I can feel them staring at me and am trying my hardest not to acknowledge it.

"Hopefully we get put together." Trix says hopefully.

Nodding I tell her, "Same I don't really know anyone but you, the boys, and that jerk Lilthe."

"Alright, I want everyone paying attention. We're going to start listing the groups so pay attention." Professor Latman bellows.

I start to zone out as he is calling names when I hear him say my name and sit up straight.

"Next group is Liora, Lilith and Aurelius. Then lastly our only group of 4 will be Trixie, Zaiden, Ryder and Jasper. No one gets to change groups. I don't care that your bestie isn't with you. Groups are final. Go find the other members of your group and start practicing." Professor Pyran claps dismissing us to find our groups.

I'm frozen because godsdammit. Of fucking course, I get stuck with that bitch. I have the worst fucking luck.

"Hey sugar too bad we aren't in the same group You know I would have protected you." I hear from behind me.

I know it's Jasper, but I'm mad at them.

"Oh, come on bunny don't ignore us we know you know we're behind you it's rude." I hear Ryder and almost turn but instead get an idea.

Leaning over to Trixie I say acting confused, "Trixie did you hear that noise? Maybe the school is haunted. Anyways I am going to go find whoever this Aurelius person is, maybe he is cute."

She grins wickedly at me, "Hmm I don't think I heard anything. You go girl get yourself a hot new man." she says.

Walking away but not before I hear a couple growls and was that a whimper I heard? Nope. not falling for it. Just keep walking Li.

Getting off to the side I see Lilthe arguing with the professor I'm sure to try and be switched. God, I hope so. A smoking hot guy with blue hair walks up to me.

"Hey, you're Liora right? My name is Aurelius." he says holding a handout.

Hot damn this man is so pretty.

Fuck no you can't think like that. He really is pretty, but he isn't as hot as Malrik, Ryder and Jasper. Although I don't think they would touch me with a 10-foot pole.

I wonder if I will feel the weird tingles that I feel sometimes when I touch the guys and even Daemous.

Grabbing his hand I'm slightly disappointed that there isn't that warm sparky feeling. Just a normal person. He smells like the ocean mixed with someone masculine. I wonder what he is.

"H-Hi yes I'm Liora nice to meet you Aurelius." I say dumbly before shaking his hand.

He smiles slightly at me, "So, should we say what we are so we can plan how to work better as a group?"

Before I answer I see Trixie across the gym wiggling her eyes at me and giving me a thumbs up while she has 3 glaring figures next to her. Man, if looks could kill either I'd be six feet under or Aurelius. Hmm can I make them jealous?

"Sure, I'm not anything fancy or special so I'll apologize in advance for that." I tell him sheepishly.

"Just because your powers are something huge doesn't negate what you can do or bring to the team, don't be so hard on yourself. Everyone has something they are good or bad at." he tells me firmly.

I smile at him, "I'm a telepath with some telekinetic tendencies but I can't do too much." I explain.

When he smiles it's blinding but not in a way my panties are melting like I have read in books. More like a crush that may turn out to be more or someone who is more of a piece of art to admire.

"I'm a siren who prefers to be on land so you're not so weird. I'm still strong and capable on land but my power is stronger in water and for the most part sirens are the bigger predator in the waters." he tells me.

A siren. A freaking siren, so basically a mermaid, right? Would it be insensitive of me to ask that. I wonder what he looks like shifted. I bet he looks God-like.

"Wow, that's so cool. I'm trying so hard not to ask all the different questions running through my mind. But like you're so fucking cool now in my eyes." I tell him amazed.

I think he felt the stares because he turns and looks at them before looking back at me with a glint in his eyes.

"So, is there a reason I am being glared at like their stare will trigger my death? Are you with them?" he asks.

"What? No! I'm not with them but they seem to think they have some kind of claim on me probably just from knowing me as a child and nothing more." I say, shaking my head.

"Ok. So, do we care what they think? Or are we ignoring their existence?' he asks.

"Um a bit of both? I want to make them jealous. I guess Malrik and Lilthe were a thing or something I don't even know but that's why she doesn't like me and I don't know they act like I'm their possession so I want to rebel and show them I'm not something to be owned if that makes sense at all?" I explain.

He nods before saying, "I can help you make them jealous if you want? It's not like it would be hard, you're a pretty girl and with the way they're glaring it probably wouldn't take much to push them over the edge and blow up."

I stare at him in wonder before an idea comes to me thanks to the 3 glaring assholes still staring almost like they are daring me to do something. Deciding what the hell? Aurelius is cute even if I don't feel the same way I do when the guys touch me.

"Alright deal! We can spend this class making them jealous and we can go grab drinks after?" I ask.

"Sure, that's fine with me." he replies.

Before we can do or say anything else to each other Lilthe comes stomping over like someone shit in her cheerios. She glares at me like this is all my fault before Professor Latman's voice bellows, "I will say it again we will not allow any group changes! The groups are final! Start practicing and working together on everything with your group and come up with a game plan. Your first challenge is a team obstacle course this Friday!"

"Well why don't we go in a circle and introduce ourselves and come up with a gameplan?" Aurelius asks.

"Hmmph I don't care what that loser wants to do I don't even know why they let her in, she's just a puny telepath and what even are you? Something pathetic as well?" Lilthe states haughtily.

I really don't know what the fuck I ever did to her, but she really hates my ass, and I don't understand it.

"Anyways, I'm Aurelius and I am a siren, and you already know Liora and that she is a telepath." he says.

Her eyes light up in what looks like victory at what he says about what he is. She looks like she just won the lottery.

"So, like if my pheromones affect you, you can use your powers to bring down someone else?" she says sweetly twirling her hair around her finger.

He looks uncomfortable and just gives her a short maybe. Hmm is that why she looked excited? What exactly is she planning? This can only mean trouble for me.

"Anyways let's start sparring and seeing who works best with each other." I try to say before getting cut off.

"Yea sure whatever Lino." Lilthe says, still staring at Aurelius.

"It's Liora" I tell her, amazed at how strong my voice is.

"Ugh whatever I don't have time for this y'all figure it out and just make sure to protect me during the challenge because I swear if I break a nail there will be hell to pay." she harumphs before stalking off.

"Well, isn't she just a ray of fucking sunshine?" Aurelius says, causing me to laugh.

We decide to spar a little bit so he can help me with my stability and doing so he has been cracking dad jokes that have had me laughing so hard I can barely keep up.

"How many tickles does it take to tickle an octopus?" he says, trying not to laugh at me.

"I-I don't know." I say trying to catch my breath.

"Ten-tickles." he says with such a straight face I don't know what makes me laugh harder, the joke or his expression.

"O-Oh M-My G-God you have got to s-stop. I-I can't b-breathe." I tell him between giggles.

I end up leaning on him trying to catch my breath but one look at him and we both start laughing and at this point he is basically holding me up because I can't stop laughing.

"Hey Liora, what's so funny?" Trix asks with the 3 stooges following behind.

Of course, they followed her they are so fucking noisy. Like I'm not a whole ass adult who can take care of herself.

"Huh? Oh, nothing Aurelius was just telling me a funny joke. At least one part of my group is great." I tell her pointing at him.

"Oh, that's good, well are you ready to head out?" Trixie asks.

"What was the joke? I bet it couldn't have been so funny you ended up all over him."Malrik snarls out.

"It's none of your damn business. And I wasn't all over him, if I was you would have known." I state back giving him a look.

What a damn asshole. He hates me then he's worried about me then we're back to hating me like dude pick one.

"Alright well Liora I'll see you later yea?" Aurelius asks.

"For sure. Can't wait. See you there." I tell him before giving him a smile and a peck on the cheek.

"Come on Trix lets go change." I say attempting to link arms with her but am stopped.

"This isn't funny bunny, you're playing with fire, and it will come bite you in the ass. You better not go and see him outside of class or I will make you regret it." Ryder says pointedly.

"I will see him if I so please Ryder. You don't own me or rule me and the more you push the more I will resist." I tell him poking a finger at him to get my point across.

He steps into my finger and growls lowly, "You don't understand how wrong you are."

"Okay that's enough let's all go cool off." Trixie says pulling me away from the brooding assholes.

We make it into the changing rooms and get changed before leaving the gym. Since we have time, we decide to stop by the coffee shop for a drink and maybe a snack.

At least I ate breakfast today thanks to Trixie. Progress.

Chapter 30
Liora

The week flies by in a rush. The closer we get to Friday the more my anxiety amped up. Before I knew it or could fake a sickness it was Friday morning, and Trixie was trying to overload me on sugar so I wouldn't be so anxious.

"Come on Li, it isn't going to be that bad plus the sooner we get it over the sooner we can go out and celebrate with drinks. On me." she says cheerfully like it will help.

"Okay okay. You're right the sooner it's over the better. But I'm going to need a pick-me-up." I tell her grabbing an energy drink.

Since it's Friday and a challenge day it's our only class of the day. To let students prepare and go to the medical building if needed to be healed by healers.

We're already in our work out clothes for class so that we don't have to worry about changing or not getting the chance. Trix flirted with an upperclassman to get the scoop on how the challenge is going to work so we could be somewhat prepared.

She didn't get much out of them other than the challenges are never the exact same so people can't become accustomed to them and that the Professors can be sadistic.

Apparently sometimes they wouldn't even let them change and they had to go through the challenge in whatever they showed up in as a way to make you prepare better.

Which I mean makes sense because if you're ever in a battle you won't have time to change into easier clothes to move in. It really is a smart way to always make sure you can move in whatever you're wearing.

On our way to the gym, we of course run into the 3 stooges who just happened to be waiting for their group partner. Let's be honest that wasn't why they are probably waiting but whatever.

They're like a bad smell that just follows you around. Ugh I roll my eyes and walk past them trying to ignore them. Drinking my energy drink as I continue on towards the gym.

It doesn't take long before one of the stooges speaks up finally and attempts a conversation.

"So, sugar, how is your morning going?" Jasper attempts.

"Wow these flying bugs are really starting to bug me." I say to Trixie.

She barely covers a laugh as she lets out a cough. I hear a growl behind me and something that sounds like "fuck this." I wonder who said it and what it could mean. I find out shortly after I think that because as we make it to the gym doors, I'm suddenly stuck to it.

What the hell?

I start struggling and trying to dislodge myself from the door but it's like gravity has me suction cupped to the door. I stop struggling to see Jasper shove Trixie through the other door and away from me.

Looking down at my body I see.... Is that fucking handcuffs?

What the hell?

Who the hell handcuffed me to the door?

Looking at the 3 stooges, I see varying expressions in their eyes, but they all have a smirk on their faces. Ryder is smirking and his eyes show mirth, Jasper may be smirking, but he looks like a kicked puppy, and Malrik has a smirk, but his eyes are clouded in anger? Worry? I can't really pinpoint one or the other.

I glare at them but do my best to not talk because I have a feeling me pretty much pretending that they aren't there and ignoring them when they talk is what got me in this predicament.

Who has the power to do this?

I know Malrik is a dragon although I don't remember what kind but Jasper and Ryder, I'm not sure. Maybe Jasper? No, I think he is too sweet to do this especially since he looks worried. Ryder? He would be my best guess. He would be kinky fucker to like this.

"So, bunny, are you ready to talk to us or keep ignoring us?" Ryder asks.

I don't say anything and just stare past him like he's not even here when I spot Aurelius coming up to the doors. When they see my smile, the guys look at each other before looking behind them where low and behold Aurelius is.

"Well, hey Li, how's it going?" he asks, ignoring the guys.

"Oh, you know just hanging around." I reply to him then giggle at my own little joke.

"Cool. Cool well I will see you in there. Don't hang around too long or you'll miss the beginning." he says before giving me a wink that I know the guys don't miss.

"Really that guy makes you smile with something as corny as a wink to you?" Malrik growls.

I just ignore them and look around for someone to help because now this is getting annoying. I think that may be Ryder's breaking point because I feel the cuffs tighten, not enough to hurt just enough to make me drop my drink and gasp out loud.

"Alright bunny enough with the games you need to stop ignoring us and stop with the stupid attempts at making us jealous. Keep it up and I will punish you for your bratty attitude." Ryder says lowering his voice so only me and the guys can hear him.

"No! I will do as I please for once in my life no one will tell me what I can and can't do." I finally reply.

"You can't ignore the way your body reacts to us bunny. I can see it and so can they. You are the only one who doesn't. Now be good and don't get hurt today, okay?" he says.

When I don't answer at first purely out of pure stubbornness, he tightens the cuffs enough to make me let out a soft moan of surprise before I let out a reluctant okay.

He lets me go but not before he has the dirtiest fucking smirk because I know he heard it. Dammit he really didn't need any more ammo to hold over me. What the hell body? Normally being constricted would make me panic but with him I'm fine?

I just dart around them and into the gym straight over to Trixie. I need to be away from the guys for a second to get my head on right. Oh, shit it's almost time for the challenge.

"Hey girl everything okay?" she asks when I make it to her.

"Um yeah, no, yes everything's fine. They were just upset that I have been ignoring them." I tell her with a smile.

"Lol it looked a lot kinkier than that. Maybe you shou-" she gets cut off by the professors clapping.

"Alright everyone find your groups and get ready as we are about to begin the first challenge of the year." Professor Latman states.

I say bye to Trixie and head over to where Aurelius is standing with a smile. I reach him just as Lilthe stomps over and huffs while crossing her arms.

"Ugh this is all so stupid." she grumbles.

"Let's hope we can do well with Debbie Downer on our team." Aurelius stage whispers to me.

I giggle at him. I can see us being such great friends. It's like he just knows how to lift my spirits up when I'm down. I can feel them staring at me again and I don't get it, what is their problem with their insane hold over my head?

"Alright before y'all head through we need y'all to listen closely. You may not use magic to get through the obstacles. The course will know and can detect the slightest use of magic and will alter itself accordingly, so you need to be vigilant and pay attention." Professor Pyran states.

"Yes, as Professor Pyran said you need to be vigilant however should someone get hurt we have the healers on standby in case anyone needs any help. The first group to make it through without any issues and abiding by all the rules will not only get to sit out the next challenge but will get to decide between 2 different kinds for everyone else to make it through. So, with that said good luck to you all and we will see you on the flip side." Professor Latman says using slang.

Even though I'm as nervous as they come, I can't help but giggle at the professors and their antics. They just have a way of making everyone relax.

Everyone starts moving towards the weird shimmery looking door and disappearing through it?

Oh hell no.

Nope. not going through there.

What if I get all torn up?

Are doorways even supposed to shimmer?

"Hey, it's all okay. I'm right here. Look we can link arms and go through together that way you aren't alone sound good?" Aurelius asks.

"U–um s–sure. B–but like we're g–going to be f–fine right?" I stutter out nervously.

"Yes, we'll be okay. I've gone through these before and haven't had any issues." he reassures me.

"Ugh of course you're scared, how pathetic. Wow I can't wait to tell everyone how completely scared and pathetic you look right now." Lilthe says sassily.

"Come on, let's get this over with before Filthe leaves us behind." he says, tugging me along through the portal after her.

Chapter 31
Liora

When we first step through it's like being transported into a beautiful galaxy of colors. Blues, greens and purples swirl all over and around.

Am I glowing?

Wow what's that sound I hear?

Before I get a good listen to it, I'm spit unceremoniously out onto the mossy floor. I don't land on my feet. Of course not. I land in a heap of patheticness and the way Lilthe is sneering down at me tells me I look as pathetic as I feel.

"Wow, you're so fucking pathetic falling into a heap on the floor to distract our teammate here. How desperate can you be?" she sneers.

"Don't listen to her, she fell too. She just recovered faster than you did so you didn't see it." Aurelius whispers to me after helping me up.

"It's ok sorry for being desperate." I say with the roll of my eyes and give him a small smile.

"Well let's go already the sooner we get this done the sooner I can get away from you." Lilith states.

I just roll my eyes and start the trek through whatever hellish place we have transported to.

It's terrifyingly beautiful here. Like the trees are so tall it looks like they rise to the sky and the grass is so plush and green you could fall asleep anywhere and possibly have the best nap of your life.

We follow the track in front of us down a steep hill. We start out slowly but because of the steepness you gradually gain speed so if you aren't careful you will fall and just roll down.

Just as I think that someone trips and lets out a shout as they start rolling. If it weren't for Aurelius' quick thinking the roly poly would've taken me down with him. By no means is this a short hill.

Looking up away from my sneakers I see the majority of the class making it down this hill all in various forms between slowly walking, to running and then there's the roly pollies rolling down to the bottom and taking out whoever doesn't get out of the way.

I don't see Trix and the guys anywhere, so they probably already made it past this part. Hopefully but a small part of me wishes someone fell and went rolling.

We're almost to the bottom when someone tries to use magic to fly themselves and their team down the mountain to bypass the struggle. Right as they make it past us a tree smacks them down onto the hill and they roll the rest of the way down landing in an unmoving lump.

"Omg. Are they okay?" I ask no one in particular.

"They'll be fine. The professors will come and get them if they don't get up and finish the simulation." Aurelius reassures me.

Nodding at him we finish the trek and make it to the bottom where we stop and catch our breaths.

Fuck my legs burn.

Ugh how many more obstacles do we have to make it past?

We don't stay there for long just enough to catch our breath before we start on to the next obstacle. It doesn't take too long walking down the path to come across the next one.

It looks like something you would see on an elementary playground or on an epic fails tv show. What the fuck. While we await our turn we watch most of the fails. There's a gate at the end that doesn't open until you complete the course.

You start on a balance beam of sorts that has stepping stools you can use to get across but if you stop on one for too long it disappears right out from under you. Then the next one you need your team to get through so at least one person on your team can either do it twice or attempt it by themselves.

Essentially you take each other's arms and swing each other around on the steps in the platform until you reach the other side. As long as no one falls you can make it without any issues.

Seems easy enough, right?

Not.

God help me. Please don't let me fall and make a fool of myself. Lilith goes first and she only slips once before making it to the other side of the first part and flips her hair like she's just that bitch.

"You go first and I'll be right behind you to catch you if you fall, ok? So, try not to worry." Aurelius says before nudging me forward.

Right as I start going, I already know this is going to be hell. You got this Li. Just breathe and keep going. Okay step, step, step, step. Shit that step isn't as close as the others. Taking a breath, I take a leap and go to faceplant off but thankfully I use the momentum to make it to the next platform where Lilthe is waiting. Aurelius joins not even a second later.

"Alright I think y'all should do this next part together and I will do it solo." he suggests.

"Ugh do we have to? Why can't me and you do it together and the trash do it on her own?" Lilthe complains.

"I'm bigger than both of you and could drag my weight down. Plus, you two are about the same build. You are just a little bit taller than Liora so it should work out well." he explains.

"Come on if we do it fast it will be over before you know it and then we don't have to touch again." I tell her hoping to get going sooner rather than later.

"Fine whatever but if I get sick or catch anything from you, I am suing you." she says huffing.

"Fine." I reply.

Linking hands, we step up to start the partner pull. We get a good momentum going and I think we can do this until the end. I should have known she would pull something. She makes it to the last platform and when she goes to swing me, she lets go and I go flying. It doesn't take long before I land hard on the floor letting out an oomph. I'm pretty sure I heard a snap but I'm hoping it was just a tree branch or something.

"What the hell Lilthe now we are going to have to do that all over again." I shout at her.

"Oops it wasn't my fault your hands slipped. If you're gross, clammy hands hadn' t slipped you would've been fine besides the course counted it as a completion because the gates are open." she says sweetly like it will make me believe her.

"Come on you guys there shouldn't be much more to do, and we will be done and pass this challenge, ok?" he reasons.

Lilthe rolls her eyes and just stalks away through the open gate. Right as we make it past the gate the heavens open, and it just starts downpouring on us. Because that's just what I fucking need.

I hate this.

Plus shit it hurts to breathe.

Fuck small breaths Li.

I will not let on that I'm hurt Lilthe will never let me live that shit down. Plus, I don't want to be known as the weakest link even though I probably am.

I can do this.

We trek for what feels like 30 minutes but it actually only like 5 or so minutes before we come up on our next obstacle. A jungle gym of sorts.

You have to make it through the monkey bars that drop constantly. If you aren't paying attention to the pattern of movement then you have to make it up uneven stairs where you will then go down a slide.

What the actual fuck?

And this is the easy course?

Shit I haven't been on a playground in years.

It's fine.

Everything's fine.

We decide to let Aurelius go first so he can help pull us up if needed and I go last because I'm practically shoved out of the way by Lilthe since she refuses to be last but whatever.

Aurelius only slips once before making it across the monkey bars and gesturing for

Lilthe to start. When she goes, she just tries to rush through it like the first obstacle and ends up falling face first into the mud. It takes everything in me not to bust out laughing.

It's when she turns to get behind me to try again that I let out a smile before I start my turn. I watch the pattern movement and take my time while also keeping a good motion going. Swinging my body back and forth to get in the momentum.

There's a burn in my back muscles and on my right shoulder, but I power through and do my best to not let it affect me. When I make it close enough for Aurelius to pull me to his platform, I'm breathing hard and sweating a good bit. But hey at least I didn't fall.

Lilthe however is not so lucky she falls 5 times trying to cross the monkey bars. After the third time I just laugh at her because serves her right thinking she's better than me but can't even do the monkey bars.

HA.

It takes no time at all to finish this part although I have started to shiver like crazy from the rain. Wtf why hasn't it let up? People are going to get sick.

Well, I heard supes don't get sick like humans so maybe not? But me however I have a horrible immune system always have. That's due to years of malnourishment and being abused.

We jog to the next obstacle hoping it will help us warm up although all it does is cause me to chaff horribly. I should've worn leggings instead of shorts. I hate being a girl. When we make it to the next obstacle it looks like a giant wooden A.

God, please let this be the last one.

Please please let this be it.

Fuck just let me get passed this one.

My body is hurting everywhere, and it is getting harder to breathe.

That's normal right? I'm just out of shape.

Another group arrives behind us, and they all sit while they wait. Must be nice but I'm afraid if I sit down, I won't be able to get back up and I want to get past this shit.

Lilthe goes first and clears it with only a little bit of struggle which is frustrating. Then Aurelius who just stands in the water puddle on the other side. When I asked him why he said the water helps him heal which duh that makes sense since he is a siren. Lucky asshole he looks refreshed and like he could do this all again.

When it's my turn I have to psych myself up because fuck I just want to lay on the ground and not move.

Ok Li last one you got this.

Just think about taking a nice hot shower and going to bed after this shit.

Blowing out a breath I grab the first woven rope square and start my climb up. Slowly I make my way up, my foot slips on the rope a couple times but thankfully I'm able to hold on. Gritting my teeth to push through the pain because I'm determined to make it through this stupid challenge.

Getting to the top I see Lilthe checking out the guys from the other group. Rolling my eyes I balance at the top of the A and catch my breath. Looking at my red swollen looking hands, I can't help but think damn at least I finally made it.

Aurelius is still standing in the water and slowly moving his hands back and forth along the water. When I look down at him, he just sends me a thumbs up and a smile.

"You can do this Liora. Just jump and grab the rope and then swing over the water and land on the ground. But if by chance you slip, I will catch you, okay?" he calls up.

I nod my head back at him but don't make the jump just yet partly out of fear and partly out of exhaustion. Just as I go to scrounge up the courage and jump, I feel the A start to vibrate and there's this rumbling sound.

What the hell?

Everyone starts to look around to figure out the cause when all of a sudden, the A disappears out from under me and the next thing I know I am falling.

I hear screaming.

Who is screaming?

What is happening?

I open my eyes and wish I hadn't because holy fuck the ground is coming in fast and we aren't supposed to use our magic during these, not like I could anyway my magic wouldn't help me in this situation.

Oh god.

Please don't let me go splat on the ground.

"Liora!" I hear someone shout.

I attempt to put my arms out to fuck I don't know slow my fall? But all it does is make me start summersaulting in the air. I think I'm going to be sick. Please don't let me puke on my classmates, that is the last thing I need in my life.

Fuck the ground is so close now.

I try to turn my head to look at what and who is around me but all it does is make me start flipping feet, head, feet, head. I'm gonna be sick.

The ground gets closer faster and faster and right before I hit it head first I close my eyes in acceptance but then a body slams into me.

Huh?

We land in a lump, my head slamming against something hard the same time pain racks my whole body. Opening my eyes I look up and see Aurelius. Thank God it was him and not someone else but why did the A disappear?

"Hang on Liora. I'm going to pick you up and run to the end, challenge be damned so I can get you help." he says.

When I slowly nod, he leans down to scoop me up bridal style. I can't stop the small screech of pain when he picks me up and he apologizes about it.

As he is running I can't but slowly close my eyes as my head rests on his shoulder. I'm just so tired.

"WHAT THE FUCK DID YOU DO TO HER?"

"I' LL KILL YOU!"

"OH MY GOD LIORA"

I try to open my eyes to see what is going on and who is yelling. My eyes barely open and all I see are black spots before I feel everything go black. Whelp shit.

Chapter 32
Jasper

The absolute horror I felt when I watched the wooden A disappear out from under Liora. We tried to run back through the door to help but the professors stopped us stating we couldn't go back in and help since we had already crossed the finish.

"GOD DAMMIT." Malrik growls out.

"Guys she closed her eyes." Trixie says, causing all of us to snap our heads back to the screen.

It feels like we're all holding our breaths watching her fall towards the ground. Fuck atleast she will land on her legs or ass better than her head. As if my thoughts conjure up what I was thinking her head moves and it sends her flipping through the air.

She stops flipping head down, still careening towards the ground at what feels like an abnormal speed. We watch as that guy on her team crashes into her and sends them to the side in a heap. At least she's back on the floor.

"Why did that obstacle disappear like that?" Ryder asks the professors.

"We aren't sure the challenge is set to detect any use of magic and adapt to make it harder. That is probably what happened. Someone used magic and so the course adapted not realizing someone was in the middle of doing an obstacle." Professor Latman explains.

"Well, that is stupid someone should monitor it better. Someone needs to get to the bottom of who used magic, and they had better be reprimanded accordingly." I state.

"Once everyone has completed the course all of the data will be sent to us to review and go over. It will tell us whose magic was detected and what it did to adjust the course. We've never had something like that happen before during a challenge." Professor Pyran explains.

"Oh my god she's bleeding. Why is she so hurt? Him tackling her out of the air shouldn't have hurt her that bad." Trixie says on the verge of tears and watching the screen as the guy stands up with Liora and starts running past the obstacle.

"WHAT THE HELL HAPPENED?"
Malrik shouts.

Scales start rippling along his body as multiple students take a step back and give him a wide berth. We're trying to calm him down and it works slightly until Trixie comes and flicks him in the nose saying, "You need to calm down, or you will be of no use to her."

I'm pretty sure it only works because he is stunned that someone had the audacity to do that but before he can say or do anything the door ripples and through it comes Liora and that guy.

We're barreling towards her before we can even really consciously think about it. Malrik shouts, Trixie sounds like she is crying and Ryder is threatening to kill someone. Me? I just feel like I'm underwater and when she opens her eyes slightly before going limp I almost go nuclear.

"She needs the healers!" the guy shouts, ignoring us completely.

"Here lay her on the floor while we send for them," Professor Pyran states.

He lays her down and I listen carefully to hear her heart because I can't focus my eyes enough to watch her chest rise and fall.

Thump- Thump

Thump- thu

Her heart is slowing down and getting faint enough I can barely hear it and she sounds like she's wheezing in pain. Looking up at Malrik to see if he notices as well when I see him nod at me.

Fuck

"How much longer until the healers get here?" Trixie asks exasperated.

"They're swamped helping the other students who got hurt, they said it'll be 10 more minutes." another student says running back in.

She doesn't have that long. Her heart is getting fainter. Fuck.

"Jasper, you take her. You will get there the fastest. Your magic is topped up right or do you need a boost? If you're good then we will be right behind you, go get her to the healers and make one of them help her even if you have to threaten to drain someone." Ryder says.

Nodding, I slowly pick her up whispering apologizes at her hoarse wheeze when I jostle her before I start running. I use all of the magical reserves I have to run faster than I have in a while and when I slam into the medical wing, I shout eyes glowing, "SOMEBODY HELP HER NOW!"

"O-ok s-sir lay h-her down r-right here." a healer says pointing at the bed next to her.

"Her heart is growing fainter by the second. If she dies, I will drain you of all your blood." I threaten causing her to go pale and start shouting for help.

I go to follow them into a room when I'm pushed out and told I have to wait out here while they check her out. I don't get a chance to flash my fangs because the person is already back in the room, and the door is slammed in my face.

I don't know how long I stand in that hallway before I slide down the wall and wait. I'm staring at the door that healers keep rushing in and out of when I hear a stampede of feet running down the hallway. Looking up I see my brothers, Trixie and that dude that was part of their group.

Why the hell is he here?

I stand back up and go to go after him when Ryder stops me and is holding me back.

"Let me go, she's in there because of him!" I shout.

"It wasn't his fault J." Ryder says

"Bullshit! Malrik, why haven't you barbequed his ass or let Malice out?" I shout.

He looks away before looking back at me and saying, "It wasn't his fault. We didn't see everything he did his best to help and save her."

When Ryder lets go of me, I attempt to go and throw a punch his way but Trixie steps in front of me effectively stopping me.

"Come on please, she wouldn't want this. She thinks of him as just a friend, nothing more okay." she explains.

It does help with my mood a little bit but not a lot. I need her to be okay. We can't lose her.

"What have they said?" Ryder asks.

"Nothing healers keep coming and going, shouting every now and then before going back to working on whatever they are doing for her." I explain.

We stay in that hallway, Malrik paces up and down while the rest of us lean against the wall. Just as it looks like Malrik is about to barge into the room the door opens.

Slowly all of the healers file out leaving one in the room and one in the hallway with us.

"Are all of you here for the young lady?" the healer asks.

"Yes, we're her mates, what's her condition? Is she okay?" Ryder explains ignoring Trixie's gasp.

"Well, her body is past the point of exhaustion, and her magical reserves are really low. What was she doing to cause this?" he asks.

"It-it was just our first chall-challenge. I-I do-don't und-understand why sh-she's s-so h-hurt." Trixie says between sobs.

"Ah I see. Well getting some bumps and bruises is normal during the challenges especially if you aren't listening to all the rules or being careless during it." the healer pauses and that Aero guys interject, "she wasn't careless she was really cautious and was watching everything to get the timing right. It wasn't until the last obstacle that it just disappeared out from under her."

"Well a fall like that can explain her injuries. How did she fall? Did she land on her head or back?" he asks.

"I caught her before she went splat but when I tackled her out of the air, we landed on the ground hard, and she hit her head on something hard on the ground." Aero says.

"Hmm okay that makes sense, but the broken rib and clavicle don't really add up in that fall. It is possible that her body was just weak and when you tackled her out of the air, she landed like that, but the broken rib had punctured her lung." he explains.

"No, I didn't hear any snaps or breaks when we landed so it's not possible that she got those from me catching her...... wait the other obstacle.... The partner swinging one... Lilthe was her partner and right as they got to the end Lilthe let go claiming she lost her grip, but it sent Liora flying before landing hard and rolling on the hard dirt a couple of times. Could she have broken something then? But why didn't she say anything? She just got up and continued the course wincing here and there, but I just assumed it was from walking and all the courses. How could I have missed that?" Aero says looking sick.

"That would make sense and with how weak she is her magical reserves couldn't be refilled to help her heal. I noticed she isn't marked yet which would've helped as well since she would've immediately pulled on her mates reserves to help her. Additionally, her x rays show multiple old breaks that didn't heal correctly. We have her on iv and antibiotics that should help with the pain soon but because of the wound on her head we aren't sure when exactly she will wake. Best guess is once her magic feels she is safe to wake she will." the healer explains.

"Um ok that was a lot. Can we go and see her now?" I ask because I'm a little shell shocked about the info dump.

"Oh yes of course just keep the noise level down and if she wakes you need to let us know immediately." he says, stepping aside and allowing us to enter the room.

Chapter 33
Ryder

We all file into the room taking up seats or leaning against the walls around the bed. No one says anything for a while, we all just sit in a sort of stunned silence. It's Jasper who eventually breaks the silence.

"She had old breaks on her x-rays? What has she been through? Oh, sugar I'm sorry." he mumbles sullenly.

"She's had a hard life. But she is still one of the sweetest people I have ever met. None of you assholes had better make fun of or abuse any of the information you have been told because she would rather die than y'all know any of her weaknesses. I will kill you with an icicle and then toast your asses to dust before turning you into a calming bottle so anytime I'm mad I can shake your dust particles up so no one will ever find you." Trixie threatens.

Well alright then. I think.

Who would've thought someone would threaten us like that. Jasper thinks

I don't care who she is, as if I won't just bar b que her ass. Malrik says.

Oh, calm down at least someone cares about her and is willing to threaten for her sake. I say

What are we going to do?

"I just don't understand why she tried to finish the course if she was that injured." Aero says.

"Listen Aero why are–" Jasper starts but is cut off by him.

"It's Aurelius not Aero asshole and I'm here because I was on her team and am her friend." he growls out.

Tilting my head because what is he? He smells like the ocean but the fact that he isn't afraid to stand against us is odd. Plus, it's the way he is releasing some intense alpha power into the room. It's even affecting Trixie because she is trembling like she is trying to stay standing.

"That's enough asshole." Malrik says before his alpha power surges through the small room.

Fuck I hate when he uses his. It affects everyone. Their alpha signatures battle before

Malrik eventually overcomes Aurelius and keeps pushing on him. But it's when Liora lets out a whimper that it dies down immediately.

We all turn our heads to look at her, but nothing happens. We all let out a sigh before Trixie turns and glares at all of us.

"If you can't stop the dick measuring contest then you don't need to be in here before someone hurts her more than she is." she says.

I wasn't even a part of the shit between Malrik and Aurelius and I feel like I have been scolded. The balls on her are bigger than most of the guys I know.

We all just settle down and wait for her to hopefully wake soon. I'm not sure how much time has passed when a healer comes in and does another bag of fluid on her iv. I'm just observing everything so that I can help her if I ever need to.

Would marking her really help her?
I'm not sure.
We're her mates I don't see why not.
She will skin us alive and that's if she doesn't just sic Trixie on us for doing it without her consent.
I don't want to mark her yet.
What if we hid the mark from her?

Are you insane?

Jesus, are we really considering marking her without her consent? I scrub my hands down my face exasperatedly. She will kill us. She doesn't even realize we are mates yet. How hurt will she be when she finds out we knew and didn't say anything.

"How sure are you that you are really her mates? I really thought you all just said that last time to get in the room." Aurelius asks.

"Is the sky blue? Of course we are her mates." I deadpan.

"She hasn't said anything to me about it." Trixie interjects.

We don't say anything because of course she hasn't said anything to Trixie about it. She has no idea what we are to her. She still believes we are just old childhood friends.

"She doesn't know, does she?........ Oh my god. How could y'all keep something like this from her?" Trixie says starting to get hysterical.

She stands up to start pacing and mumbling to herself that I notice the purple sparks along her hands. She lets a maniacal laugh before looking at us crazily. Her hair starts lifting up and she goes to step towards us before she trips heading straight for the end of Liora's bed.

"Oh shit."

"Someone catch her."

"Aaaah."

Everyone shouts something and reaches out at once, but Aurelius is the one that catches Trixie and pulls her back into his arms. We all breathe a collective sigh of relief.

Looking back at the guys I ask, "What do y'all think we should do?"

"Fuck dude I don't know. I just want her to get better." Jasper says panicky.

"I agree with Jasper, but I can't and won't mark her. I don't even know if she is who I really want. My dragon yes, me? I don't know I still feel very confused but seeing her laying here and hearing what is wrong is gutting me deeply." Malrik replies.

Nodding at them both I know that if it comes down to it and we have to mark her we have to have a huge discussion.

Chapter 34
Ryder

I'm not sure how much time has passed but Trixie still hasn't said anything after almost lighting our asses on fire. Looking over I see her snuggled up on Aurelius and them looking at each other with dreamy looks on their faces.

What the hell?

"Oi what is wrong with you two?" Jasper asks.

They don't say anything or even acknowledge him. As I'm stepping closer to them to try and get their attention they look up. Before I can even touch Trixie to make sure, she's alright Aurelius is growling at me and barring his teeth like he is guarding a bone.

Step away from him.
What? Why?
You're too close to his mate.
Mate? Are you sure?

Yes, and he will attack if you get any closer.

Putting my hands up placatingly before slowly backing away from them. It's not until I'm back against the wall does he look less aggressive towards us.

"Stop it!" Trixie smacks his chest.

"They're Liora's mates! We like Liora remember so don't cause any issues while we're in here please." she asks him.

"Fine but only for yours and Liora's sake." he agrees.

"Whew, great, glad that's outta the way. So cool y'all are mates? Well at least now we don't have to worry about you or your relationship with our mate anymore. Well, somewhat we still aren't going to like you around her because you make her smile a lot." Jasper says while rubbing the back of his neck sheepishly.

"I can't believe she doesn't know y'all are mates." Trixie says.

"Yea well she's a little ignorant when it comes to our world okay so lay off." I bite out.

"Someone has to tell her. She is going to be so hurt if she ever finds out everyone knew, and she was left out of the loop. I should tell her, right? She's my best friend; I don't want to lose her." Trixie rambles to Aurelius but it's when she mentions telling Liora that I snap.

"Under no circumstances will you tell Liora anything about the mate bond do you understand? Friend or not we will dispose of you if we find out." I threaten letting some of the metal nearby start vibrating to show how serious I am.

Trixie nods quickly while she mumbles something about stupid males. I glare at her but all she does is looks away. I can't be too mad because if the shoes were on the other fit, I would be pissed too.

"Can you go grab her some clothes and some of her things? I think it would help when she wakes up if some of her things are nearby. Please Trixie, it would mean a lot to us." Jasper reasons.

"Oh! Yes! Totally! I can do that. I will go to our dorm and get a bag together. If she wakes up before I'm back let me know immediately, okay? I will zap you if you don't." Trixie attempts to threaten.

Aurelius follows out the annoying witch like a lovesick puppy but at least he's gone, and we can have a moment with our mate. I look around the room at my brothers and our mate and just think about all the possibilities of what happened to Liora. What happened to you bunny?

Jasper goes to open his mouth when suddenly Liora lets out a scream that startles the hell out of us. Jasper goes to her first, shaking out of the shock first and tries to console her. It doesn't really help, she just keeps screaming and thrashing around.

A healer bursts in and chants some kind of spell to sedate her so she will calm down and Liora's last words before going silent again were, "please mom, I don't want to do it anymore it hurts."

What the hell?

My poor bunny, what happened to you for you to scream in your sleep like this? The healer leaves the room quickly and returns with the main healer in charge of Liora's care.

"So, we just gave Miss Liora a mild sedative to get her to calm down and help her continue to heal," he explains.

"But what doc?" Jasper asks.

"She had the episode when we were hoping for her to wake on her own. We can attempt to wait for her to hopefully wake on her own without any more episodes or...." he trails off looking at us.

"Or one of us can mark her right?" I ask.

"Precisely, it wouldn't be a complete bond as that involves marking and mating but even just one of y'all's mark can help her heal tremendously. With the power of each of you it would speed up the healing and keep her relaxed enough to wake up with hopefully no more episodes." he explains.

"We will discuss among ourselves and will let you know what we decide." I dismiss him.

He leaves quickly after that leaving just us left in the room.

"Are we really going to mark her without her knowing?" Jasper asks.

"I'm not marking her." Malrik says firmly.

"We get it. You won't mark her." I tell him.

"So that leaves me and you to mark her?" Jasper asks.

"Who else?" I reply snarkily.

"Jeez what crawled up your ass and died?" Jasper asks.

"Nothing or have we all forgotten our mate has endured years of abuse while we lived it up huh." I replied.

"We looked for her." Jasper replies meekly.

"But not hard enough. And what was with her reaction to saying she knew Malrik after the last time she ended up here."I say effectively shutting him up.
I look over at Malrik who refuses to meet my eyes.

"Mal?" Jasper whispers.

Malrik tries to go around Jasper and leave the room still not signing anything. I block the door but I'm no match for shifter strength and he pushes me aside. Before he can completely turn the handle of the door I melt it. Then for extra precaution I manipulate the metal on the hinges and part of the door so he can't leave.

He rounds eyes wild and looks at me accusingly.

"Undo it Ryder."

"No, not until you talk."

"Undo it."

"No"

"Yes, undo it NOW."

"NO, not until you talk. You can growl and puff your chest at me, but I'm not intimidated."

Fuck he might actually roast my ass.

Why is he being so defensive about it all?

Malrik starts mumbling to himself while pacing back and forth and letting out a snarl here and there. What is going on? Is he arguing with his dragon?

Jasper grabs my shirt and pulls me back a little bit so he can talk to me. He asks the same questions I am asking myself. I'm not sure how much longer we watch him before he turns and looks right at us eyes glowing and baring his teeth.

Is he about to roast us?
No, I don't think so
He looks like he is about to barbeque our asses
Maybe he just feels trapped because I melted the door
So, use you as a shield gotcha
This isn't a laughing matter
I'm not laughing man I will use you as a shield if he tries to barbeque us

Rolling my eyes at the shit Jasper says because what the fuck. He would use me as a shield when he can just run away fast.

"Hey man, let's all calm down. You don't want to do anything that can harm Liora right?" I placate.

When he looks over at her it's like some of the tension bleeds out of his body. But when he goes to take a step towards her, we block his way. I know he isn't happy about it because his eyes glow brighter.

"Mate, my mate." his dragon says in a gravelly voice.

"Our mate." Jasper chimes in.

"No hurt mate..... Just want to touch mate...... Smell mate." his dragon says.

He doesn't speak well but he can get his point across if he really tries to communicate.

"I will let you near her if you promise not to do anything to hurt her and absolutely no marking." I tell him.

"No hurt her... no mate her....M says no." he grumbles almost sadly.

Nodding I step aside to allow him near Liora. He leans down and takes a big sniff of her before looking almost serene.

Chapter 35
Malrik

I'm pacing and arguing with my hardheaded dragon one minute and the next moment I'm sitting passenger in my own body. I hate when he does that. Pushes me out of the driver seat so he can run the show, and I can do nothing but watch through my own eyes as he does as he pleases.

I should've just been honest and told Ryder the truth. Then I wouldn't be here in this position. It's not until my dragon turns and starts staring down the guys that I try to gain control back.

It doesn't work and I'm worried my dragon might do something when Ryder tells him Liora's in the room. That seems to snap him out of it. He tries to go towards her, and they step back in front of him causing him to growl.

Jeez he's such a meathead.

"Mate, my mate." he says gravely.

"Our mate." Jasper says unhelpfully.

"No hurt mate…… just want to touch mate…. Smell mate." my dragon says.

He's not the best communicator and sometimes he won't say anything because he is stubborn and just refuses. It used to get me into so much shit growing up.

Sometimes he will flat out ignore the guys so they can't always help either. And since neither of them is a telepath, speaking telepathically with him doesn't work.

Ryder tells him that he will let him near Liora if promises not to hurt her or mark her. I have to start yelling over the no marking because he will and there will be nothing, I can do about it once it gets started.

You can't mark her.
Mate
If you mark her I will make sure to avoid her and then you won't get to see her anymore
My mate
I don't care if she's your mate if you mark her. I'm telling you right now I will get someone to kill me.
Fine no mark mate
Thank you.

"No hurt her.... No mate her...... M says no." he grumbles back to Ryder.
NO MARKING HER EITHER I shout at him

He huffs but doesn't say anything while Ryder steps out of the way to allow him near Liora. He leans down and sniffs her. Because that isn't weird at all. Thank god she isn't awake she would be so weirded out.

She starts whimpering and that's when he reaches out to grab her hand. When our hands touch, I'm momentarily pulled into her mind. What the hell? She's a telepath?

We're in a dark room and it's cold. Cold enough I can see Liora's breath when she breathes out. She's shivering and covered in bruises. What happened to her? She's holding her stomach and silently crying.

Why is she down here?

Who did this to her?

How old is she here?

She looks around before whispering "I don't want to live anymore. I miss my friends. Daddy I'm sorry."

That's the last thing she says before slumping over and closing her eyes. Is she asleep?

I'm yanked back out of her mind and shoved back in my own roughly,so rough that it is jarring. I'm back in the driver seat so at least there's that. I fell onto the floor when I was shoved out. What was that? God please let that be a bad dream and not some twisted memory.

"Yo Mal are you ok?" Ryder asks, helping me up and onto one of the chairs nearby.

"Yea I think so. The weirdest thing just happened. I was pulled into Liora's mind and then roughly shoved back out when she slumped over." I reply.

"Hmm I wonder what happen-" Jasper is cut off by a long beep.

"What the fuck?" I exclaim.

"Her heart monitor, it,s just a long line now." Ryder says.

"Guys I can't hear her heartbeat anymore." Jasper whispers.

Chapter 36
Ryder

Before we can say anything, healers rush in all shouting over one another. I can barely make out what they're saying. I think I hear heart, charm, chant, and spell maybe?

Fuck it is so hectic in here now.

There's a commotion by the door and when I look over, I see it's Liora's witch friend Trixie and Aurelius. There's a bag by their feet that must be Liora's. Trixie starts crying at the sight before Aurelius turns her into his chest and pulls them out of the doorway.

"Get them out of here." someone shouts before me, and the guys get herded out of the room and the door slammed in our face.

"What the hell?" I mutter.

Why did her heart stop?

"What did y'all do to her? She was fine when I left." Trixie asks accusingly.

"What makes you so sure we did anything?" Malrik asks.

"She was fine. And I come back and there are healers shouting and surrounding her and you three off to the side. So, I ask again, "What did you all do?" she says as her hair starts floating around her and I can feel the electricity buzzing.

The hairs on my arms start to stand up and I know I need to diffuse this before she goes nuclear.

"I swear we didn't do anything; we were just off to the side talking when her heart stopped okay." I say.

"Her heart stopped?" Trixie asks sadly, still floating slightly.

"Yes, and we didn't do anything." Jasper says.

"Hey, hey come here love." Aurelius says soothingly.

As soon as he touches her it's almost like an immediate clam washes over her and she breaks down in his arms. Hmmm is it the bond that does that or is it his magic?

"What did you just do to calm her magic?" Jasper asks.

"Hmm?" he hums.

"Trixie she was about to get out of control with her magic, but you just calmed it like a calm wave washing over her." I explain.

He chuckles a little which leaves me confused but I don't get to say anything else because Liora's door opens and healers start streaming out of the room before the same healer in charge of Liora's care stops in front of all of us.

"Miss Liora is stable, but her energy levels are still extremely low. We will continue to monitor her, but we are unsure of how else to help her." he explains.

"How did it get this bad? Why did her heart stop? Why isn't she getting any better?" I fire off questions.

"We are unsure of why her heart stopped. Our working theory is that she is giving up possibly. That may not be the case, but we aren't sure what else to say. We are still giving iv for hydration. That's all at the moment you all may go back in." he says before walking away.

"She wouldn't give up, I just know it." Jasper says.

"I don't know man, we don't know what all she has been through, for all we know she could." Malrik says unhelpfully.

I glare at him to shut him up. He gets the gist because he puts his hands up placatingly before sitting in one of the chairs. Fuck I don't understand why her levels are so low.

"We're going to have to mark her to help her, aren't we?" Jasper asks.

"You can't!" Trixie says.

"Listen we will if it is the only way to help her. Do you want her to die huh?" I say.

"No, I don't want her to die but marking her without her consent is horrible and not okay." she argues.

"How about you go get some coffees huh then you aren't complicit in anything." I barter.

"No, how can I trust you won't do anything else." she argues.

"How about because we aren't fucking rapists. Is that good enough for you?" Malrik snarls,

"Hey, I could really use a coffee no one wants to see how cranky I get without my caffeine." Jasper says jokingly and effectively helping lighten the mood.

"Come on love, I could use a coffee too. I'm beat." Aurelius says ushering her out the door before giving us a look as the door closes behind them.

Okay now that they are gone, we need to figure out what our next move is in regard to Liora and her getting better. We tried to let the healers work their magic, but we're stuck with our last resort..... Marking her.

Then begs the next question…. Which one of us is going to mark her without her permission?

Malrik refuses plus his surly bastard of a dragon would probably want something big so he's out of the question. Jasper is the one who will have to bite her and use some of his blood magic and mix their blood together to seal the mark onto her. Then there is me. It's just a quick spell and I basically brand her with a metal mark but I'm ok if mine isn't always seen. Oh, who am I kidding I would love to mark my bunny first.

"Ok we are really marking her." Jasper says.

"One of you two fucks is doing it." Malrik states.

"Oh man she is going to be so mad at us." Jasper says worriedly.

"She'll get over it, we're doing it to help her." I state firmly.

"You're right….. So, I guess I can do it. I just have to bite her and mix our blood before chanting a spell." Jasper says, looking at me.

"No, I will do it. Bunny can be mad at me all she wants. Plus, all she has to do is give you sad eyes and you will fold. I can hold out." I explain.

"I wouldn't fold that fast." Jasper tries to argue.

"Yes, you would." Malrik and I say at the same time.

"Whatever assholes." Jasper says, rolling his eyes.

"You had better do it quickly before the witch and her tag a long get back." Malrik says.

"Yeah, yeah leave me alone." I grumble.

Now where should I mark her? It has to be somewhere she doesn't look at very often.

Boob.... No.

Thigh?... no.

Back?....... no.

Hmmm..... Oh, I know.

I get the guys to help me sit her up and move her hair out of my way so I can put my mark. Chanting a spell, I watch the grey and green smoke flutter around before becoming a symbol. Lastly to seal my mark I press a soft kiss to the back of her neck.

Once done I step back to take a look at it. It's amazing. It looks like our initials intertwined with what looks like a grey and green smoky swirl around it. Now to hopefully not let it fade off of her skin completely so that I always have a way to check on her if needed.

We gently lay her down and wait and hope this helps her.

Chapter 37
Jasper

Before we can do or say anything Trixie comes back in. I'm pretty sure she knows something went down because she just stares at us. I do feel a little bit bad, but it was the only way to help her.

Ryder slowly sits down looking exhausted. Is it that draining power sharing? Or is it that her levels really were that low. How does her magic work so we know how to help her.

Hey, are you ok?
Hmm yeah, fine, just sleepy now.
See this is why I didn't want to mark her.
Oh, shut up it's probably only this bad because of how low her levels are.
Yea well let's hope this helps
.....

So, like how does it feel to have marked her?

Good I can feel how low her levels are and she's weak enough that her magic didn't latch onto mine until I pushed some of my energy into her.

She's greedy just like Lilthe? I knew it.

No dumbass if you would listen to everything, I said her levels are just that low and even though I'm powerful it's taking a lot out of me.

Doze off man and get some sleep.

No, I don't want to miss her waking up.

You won't, I'll wake you at the slightest finger twitch, ok?

Promise?

He asks but is already dozing off before I can really reply. Ah poor dude. I wasn't kidding the slightest movement, and I will be shaking him awake. Now it's just a waiting game at this point.

We settle into our spots and bask in the silence. It doesn't last long because of course not why would it?

"Did y'all actually mark her while she is asleep?" Trixie asks, sounding hurt for her friend.

Malrik and I exchange looks unsure of if we should tell her the truth because she could blab to Liora and we can't have that.

"And what if we did huh what are you going to do about it?" Malrik asks, smirking at her.

Jeez does he always have to be such a dick.

"She deserves to know." she says.

"And when WE decide to tell her WE will but NO one and I mean NO one will take that decision from us. WE are her mates so no you WILL NOT utter a word to her, or I will find a spell to permanently shut you up and cause you to dive into madness." Malrik growls eyes glowing gold.

I think he makes his point because Trixie actually looks scared of him and what he might do but doesn't bring it up again.

"You don't have to be such a dick about it Malrik, she's just worried about her friend." Aurelius says glaring at Malrik.

"Her friend or not, she is our mate. We don't tell you how to manage your mate, don't tell us how to do ours." Malrik bites back.

They both back off slightly and just sit to the side with Trixie on his lap. She sniffles slightly and he rubs her back. About 10 or so minutes later Trixie droops over and falls asleep surrounded by the heat of her mate.

Malrik leans back against the wall and falls asleep or at least looks to be asleep shortly after them. It's been about 30 minutes since I have just stared at her heart monitor, and I notice her finger twitch.

Sitting up I stare switching between her fingers and her face. Just when I relax back into my chair thinking I imagined it, it happens again. I rub my eyes and watch. I need to be sure before I sound the alarm.

When she mumbles I start smacking Ryder's arm to wake him up and just as he wakes up her eyelashes flutter.

Chapter 38
Liora

Where am I?
Why is it so dark?
What happened?
I'm so tired..

Mom tossed me into the dark basement after punishing me. Although being stuck in this cold basement is more of a punishment because in her own words "Sluts don't deserve nice things." so the barely there thin as hell mattress with sharp springs and stuffed poking through is my bed here.

I haven't even been allowed to go to the school here. I went the first week but the moment it seemed like I was making friends I was banished here and told I didn't deserve to go to school if I was going to whore myself out.

Not that I was doing anything like that but all it took was moms boytoy saying he saw me walking with a boy and that's it I was immediately flagged as whoring myself out.

Oh, and the guy he saw me with lived a couple houses down and we just happened to walk the same path. But did it matter when I tried to say that? No, because me.... Her daughter..... Is worthless and a liar in her eyes.

I'm not sure how long I sit down here before her boy-toy pays me a visit. I know mom isn't here at the moment because I heard the car leave. Dread coils in my stomach. He's carrying a bottle of water.

Is it for me?

Is he just toying with me?

Is it poisoned?

What's his end game?

"Hey sweetie you look thirsty, want some water?" he asks

I don't react or move. The first slap is a surprise.

"What do you think you are too good for the water I so graciously brought down to you?" he snarls.

"N-no s-sir. I'm-m s-sor-ry." I stutter out.

"Much better. Now let's try this again. Want some water?" he asks semi nicely.

"Yes s-sir t-th-hank y-you." I stutter my reply.

"Good girl." he says, giving me the water.

I take a sip unsure if this is all a trick. When he doesn't do anything, I continue drinking until half of it is gone. Putting the lid back on and setting it aside I go to say thank you again when I see how close he is to me.

"Ok since I gave you a treat it's your turn to give me a treat. Lay down." he says, pushing me down.

I try to resist it but a quick punch in the face and I lose consciousness. I wake up as he is groping my chest. I start fighting and trying to kick him off but he is stronger than me. He starts trying to take my pants off as I am crying and begging him to stop.

The basement door opens and my mom rushes down shrieking in outrage at both of us. I thought she was there to save me, but I should've known better because all it takes is him telling a lie.

"I'm sorry sweetie, I just brought her a water, trying to be nice and she came onto me." he says.

That's all it takes for my own mother to turn against me and start her assault.

"YOU LITTLE WHORE!" she shouts as she starts punching and smacking me. She also yanks on me hair and rips part of my shirt. Just when I think she is done she deals her final blow.

"I should've aborted you." she says before kicking me hard enough in my stomach to leave me gasping for air.

After that she leaves me and walks out of the basement with her boytoy where I'm sure they're going to go and fuck upstairs before drinking until they pass out. How long will she forget about me down here?

Slowly but surely, I manage to get into a sitting position silently crying at how bad the pain is. It is so cold down here. I can literally see my breath puff out with each breath.

It feels like there's another presence down here with me. Is it my dad finally taking me to be with him? It doesn't feel so cold anymore. I don't know if that is a good thing or a bad thing.

"I don't want to live anymore... I miss my friends.... Daddy I'm sorry." I whisper into the silence.

I'm sorry I wasn't stronger is my last thought before it goes dark

Ugh my body feels like there's a million pounds sitting on it. What the hell happened to me?

Am I safe?

Come on Li wake up.

I try to move my fingers but nothing.

Taking stock of everything around me I use my telepathic abilities to search for a mind around me and notice how easy it is to latch on.

Um Hi?

Hello? Are you awake?

I don't get an answer which means they're probably sleeping. I wonder who it is.

Okay Li time to use all your strength and wake the fuck up.

I try really hard to move my finger and I think it twitches because I feel pins and needles all up my arm.

Ugh I hate that feeling, it's like when part of your body falls asleep.

Pushing through the sensation I keep trying until I know it moves again.

I can somewhat hear some noises around me so I can't be alone I don't think.

The longer I am pushing to wake up the more sounds I can hear. There's an annoying beeping sound, what sounds like people breathing, and I swear what sounds like a smack.

But every time I try to open my eyes nothing happens.

Reaching into the same mind again I try to communicate with whoever it is.

Hello?
Oh, thank god bunny.
Bunny?
Yes bunny, Liora those are your names.

The only person that has ever called me bunny is Ryder. But there's no one I linked to Ryder's mind, right?

I had better be the only one calling you bunny.
Ryder?
The one and only bunny.

What happened?
Why am I linked to your mind?
And why do I feel like I'm getting stronger?

He doesn't say anything back at first, but I felt a trickle of unease from him. Oh god am I missing a limb? Do I look weird?

Open your eyes bunny.
I can't.
Yes, you can.
No, I can't, I'm not strong enough.
Yes, you can
If you don't wake up, I'm going to let Malrik burn all your books.
You wouldn't dare.
Try me.

He had better not have touched any of my books! Why the hell are they even in my dorm room? He wouldn't let Malrik do that right? Thinking back on when we were all kids if I was being stubborn on something either Malrik or Ryder would fuck with something.

It's that thought that has me using all the strength I have to open my eyes. I can't stop the very unladylike groan that escapes my mouth, however.

Chapter 39
Liora

The first thing I notice when I open my eyes is how fucking bright this place is. Jeez, groaning I close my eyes again when I hear the voices clearer around me. I think I hear Trixie, Aurelius, Ryder, Jasper and is that Malrik?

"Come on Sugar let us see those pretty eyes of yours." Jasper says.

Ugh he sounds so sweet. But I'm still mad at them. Opening my eyes slowly it's still bright as fuck so I squint and try to talk but my throat is so sore.

"Turn the damn lights low, it's too bright in here for her." Malrik growls out.

Hmm Malrik coming to my rescue to help is odd. I thought he hated me. Once the lights are dimmer it's easier to open my eyes. I try to sit up but end up groaning from how sore everything is. What the hell?

"Hold on, let me help get the bed sitting up." Trixie says.

Slowly but surely, she helps me get into a sitting position. Ugh how long was I out? Back in the medical building again? Wow I knew I was accident prone, but this is crazy.

I don't even have to ask and there is already a straw heading towards my mouth. I gulp down some water. Sighing at how amazing it felt. God Trixie is a godsend. If I swung that way I would totally choose her as a lifelong partner.

Careful Bunny, you're ours.

Dammit my walls are still down. How is he talking back into my mind that's weird no one has been able to do that before. What happened to me and why is he in my mind.

Putting my walls up I hope this works. However, looking over at him he is smirking at me. Hmm can he still hear my thoughts and talk back to me?

Hello?
Ryder?

When I don't get a response, I know my walls are back in tack. Thank goodness. Hmm I don't like how cocky he looks or how they are in my room as well Trixie and Aurelius I understand because they're my friends, but I don't understand why the guys are here.

"Hey Sugar, how are you feeling?" Jasper asks.

Looking at him, I tilt my head and ask confused, "Who are you?"

The bewildered look on their faces almost makes me laugh, almost. I stand firm though and just look confused. Ryder narrows his eyes at me looking perplexed and trying to see for deception.

"Bunny, this isn't funny." Ryder says still looking at me with his eyes narrows.

"Bunny?... Why would you call someone bunny?.... Are you okay?..... Do you have a fascination with bunnies?" I ask him, furrowing my eyebrows.

"Wha- what? No, I don't have a fascination with bunnies, well I do with one." He splutters out incredulously.

I look away from him, still remaining in my confused exterior. Hmm this is fun and not even everything they deserve.

"Liora hey it's me Jasper." Jasper says, trying to get my attention.

"Jasper?" I ask.

"Yeah, yeah and Ryder and Malrik are here too. So are your friends Trixie and Aurelius." he explains.

"Trixie!" I say excitedly when I look over at them.

"Hey girl, don't scare me like that." she says.

"Sorry but umm I have a question." I say leaning over towards her.

"Yeah, what's up?" she asks.

"Um, who are the 3 weird guys that are staring at me?" I ask completely confused.

Aurelius can't contain his chuckles and Trixie? Trixie full on belly laughs but when there's a growling noise she attempts to sober up. She is still smiling and looks back at me and says, "You don't remember? I thought you didn't hit your head."

"Hit my head?" I ask.

"Ok that's it where's the fucking healer. He didn't say anything about possible memory loss." Malrik says getting up to stomp towards the door of my room.

"How long was I out?" I ask Trixie.

"Um about 2 days." she replies.

"What all happened to me?" I ask.

"Ummm maybe we should wait for the healer?" she replies, shooting nervous looks towards the guys.

What the hell?

What happened while I was out?

And why does she seem so nervous?

Also why does she keep looking at the guys like they're my keepers somehow?

"Why do you keep looking at them?" I ask her.

"Wh-what do you mean?" she asks, stuttering.

"You keep looking at those guys like they're my keepers or something. Why is that?" I ask more pointedly.

"Oh, they've been here waiting since you got hurt so they have been the point of contact for everything. That's all." she replies, looking away from me.

Hmm why don't I believe her? Would she really lie to me about something like this? How long should I keep the ruse that I don't know the guys up? Malrik reacting like that was funny but the look on Jasper's face makes me feel bad. Before I can stew too long on it Malrik comes rushing back in with a harried looking healer.

"Oh, hello miss I wasn't expecting you to look so alert. The growly boy over there didn't tell me much, just started dragging me along while muttering and growling." he says a little panicky.

I just stare at him because um wtf.

Why is he panicking?

Also, I have to contain my giggle at the fact that he called Malrik a growly boy. I'm totally going to start calling him that. I wonder if he would growl at me? Would I like it?

Focus Li, we can't think of him like that because he hates us.

"I'm okay, when can I leave?" I ask.

"Oh um, well we have to do a couple checks and look over you but I'm not sure we will release you today. That was quite the fall you took, and you were severely dehydrated and malnourished. So, if it's okay with you I will get started checking you over, okay?" he asks.

I nod because the faster to get this over with the better. He comes and looks at the monitor next to me before laying a hand on mine. He hums and mutters things while doing all of it checks.

His eyes do get wide at one point when he says a spell? Before a light glows around my body. It gets really creepy, and I have to resist the urge to jump away and scream.

"Hmm wonderful. Your magical reserves are almost full, and you don't seem to be so dangerously low on magic. It seems one of the gentlemen finally gave you a ma-" the healer gets cut off by Ryder.

"Made sure you were looked after and that you weren't left to wake up alone right sir?" Ryder says sending the poor healer a glare.

Um that's weird.

What the hell is going on?

I don't think the healer was going to say that and the fact that Ryder shut him up is fishy.

"Oh, um yes what the boy said. With your energy levels being better I don't see why we can't release you tomorrow after some more observation." he says heading towards the door.

"Please let me go now, I don't want to stay, I want to just go to my dorm and sleep. I will sign whatever I have to." I plead.

I will do anything to not stay here in the fucking hospital. I don't like them and would rather die than stay in one longer than absolutely necessary, since my dad died it makes my skin crawl.

I have always hated them even before he died but at least now I can definitely say it was my dad.

"Someone needs to watch you for the next 24 hours to make sure there aren't any drops or issues," he says.

"My roommate will be there so she can check on me." I plead again.

He looks over at where I point towards Trixie before saying, "fine if your roommate agrees I will allow you to be released into her care."

"I will take great care of her." Trixie says with a smile once again being my savior.

Chapter 40
Liora

I sigh in relief.

Thank god.

Thank god the healer is releasing me. I don't like hospitals. I never have, my dad died in one and then my life went to shit.

I still don't understand why the guys are here. After the shit they have pulled, why? The healer mentioned a fall, what fall?

Just as I mentally ask that question it pops back in my head. The A disappearing out from under me, Aurelius waiting in the water to help or catch me if I fell, Lilthe twirling her hair and flirting with someone from the group waiting for us to get done, me falling and desperately trying not to land on my head, Aurelius catching me and then everything going black.

Gasping because holy shit I almost died.

I could've died.

Omg.

What the hell?

Why would that happen?

Are the professors trying to kill us?

"Are you okay sugar?" Jasper asks.

I don't answer him because he could be in on it. Did it happen to him? Is it just because I'm weak?

"Li are you okay?" Trixie asks.

"Mhm I just remembered the fall is all." I reply.

"Could she have amnesia?" Ryder asks the healer.

"She did hit her head, so it is possible, but I didn't sense anything when I did my scans.... Could you tell me what your name is?" he asks.

"Liora Morgan." I reply.

"How old are you?" he asks.

"21." I reply.

"Can you tell me who is all in this room?" he asks.

"Trixie, Aurelius, Malrik, Ryder, and Jasper." I reply.

"You were faking that whole time, weren't you?" Jasper asks.

"Faking? What are you talking about?" I reply to him.

"You asked Trixie who we were." Ryder says.

"I have no idea what you are talking about. Trixie can confirm that I know you guys. Right Trix?" I ask.

"Right. She knows who you all are." she replies, sending me a smile.

Girlhood is great. Knowing that she will go along with whatever I am saying is amazing. Plus, the guys deserve this and so much more because one way or another I feel like this is their fault.

"She seems to have her memory all in check so if you will excuse me, you're free to leave once you get dressed." the healer says before leaving the room.

When the door closes the room becomes silent with no one speaking as they all just glance at each other.

"Y'all are acting like someone died jeez. You're killing the vibe." I say jokingly.

Everyone except Malrik let out nervous chuckles. Hmmm I wonder what that's about? Meh, who cares. I just wanna go home and shower. Groaning as I slide my legs over the side facing Trixie I ask if my clothes are anywhere. She smiles before putting a duffle bag on the bed next to me.

"I brought you a change of clothes from the dorm. Do you want some help to the bathroom so you can change?" she asks.

"Nah I've got it thank you though." I reply before standing up.

Woah head rush. Surprisingly I feel pretty good considering everything that has happened. I grab my bag and head to the bathroom to change.

Shutting the door behind me I can hear talking but it's all muffled enough I can't decipher what all is being said. Hmm, are they talking about me?

Getting dressed in the sweats and cropped tee I silently send another thank you to Trixie for bringing me comfy clothes. I pull my sweats up so you can't see much skin between them and my tee because while I like to walk around at home like that doesn't mean I want to walk around in front of the guys like it.

I can still hear talking so I decide to put my ear against it and see if I can hear anything. I know I could just let down my walls and listen in that way through someone's mind, but I don't like how Ryder was able to talk in my mind. That was weird. I don't think he is a telepath.

You know I wonder what the guys are actually. I know Malrik is a dragon, but I don't know what kind, and I don't know what the other 2 are. Is it rude to ask? Maybe Trixie will know.

Li. focus.

Oh, right I'm supposed to listen through the door. I can pick up snippets like she's going home and she deserves but I can't really pick up much else.

Deciding I have stalled enough I walk back out, and all conversation stops when I walk out. Hmm so they were talking about me. Frowning because what could they have been saying that they couldn't talk about in front of me?

"Why are you frowning? Are you ok? Do I need to get the healer back in here?" Jasper asks heading towards the door.

"No, I'm fine, just lost in thought." I reply, stopping him from going and getting the healer and me having to stay here.

"You ready to go?" Aurelius asks.

"Yes, I wanna go take a shower and go to bed." I reply.

"Then let's go." Trix says, looping her arm through mine.

"She can stay with us. We all share classes with her so one of us can watch her tomorrow. You can't miss any classes, but we can." Ryder says sternly.

"It's the weekend so there aren't any classes tomorrow. So no, no one has to watch me." I state

"No sweetie, you were out for 2 days. It's currently Monday so we do have classes tomorrow." she tells me softly.

What?

It's Monday?

Well, I guess that would make sense.

Damn its already Monday.

Omg I missed classes today.

The challenge was on Friday and now it's Monday.

Holy hell.

Do my professors know I wasn't just skipping class to skip? Wait, what about the guys and Trixie did they go to class today? No, they wouldn't have because they've been here all along.

How sweet of them.

Wait, will they get in trouble?

"What about you guys? Will you be in trouble for missing class today? Am I in trouble for missing? Will I get in trouble if I miss tomorrow? On second thought it's fine I can go to class tomorrow then no one has to miss class. Yeah? Yeah?" I ramble.

"Hey, hey breathe sugar. No one is in trouble or will be in trouble. The healer has let the professors know your condition and we have all gotten excused today and yes you do have to stay home tomorrow healer's orders, or you can just stay here in the medical building." Jasper replies answering all my questions.

I sigh in relief but then pause because dammit who's going to stay with me tomorrow? I will feel terrible if anyone misses class because of me.

"I don't need a babysitter." I say.

"No one is saying that." Ryder says at the same time Malrik rumbles, "Yes you do."

"You're not helping." Ryder grits out.

"You can come stay with us and the 3 of us will rotate watching you tomorrow." Jasper says.

"No, I'm going to go to my dorm." I firmly say.

"No, you are going to stay with us." Malrik grumbles.

"No."

"Yes."

"No."

"Yes."

"I said no."

"Yes, you stubborn ass woman I will throw you over my shoulder and chain you to the bed." Malrik says, raising his voice as we argue.

"Ok, ok that's enough. Liora it will be easier if you just stay at our house where it will be easier to rotate the watch. Trixie and Aurelius can even come stay too if it will make you feel better. Or you can give us your dorm key so we can rotate that way."

I don't want to give them a copy of my room key who knows what they will do with it. They could give it away or make copies and come over whenever they want. Staying with them seems like the lesser of the 2 evils but I don't like it.

"Come on Li it will be fun. We can have a slumber party at their house, and we can make them watch our movies and do skin care. Does that sound good?" Trixie says. Then leans over to whisper, "We can go through their things and move stuff around."

"Yes, I guess but I'm walking and I'm not sleeping with any of you." I state firmly.

"That's fine we have 2 extra rooms in the house, and you can always take one of our rooms and we can bunk together. So now there's no excuse bunny. You will always have someone to watch you tomorrow if you're at our house." Ryder says.

"Ooo it's going to be so much fun we can make cookies and order take out." Jasper says excitedly.

Chapter 41
Liora

When we leave the medical building, we follow the guys to their house. House is crazy I would've figured they lived in a dorm like us but noooo apparently, they live in one of the houses down the student living street.

Could I just bolt and go to my dorm? No, they would most definitely chase me, and I don't think I'm strong enough to get away.

Ugh stupid brooding men.

We make it to the guy's house, and it looks like a 2-story house that is dark blue on the outside and has a porch. Hmm I wonder if the guys sit on it and drink coffee, the thought makes me giggle.

"Are you okay? What are you giggling at?" Jasper asks.

"Oh nothing, just my own thoughts." I reply.

He nods and leaves it alone. Hmm I wonder what the inside looks like. Are they tidy or will it look like a frat house? Please don't let it smell like dirty gym socks. I don't think I could stomach it.

Walking in the door after the others and Ryder being the last one in is weird. I wasn't expecting a nice and tidy place. They have a comfy looking sectional that looks like it would be the best place for naps and a giant tv in front of them. Oooh so they have money? No, it's more likely their parents paid for it. I wonder how their parents are doing, are they okay, healthy, I miss them, their parents used to be so nice to me.

Off track Li.

Oh god everyone's staring.

Why are they staring?

"Why are you all looking at me?" I ask.

"Um probably because you stopped in the walkway and haven't moved so we are seeing if you are okay. Plus, the guys asked what we wanted for dinner." Trixie answers with a smile on her face.

"Oh, um I don't care whatever's easiest." I say looking down because I'm sure my face is flaming red.

And then it dawns on me I'm probably blocking Ryder from entering all the way in. So, I quickly move and offer an apology.

"It's okay bunny, I was enjoying the view." he says smirking.

"What view?" I ask.

He just looks at me questioningly. I know what view he was talking about but I'm self-conscious and I'm in sweatpants and just know I look like a mess. Ugh how could he be enjoying the view of me? No, there's no way he must have meant the view of everyone in the living room. Yeah, that has to be it.

"Is pizza good for everyone?" Ryder asks.

Everyone says yea and Malrik walks through a door off the side of the living room area with his phone in his hand. I'm assuming he is going to go order it. I wonder what the kitchen looks like.

Shaking those thoughts away I see everyone starting to take a seat on the couch and not wanting to be the weird one out I go over and take a seat as well. I end up between Ryder and Jasper which is fine, I guess.

I see Trixie and Aurelius sitting really close and every now and then brushing their hands together. Hmmmm I wonder what's going on there? Trixie never said anything about them dating. I'll ask her tonight.

"I guess I'll bunk up with Trixie tonight in one of the spare rooms?" I say.

"Um yes sure we can show you to your rooms after we all eat." Jasper says.

I don't miss the look Trixie and Aurelius share. It's weird. Maybe she will open up once we are in the room. I'm curious and if the guys weren't here, I would totally ask.

Malrik comes back in and takes a seat on the one chair off to the side of the couch but still where you can see the tv. Jasper has the remote and quickly turns the tv on. I wonder what he is going to put on. Hopefully it isn't something dumb and boring.

Oooooo I see crunchyroll. I wonder if he would watch anime or if any of them would. I know Trixie does since we watch it at home, but would they be offended if we watched it?

"What do you want to watch sugar?" Jasper asks.

"Me? Why do I get to pick?" I ask back.

"Um well we figured since you were the hurt one you would get to pick. But if it's too much pressure one of us can instead." he replies.

"I can pick anything?" I tentatively ask.

They nod while Malrik just pretends to play on his phone. Asshole.

"Um, have you seen Fairytail?" I ask shyly.

"Ugh, it's amazing." Trixie says.

All of the guys shake their heads no.

"What is it?" Jasper asks.

"Um, it's an anime." I reply.

He clicks into Crunchyroll and goes to create an account when I pipe up that I have one we can use. He shakes his head and gets the best package, and I can't help but drop my jaw because why would he do that if they clearly don't watch anime? He just smirks at me before going to Fairytail and getting the first episode loaded up and praise Jesus. He made sure it was on English dub.

We're just listening to the opening credit song when the doorbell rings. I wonder who that is? Did one of the guys invite someone over? Omg what if it's a girl for a booty call. Would they do that with me here? The thought of it makes my chest hurt and for some reason makes me sad.

Ryder looks at me questioningly then it's like he understands what I'm feeling because he says, "It's just the pizza no one else was invited to this get together so you don't have to worry okay?"

Nodding at him I can't help but wonder how did he know what was going through my mind? Did my shields drop? I check them and it doesn't seem that I did but I don't know honestly.

Malrik comes in carrying the boxes of pizza and sets them down on the coffee table.

Mmmm it smells really good but at the same time I don't know if I should eat a lot.

"Does anyone want any drinks?" Jasper asks.

Everyone says yes and either wants a water or a soda. He nods like he's got all of it down but when he doesn't get up to go to the kitchen I quirk an eyebrow at him. He just smiles at me. Hmm I wonder what that's about but before I can ask, he just hits a button on the coffee table that I didn't even notice, and it opens what looks like a cooler with drinks.

"Rich assholes." I mutter under my breath.

I'm pretty sure they heard me however because the looks Malrik shoots me could kill. Although I'm pretty sure he would like to see me dead, so I guess the look is fitting.

"There aren't very many in here, but it is convenient when we get into a heated battle on the game console and just grab a drink. It isn't about showing off our wealth or anything." Jasper rambles out.

"It's fine, I just wasn't expecting it is all." I say.

Ryder grabs me a Dr. Pepper and hands it to me. I smile gratefully back to him. Did he remember that this was my favorite or was it just a guess?

It had to be a guess there's no way they would remember those types of things about me right?

We settle down and watch Fairytail while eating our pizza and it seems Jasper and Aurelius are interested in it. Malrik scoffed so loud when Natsu popped up and Lucy found out what he was. We ignore him because fuck him at least Natsu wouldn't be a giant douche canoe.

We're on episode 3 when I feel myself getting tired but try to stay up. I managed to eat almost 2 slices of pizza which is good and I drank like half of my soda. The next thing I know I am dozing before sleep takes me completely.

Chapter 42
Ryder

I don't think she realizes that she unconsciously allows me past her shields. I don't know if maybe it's the mate bond, our past, or the fact that I marked her to allow the power share. I can't wait until I can seal it all the way and I fuck her.

Hearing her thoughts about the fact of maybe a booty call coming was a little frustrating to say the least but at the same time she doesn't really know us and the first time she came face to face with Jasper he had just left a booty call.

She's always been a little dramatic about certain things but the way I felt a phantom ache that I know came from her at just the thought gutted me in a way I wasn't expecting.

She doesn't even know we're mates but is already feeling such things like that is a little surprising. But her not realizing why is odd. However, this is an odd situation we have found ourselves in.

Me being able to feel her phantom pain is a weird feeling and having to decipher what is my feelings and what is hers is new. I wonder if I can track her with the mark?

No, I think we have to be fully mated.

I'm lost in my thoughts but at some point, she falls asleep and ends up on my shoulder sleeping. Should I move her to a bed? No she just fell asleep she may startle if I move her.

I adjust her a little bit better to where her head is in my lap and I see Jasper move her feet into his lap while covering her up. I'll let her sleep for a little bit before I move her.

Watching this show for a little while longer because I can begrudgingly admit that it is a good show, but I won't ever tell her that. We only watch 3 more episodes when I notice everyone yawning and getting up to go to bed.

"If you show me where our room is I can wake her up." Trixie whispers.

"No, that's okay she can sleep with me." I reply.

"She isn't going to be happy about that. She will tear you to pieces." she tells me whispering.

"She can take it up with me, it's my decision." I tell her sternly.

"Whatever I guess, if you want to face her wrath that's on you." Trixie says huffing.

"Come on love, you can sleep with me." Aurelius tells her, wrapping her up in his arms. She sighs and looks at him dreamily.

I don't bother saying anything else to them. I get up and turn to pick Liora up in my arms. She sighs and snuggles into my chest, and I can't stop the soft smile that I have now.

It makes me happy to know I make her safe enough to snuggle into. She would never admit it when she is awake but her subconscious? Yea it knows I would never mean her any harm.

Leaving the living room I head to the stairs. Walking up the stairs as I head to my room. It's not much but I like it and that's all that matters. Walking over to my king size bed I lay her down thankful I hadn't made my bed earlier.

As I step away to take my clothes off and get comfy, she whimpers. It has me hurrying like my ass is on fire. I keep my underwear on since I usually sleep naked, but I don't think she would appreciate that.

Flipping the light switch before climbing in the bed with her. Just as I get settled on my back she rolls over and onto my chest.

I freeze in fear of waking her up but when her breathing stays steady, I let out an exhale of relief.

I'm absently running my hands through her hair like I used to do when we were kids when I doze off. I'm not even completely asleep when I'm pulled into her subconscious and witness something I wasn't expecting.

We're in a bleak room. No windows and just a blanket in the corner. Is this where she used to live? Please let this be a dream and not a memory. Before I can think about it too much the door opens, and a small figure is pushed before the door slams shut again.

The figure doesn't move at first but lets out a small wheezing sound. The figure moves and I see Liora's small face look out from behind her hair. Her hair is matted and is that blood in it? What the hell happened?

I try to reach out to her, but my hand passes through her. What the hell? I'm pretty sure she feels it anyway because she looks up at me before whispering, "RyRy?"

I don't get to answer because she starts sobbing and it completely guts me that she's crying. As she sobs, I can barely make out words. "No there. Never here. I miss them."

"Hey bunny it's okay I'm right here." I say trying to calm her down.

The memory twists as I'm holding her and when I look up she is a little bit older and she's not crying as bad. I'm following her from school when I listen to her talk about how much she hopes no one is home.

Why would she be like that? Doesn't her mom live at home? And what happened to her in the other memory?

Following her into a really run down house the door closes before she quietly makes her way to the kitchen. I watch her open the fridge and cupboards that are completely empty.

She fills a cup with barely clear water and sighs, "Guess this will have to do for dinner. Although I haven't eaten in a while so there's that."

"Why isn't she eating?" I say out loud without meaning to.

Her head snaps over before a look of horror crosses her face. She doesn't get the chance to confront me being there too because her mom walks in.

Her mom looks terrible and like she has aged so much. What has happened since they left?

"Why are you late whore?" her mother sneers.

"A teacher had questions about my essay." Liora replies softly.

"LIAR! You probably met up with some guy, and you don't want to tell the truth." her mom sneers before slapping her hard enough Liora's face whips to the side.

"I am telling you the truth." Liora says, speaking up.

I can do nothing but watch as her mother starts to beat her before kicking her in the head.

Liora is crying and trying her hardest not to make a sound when her mom grabs a handful of her hair and starts dragging her down some rickety steps into what looks like a basement.

She tosses Liora down the rest of them before going down and putting something around her wrists and ankles. What the actual hell are those shackles? Why would her mom do that? Why didn't she try to find us or reach out?

Before her mom leaves she sneers, "disrespectful girls get punished like the sluts they are."

Her mom leaves her in the dingy basement and shackled to the floor while she tries to wake up.

What the hell am I witnessing right now?

How did we not know how everything went wrong for her?

We should have looked harder.

I'm not sure how long we sit in the dirty basement before her eyes fly open and she looks at me.

"Ryder what are you doing here?" she asks worriedly.

"You pulled me in bunny but what is going on here? Please tell me these are just nightmares and not an old memory." I reply willingly that this to be just a dream.

The door opens above us before she cries softly and says, "I'm sorry please don't hate me RyRy."

She sounds so broken and I don't know how to help her. Because she just admitted this isn't a nightmare and there isn't anything I can do to stop this.

I'm frozen in place when I see some guy come down the stairs with a wicked smile as all get out grin. He looks crazy and like he has the worst intentions.

"Well, hello lovely. Don't you look so nice all tied up like this and completely at my mercy." he says smiling with a mouth of yellow teeth.

I'm powerless to do anything to help.

It's like I'm being held here.

I can't stop the first couple hits he delivers on her and I'm powerless to stop when he starts groping her on her chest.

When he starts ripping her clothes, she says, "Please no, no more."

I try to move and start pushing against my confines and as her shirt gets ripped all the way off, I see her body with bruises and cuts. I get shoved out of her memory and pulled into my own body again and staring at the ceiling of my room.

Chapter 43
Liora

Seeing Ryder in my nightmare was not on my bingo card. How the hell did he end up here? No one has ever accessed my dreams or mind before but somehow, he can? I don't understand it.

When the dream shifted to one of the times, I was chained in the basement I couldn't help feeling helpless that he witnessed it all and it took so much effort to shove him out, so he didn't see what happened next. I'm sure he already hates me, but I don't think I can see that on his face.

Slowly I wake up all the way and see that I'm in a room I don't recognize. Didn't I fall asleep in the living room? I guess one of the guys moved me. How nice of them. As more things become clearer around me, I notice someone lying next to me. Assuming it's Trixie I go to get out of the bed. Looking around the room, I realize there's no way this is a spare room. There are pictures of the guys and even a pc. Hmm I wonder whose room this is.

Deciding to snoop a little I open the first drawer I find and see some clothes in it. Lifting up one of the shirts and sniffing it, it smells like Ryder. Like mahogany and orange? It smells really nice, so I decide to slip it on and take off my bra and crop top.

I can change back before I leave the room in the morning, and he will never know. Lifting up and sniffing the shirt I can't help but sigh at the safe feeling it gives me, it's almost like coming home and the thought almost has tears filling my eyes.

Before they can fall a voice whispers from behind me, "Are you done snooping or would you like to look in the closet too?"

I can barely contain the yelp at one being caught but also that that isn't Trixie's voice. Rounding on him and whisper shout, "I was supposed to sleep with Trixie, why the hell am I in your room with you?"

"Because I wanted you to. I wouldn't have brought you if I didn't want to. Besides, I've missed you. Plus, it's not like we haven't slept together before anyway." he replies.

"Yea when we were like 7. And I thought y'all were my best friends back then and I had a home." I whisper.

"You always have a home with us," he replies.

"I don't have a home I look forward to anymore." I whisper sadly.

He gets up and before I can ask where he is going, he opens a drawer and pulls out something I didn't think I would ever see again.

"I haven't seen this since mom dragged me away." I say tearfully.

Wrapping my arms around it and hugging it to my chest I can't help but feel so fucking thankful to him for this.

"I've held onto it for you in case we ever found you again. It used to be your favorite and helped with nightmares." he says softly.

"Thank you RyRy." I say throwing my arms around him and starting to sob. I can't stop the tears because this has to be the best thing to happen since my mom died.

I don't think he will ever understand the level of gratitude I have towards him for this. The guys won it for me at a fair when we were kids and I was obsessed with it. I took this guy everywhere with me.. Until mom drug us away from the only home I ever knew that is.

He hugs me tight like I might run if he lets go and it's very possible because once I'm not sobbing and I realize the embarrassing position I'm in I will dart. I'm on his lap while he hugs and strokes my back soothingly.

Once I'm not crying as hard, he maneuvers us to laying down with him on his back and me on his chest. He runs his hand through my hair as I start to doze back off again. I fight it and do my best to stay awake.

"Go back to sleep, bunny you need it." he says.

"No more sleep, I don't want any more nightmares tonight." I reply groggily.

"You won't have any more. I'll be here to wake you up as soon as they start and plus, I'm just back up for your bunny." he says.

I don't reply, just snuggle closer to Ryder and attempt to wither away from embarrassment. Ryder hasn't stopped running his hands through my hair and I can't fight it anymore. Just as I'm succumbing to sleep, I hear Ryder whisper, "You're safe now bunny."

I'm not sure how long I was asleep or how much time has passed but when I completely wake up, I realize I'm alone in Ryder's bed so at least I don't have to worry about the awkward wake up with him.

Slowly sitting up in the bed I swing my legs over the side and stretch. I don't think I've slept that well in a long, long time. I won't admit that to him though because he would probably just use it as ammunition against me and no thanks.

Was he just being nice because of me getting hurt? I'm so confused about everything. At the same time if he was just an asshole then why would he hold on to this bunny all this time?

My bright blue with rainbow polka dots and floppy ear bunny which coincidentally is how I got my nickname by Ryder. Smiling a little at my bunny because I can't help it. I observe the room in daylight.

It looks a lot cleaner than your typical boy room, dark blue with steel grey accents.

There are 3 doors that I can see so does that mean he has his own bathroom? That is awesome, I wonder if he would let me take a shower? He has the pictures I saw last night on what looks like his dresser.

Looking over at the nightstand next to the bed I see my name scribbled on a note. Hmm at least he has nice handwriting.

Good morning bunny,
If you see this when you wake up go ahead and use the shower if you want,
and feel free to go through my clothes for yourself.
I'll bring food up when it's done. It's you and me today 😊
-Ryder

Hmm don't mind if I do. Getting up I trudge towards the door to the left of the bed and open it up. I got lucky on my first try it's the bathroom. It's a decent size with a bathtub that I could dream about baths in and a shower big enough for 2 or 3. Then there is a big mirror above a vanity with a sink and a bunch of drawers.

Opening the shower door, I turn the handle and wait for the water to heat up. While that heats up I open the cupboard on the side wall I didn't even notice at first and find extra towels that are a dark blue.

Shucking my clothes off and dropping them in the corner deciding I will pick them up when I get done. Getting into the shower I can't help but sigh at how relaxing the hot water feels on my muscles. This showerhead is heavenly.

Ok Li wash yourself so that you don't enjoy this too much. We aren't sure of the guys, don't get too comfortable. Even if this is the best shower you have ever had. Shaking myself to clear my head I reach over to grab the shampoo when I notice girly shampoo and conditioner next to men's shampoo. Oh god he totally has a girlfriend. And she will totally beat my ass for not only using her products but sleeping in her man's bed.

Stupid, stupid, stupid

It would be just my luck. Where is she though? I didn't see any pictures of another girl in his room. Not my monkey, not my zoo. Well, whoever this belongs to they have great taste. It smells amazing. Like coconuts and candy.

Rinsing the shampoo out of my hair I lather in the conditioner. While I let the conditioner sit, I wash my body and ughhh this smells good too. Can I be upset at whoever this is even though I'm using their products? You know what? No, I don't care.

This body wash smells like peach, lime and coconuts. It reminds me of opening up a new bag of candy. Ugh now I want some candy. I wonder if they have any here? No, probably not. I don't remember any of them having a sweet tooth. They would indulge with me sometimes but not always.

Rinsing my body and my hair I stand there a little bit longer just relishing in the shower. I would live here if I could. Nope, get that thought out of your head.

Turning the shower off I get out and wrap the towel around myself and start drying off. Opening the bathroom door I peek into the room, seeing that it is empty I walk out and towards the other door opening it and I see the closet.

Walking into the closet I can't stop the smile when I see a solo leveling t-shirt. I knew he was a closet nerd. How mad would he be if I stole this to wear? Meh oh well.

Slipping it onto my body it falls like a dress on my body. Grabbing my towel off the floor and walking back into the bathroom I gather my clothes up so I can ask to wash them.

Opening the drawers I find a brush and decide to brush my hair and then I do a messy braid before tying it off with the hair tie I found in the drawer.

Walking back into the room I go over to the dresser and steal some of the super soft boxers in the top drawer. They feel like spandex but look like boxers. Oh well they're super comfy.

Deeming myself clean enough and ready I gather my clothes up and walk out of the door towards the stairs.

Chapter 44
Liora

Making it down the stairs I stop and listen to figure out where people are. Making my way through the living room and through a doorway that leads to a dining room. I almost give up because damn it I don't know where I'm going. Walking through another doorway I come across the kitchen and Ryder.

"Oh, hey bunny I was going to bring food up for you." He says.

"Oh, um it's okay. Can I borrow your wash, or do you have a bag I can put this in until I go to my dorm?" I say shyly.

"Here hand them over and I will go get it started. You can take a seat at the bar or in the living room and we can eat the food. It's almost done." he says, taking the clothes out of my hands before walking out of a swinging door in the kitchen.

Um ok. Taking a seat at the bar because what else should I do? I know he said I could go sit in the living room but who wants to stare at a blank screen?

As I'm sitting there, I take a look around the massive kitchen. It looks like a chef's dream. While I can cook some things to stay alive, I don't know what half of the things I see in here are used for. Maybe they're just decoration? No, that doesn't make sense.

Whatever it's not like it's my kitchen anyway. Ugh I need an energy drink, I wonder if the guys have any? Should I look? No, what if they get mad and accuse me of stealing? On second thought I will wait for Ryder to return and just ask for a drink. Yeah, yeah that's what I'll do and even if it is just a water at least it's something.

When Ryder comes back in its then that I realize he is shirtless with a pair of sweats hung low on his hips and can I just say HOLY SHIT he is one fine looking man. And all those yummy looking tattoos and let's not forget about those muscles. Ugh the unholy things I want to do to that man.

He smirks when he notices me staring at him like a starving dog. Shake out of it Li, you're acting like he is the last man on earth. Maybe I just need to get laid. Yeah, that has to be it.

Shaking myself out of my own thoughts I notice Ryder has a thunderous expression. I wonder why?

"Hey, are you okay?" I ask.

"Just great." he grits out.

"Are you sure?" I ask again.

"I'm fine." he grits out.

"Ok I can see that you're pissed and obviously don't want to tell the truth so I'm just going to go. You can send my stuff to my dorm when it's done or burn it, it doesn't matter. And let me know how much I owe you for the soap I used in your shower." I tell him before sliding off the stool and heading towards the front door.

I hear him sigh like he is frustrated but I don't stop or turn around he catches me and pins me against the wall. Looking up into his heated eyes I can't figure out what he is feeling.

"What?" I growl.

"Ugh must you be so infuriating?" he says exasperatedly.

"How is this my fault? You're the one who got mad. I'm sorry I borrowed your girlfriend's soap and I'm sorry I'm an inconvenience to you and your plans." I mutter out.

"Girlfriend? I don't have a girlfriend." He says confused.

"Yea the girly shampoo, conditioner, body wash and the hairbrush I found." I say losing some of my steam.

He loses it. Just starts laughing like something is hilariously funny.

Ryder

I couldn't help but laugh at her ridiculous notion that I have a girlfriend just because there are girl things in my shower. I bought them shortly after I found out she was here at Rosepin. That way if she ever needed it or needed something I would have them.

She must not have snooped too much because we even have some feminine products in the house. Our mom's raised us to never be grossed out or embarrass someone because of it.

When she goes to turn away and storm off again, I catch her and pin her against the wall again. She refuses to look up at me, and I think I hear sniffles. Ah damn it.

"Bunny, I'm not laughing at you in a bad way, I'm laughing because I bought those for you in case you ever needed it. You must not have snooped too much because there are so many feminine things I made sure were stocked for you. And eventually I will have spare girl clothes for you as well. So no, there isn't any girlfriend or any booty call girls." I explain.

She looks at me with tears flowing down her cheeks and I have to try not to panic because now I have no idea what I did to make her this upset, I was genuinely trying to make her feel better.

"Hey, hey bunny what's wrong. If you don't like something, tell me and I can change it." I tell her.

"No one has ever made an effort to make sure I have comfort things. It makes me feel wanted and I haven't had that for so long." she hiccups while sobbing.

"Oh bunny, I will always want you around, you are always safe here." I tell her cupping her cheek and wiping her tears before giving up and pulling her to my chest and hugging her until it settles down.

I'm not sure how long we stand there, me holding her and her sobbing into my shirt. When it seems like she's done crying I offer to turn on the show she was watching last night, and she can curl up on the couch and just relax for today.

When she nods and says that would be nice, I pick her up and take her over to the couch and let her settle in a spot. She picks the corner, and I hand her the remote before running upstairs to grab her bunny and one of the comfy blankets I have stashed for her.

Making it back downstairs I hand her the stuff before going to the kitchen to plate up our things and grab her one of the energy drinks out of the fridge. It's the one we always see her with; we got a bunch for her.

Taking it all into her she lights up when she sees the energy drink but then settles down again like she doesn't think it's hers. Silly girl. Handing her the drink she beams. It's the most beautiful smile and I need to find other ways to keep it on her face.

Tucking into our food I can't help but be glad that she is eating it all. I'm starting to understand why Malrik likes to make sure the people he cares about eat around him.

Chapter 45
Liora

Tucking into the food Ryder made me I can't help but look over at him. Feeding me is the way to my heart. Plus, the fact that he has extra things in the bathroom for me and there was one of my energy drinks in the fridge.

I wonder if Trixie had brought me one or if she had told them which one is my favorite? I guess it doesn't really matter because I have one in my hands right now. We're watching Fairytail while we eat and it always makes me feel super happy when I watch. Plus, the fact that Ryder is watching it with me makes it all feel so comfortable like there's no awkwardness.

Once we're done eating, he takes the plates and goes and puts them in the sink before coming back. We watch another episode before he looks over at me.

"I know we don't know each other like we used to, but I would love to change that and be friends again?" he says.

I think about it because I have missed the guys so much but also, I don't know if I can be friends with them. Not because I don't want to but because I want more than just friends from them.

"Sure, I would be okay with getting to know each other again. I mean we have already slept next to each other sooo." I trail off smiling.

"Fair point. How about 20 questions?" he says.

Nodding at him I wonder what questions he's going to ask and which ones I should ask.

"What's your favorite color?" he asks.

"Bright teal, what about you." I reply then ask.

"Steel grey. Favorite drink?"

"Dr. Pepper. What about you?"

"Big Red. favorite candy?"

"Gummy bears. You?

"I don't really eat candy, but I guess sweet tart ropes. Favorite food?"

"Tacos. You?"

"Chinese. Favorite chips?"

"Ooh Chinese is yummy. Um hot munchies. What about you?"

"Flamin hot funyuns. Favorite thing to do?"

"Read my books. You?"

"Play games. Something you have always wanted to do?"

"Go to Disneyworld. You?"

"Travel. Comfy or dressy?"

"Comfy. You?"

"Same. favorite season?"

"Fall. you?"

"Winter so it's cold. I'll be right back," he says.

He gets up and leaves the room while I go back to watching my show. I wonder if he is telling the truth about everything. Why would he lie? I wonder if we are going to get into more personal questions or keep doing the surface level questions.

I wonder what he went to do? Should I stay here on the couch? Would he get upset if I get a Dr. Pepper from the magic drink table? He comes back into the room and says, "You're welcome to get a drink or even go look in the kitchen for a snack. I promise no one will get upset."

Getting up and grabbing one out of the table I still can't help how cautious I am about the whole thing. Once I get settled back in my spot, I gather the courage to ask, "Where'd you go?"

"Oh, I just went to change out the laundry." he replies.

Nodding we go back to watching the show for a little bit. We watch another 4 episodes before he speaks up again.

"Can I put my number in your phone?" he asks.

Nodding because why not they have been nice and taken care of me through this whole ordeal. I figure the least I can do is give him my number and get his in return. Handing over my phone I watch as he puts in his number. I glance back at the show before he gives the phone back.

"Ok I put mine and Malrik's numbers in your phone since you already had Jaspers and texted myself. Anytime you need to talk no matter the time feel free to message or call me or one of the others." he explains.

Smiling and saying okay we settle back onto the couch watching Fairytail again. I'm snuggled under the blanket when my phone pings alerting me to a message.

Daemous
Hey, how are you doing?
Heard what happened but couldn't make it up to see you.

Rolling my eyes at Daemous because I still don't know how I feel about him. But at the same time, it was nice of him to check on me. I send a quick text saying I'm fine.

Ryder

Me
Bunny's phone <3

Smiling at what Ryder sent himself so he would have my number because the name is growing on me again. I love that he still calls me that, but I almost wish that he called me something more grown up or sexy. On the other hand, at least, I know he means me when he says it, and no one can take my nickname.

I haven't felt so safe in years. Come on Liora you can't get too attached. Snuggling back under the blanket we continue watching tv and before long I can feel my blinks getting longer before I fall asleep completely again. It's so weird because I didn't think I was tired.

Chapter 46
Jasper

Coming into the house to switch out with Ryder even though he didn't need to stay today he is just using the fresh mark as an excuse to stay close, before I can yell or say anything Ryder speaks into my mind.

Be quiet when you come in, she just fell asleep.

Gotcha, how was she today?

Walking into the living room to set my shit down and I see that she is laid on him again. The lucky bastard. He must notice my expression because he whispers, "You wish this was you huh.?"

"Whatever man. I'm here to switch out with you so you can go to class for the one y'all have together." I reply back softly.

"You think I'm moving now? Hell no. Trixie can tell us what happened and what we missed anyways." he replies.

"Ok well I already told my professors I wasn't coming back the rest of the day, so I guess I'll chill here." I tell him.

"Ok sure. I'm going to let her sleep for as long as she wants. She's obviously tired." he says, running his hands through her hair.

"That's fine, we can work on homework while she sleeps. She deserves some uninterrupted sleep. Do you wanna watch something else or we can play games?" I suggest.

"I'm down for games. Load up the system and hand me a controller." he says.

Grumbling about how he gets to sit and snuggle while I have to get everything set up. I can't help but flip him off when he smirks at me from the couch.

Tossing him a controller before settling back onto the couch. He helps me shift Liora so that she is between us like last night. She doesn't wake up, just snuggles back into Ryder before a slight glow takes over her and disappears.

Blinking because did I see that right? I look at Ryder to see if he saw it and he nods at my silent question before shrugging. Well okay then. Maybe it was the mate bond?

We should probably look more into the effects of the mate bond so we know what to expect. Something to think about when we have the extra time.

We load up into Call of Duty and start playing.

Malrik

Getting back to the house I can't decide if I want to groan or rage at the fact that the whole place smells of her sickly-sweet scent. My dragon loves it; he would bottle it up if he could. How am I supposed to get to know her again and make my decision of the whole mate bullshit when I can't even get a break from her or her scent?

Storming past the living room towards the stairs I can't help looking over to get a glimpse of her. She is nestled between the guys again and she appears to be sleeping so at least I don't have to worry about her talking to me.

Closing the door to my room my dragon fights for control when I go to open a window to air it out because it smells like her up here as well. It is fainter compared to the living room and I'm sure Ryder's but still.

Quickly changing I decide to head to the kitchen to cook. It always helps with the stress and maybe I'm just hungry. Yeah, that has to be it. Walking back downstairs I go to turn towards the kitchen when the doorbell rings.

Fuck who the hell could that be? Opening the door is the last person I want to see.

Chapter 47
Liora

Yelling nearby is what wakes me up, when did I fall asleep? How long have I been asleep? Sitting up when I hear a slap ring out my body is already going into panic mode in fear of my mother coming.

When nothing comes my way, I slowly peak my eyes open and see that I am by myself on the couch. You're safe Li, you're at the guy's house and your mom is dead.

Blowing out a breath I get up and head towards the yelling to try and figure out what is going on. Because why are the guys yelling and who has pissed them off enough to yell?

Coming around the small wall towards the front door I see all 3 of the guys' backs. I can't see who they are yelling at because they are so tall. Ryder notices me first and reaches a handout towards me.

Grabbing it he pulls me to him and gives me a kiss on the head. It takes everything I have not to swoon like cartoon character. That's when I hear the voice of nightmares.

"What the hell is she doing here?" Lilthe screeches.

Dread pools in my stomach. Why is she here? She doesn't like me, and I don't understand why. I haven't ever done anything to her, so I really don't understand the hate and if it really is all over Malrik of all people she needs to grow the fuck up.

"She is always welcome here, however you are not. Go away no one needs your desperateness around here." Ryder states.

"Mal baby come on, it was a little mistake. You know how my magic works. We had such a good thing together before your friends got in the way of our happiness." Lilthe pouts.

She reeks of desperation.

I notice Malrik looks uncomfortable and shaking slightly.

I wonder what happened between them?

Did she cheat?

Did he?

Would he get mad if I ask?

Probably, shaking my head to get that thought out because he would bite my head off.

"What the hell are you shaking your head at bitch?" Lilthe follower number 2 says.

"Who even are you?" Ryder growls out.

"R-Ryder you know my name we shared a special night." she stutters out.

"Mmm no. must not have been very good if I can't recall." he says rudely.

She starts crying and I do feel bad for the girl but at the same time none of them are getting the hint from the guys, so I don't feel too bad about how they're being treated.

I try to walk away but Ryder has a firm grip on me so I can't go anywhere. It almost feels like he is using me as a shield from the trio of thirsty bitches.

"Why are you even here? Are you trying to steal the guys? Oh my god, do you think they will sleep with you? You're such a filthy slut trying to get into their pants. No one wants you around for more than a bed warmer, but you'll never be worth more than that." Lilthe sneers before laughing in disgust at me.

"I'm not trying to sleep with them but even if I was it isn't any of your business to know anyway. It looks like y'all showed up uninvited and are basically harassing the guys in their own home. It's you who is desperate for dick and status from guys who want nothing to do with you." I say standing up to her.

I don't know why it gets on my nerves so bad when girls come onto the guys. Maybe it's because of my history with them or how uncomfortable they seem. I don't know but it is infuriating that they won't get the hint on what the guys have said.

"Shut up bitch you don't own them." Lilthe sneers.

"Enough Lilthe I don't know how many fucking times I have to tell you that I don't want you for it to stick but damn. You are like a fucking leech hanging around and lying to everyone that we are still together. Get it through your stupid fucking mind that I don't fucking want you. I would sooner fuck Liora than you again." Malrik growls out at her.

Damn that was harsh and I wasn't even the intended victim.

"I rejected my mate for you! How could you do this to me?" she screams before running away crying.

Her followers run after her while shooting the guy's nasty looks.

She rejected her mate?

What's a mate?

Like she rejected a friend for Malrik?

That doesn't really make sense but whatever.

"I need some space." Malrik growls out before stomping through the house.

I hear a door slam and can't hide my jump at it. Ryder and Jasper lead me back into the house and away from the passerby's looks. I want to ask them about what she said but it sounds ridiculous.

"She is a menace and needs to leave Malrik alone. She knows he won't do anything to physically hurt her and it's not okay." Jasper rants.

"Does she corner him a lot?" I ask.

"She basically stalks him and even though he isn't interested in seeing anyone else she threatens and scares everyone away. She thinks she has some stupid claim on him." Jasper says.

"Girls don't get the hint unless another girl drives it in." I tell the guys as we walk back into the living room.

The guys sit down, and I debate what to do.

Do I sit back down and hang out?

Or go ahead and go to my dorm?

I see that they had a game loaded up and I don't want to interrupt that but also don't want to overstay my welcome.

"Hey um where's my bag at?" I ask the guys when I notice them looking at me.

"Why? Are you looking for something in particular?" Jasper asks.

"Um no, just so I can head back to my dorm since I have been okay all day, and classes are almost over so Trixie will be home soon" I tell them while nervously wringing my hands together.

"You want to leave?" Jasper asks sadly.

"Well, I figured y'all would want to do your own thing and this way I'm no longer burdening anyone." I say softly.

"If we wanted you to leave already, we would have said so." Malrik's gruff voice comes from behind me.

I jump and turn around startled because I didn't hear him come in. How is he so quiet when he is so fucking big.

"Um, well are you sure?" I ask him.

"Yes, now go sit down, I'm about to make dinner." he grumbles out walking towards the kitchen.

"Come on sugar, you can have a turn too. I'll show you how to kick Ry's ass in this game." Jasper says, wrapping an arm around me and tugging me towards the couch.

Chapter 48
Liora

As we play the game, I quickly learn I absolutely suck at video games and poor Jasper has tried so hard to teach me the controls, but it isn't clicking in my head.

"Ugh fuck this game and fuck you both for trying to get me into gaming this is so stupid." I rant.

They chuckle at me. It's like they love making fun of me. That was dramatic. I need to chill.

You know what I don't even care, it's just a stupid video game anyway it's not like I play them anyway. I would rather read a book or watch tv. I wonder if there's a cozy type of game maybe?

Nah I don't have time for all of that. I'm a busy girl what with my schoolwork and juggling my crushes and finally having a friend.

The doorbell goes off again before they start the next round. Hmm I wonder who is at the door? Oh no, is it Lilthe again? Please not again she really needs to take the hint.

I don't get up to see who it is, but I do try and listen when Ryder gets up and goes to answer it. I can hear voices but can't make out what is being said or who it is.

Damn I wish I had some super hearing right about now. I'm pretty sure I pout out loud and not just in my head because it has Jasper sitting up and getting my attention.

"Hey sugar are you doing, okay?" he asks.

"Hmm? What? Oh, I'm fine just thinking and maybe being a tad dramatic about something I can't do." I reply.

"Is it about your terrible hearing?" he says cheekily.

"What? How would you know what it's about?" I question.

"You used to always get mad at us because we could hear better and could whisper to each other and you didn't know. You used to get the maddest at Malrik because he could even hear who was coming." he replies leaving back onto the couch.

"Oh, so I have always been pissed about that? That's great to hear. It is a lifetime old thing I have been upset about with cool beans." I reply to him snarkily.

"Ah come on sugar you know it's not like that. Do we need to turn your frown upside down." he says while tugging my lips up into a smile.

"Stop it, you're being ridiculous." I tell him while shoving his hands away and trying not to smile.

"Oh yea?" he questions while going to start tickling me. Immediately my body starts spasming from it and I can't help the loud laugh I let out. I'm trying to halt his movements, but he is a lot bigger and has a wider arm span than I do so it's futile.

"If you don't stop, I'm going to knee you in the balls." I attempt to threaten but all it does is make him smirk at me.

"Oh, sugar if you wanted to touch my balls all you had to do was ask," he says.

"W-what? No, that wasn't what I meant. I just meant to stop tickling me." I huff.

We start grappling on the floor. Me trying to stop his hands and him keeping me from bucking him off. Wait Li, we learned a move on how to overturn our opponent off of us.

Planting my feet on the floor I use his body as the momentum to roll and because he is more interested in tickling me, I actually manage it. We roll and I can't help but cheer in victory when we roll and I end up on top of him.

He has a look of surprise on his face before he smirks at me. Hmm I wonder why he is doing that? Well, I guess it is because I'm sitting on him, but we are clothed so I don't think he would look at me like that.

"Sugar, I need you to stop moving." he says as I stop bouncing from my victory.

Tilting my head in confusion because why would he say that? I don't think he is attracted to me, but I do feel something poking me in my thigh. At the same time though it could have just turned him on because of the motions. Yeah, that has to be it.

"Aw, are you okay?" I ask him, enjoying the way he reacted to me.

"Oh, you think you're so tough?" he taunts.

I attempt to shake my head because there's no way I'm going to win against him, but he has us flipped so fast everything is a blur. What the hell? I gasp in the sudden shock of it all. Opening my eyes back up to look at him, I notice how close we are to each other.

Wow his eyes are so pretty up close. It almost looks like there's a bit of red swirling in his eyes. How unfair his eyes are so pretty and dammit he actually smells so good as well. Does he not have any unattractive attributes? Jeez how come he is god's favorite?

I don't get to ponder on everything much longer because his eyes shift from mine down to my mouth and back up again. He slowly leans in closing, and I unconsciously lean in until our lips touch.

It starts off sweet and a little unsure like neither of us wants to pressure the other. It doesn't take long before he groans into my mouth and starts moving his mouth with mine with urgency. Almost as though he is afraid this is all a dream.

I'm thinking the same. Deepening our kiss, I open my mouth to let him in, and he explores my mouth. I don't normally like kissing another person like this but with Jasper? I can feel myself getting wet with need.

He nips my tongue with his teeth, and I can't help the moan I let out at the sharp prick I feel on my tongue. Who knew I would like a little bit of pain when kissing?

A throat clearing has us breaking apart breathlessly. Jasper rests his forehead on mine while we catch our breath and I can't help the way my cheeks flame with heat.

Oh my god.

Oh my god I just kissed Jasper!

OH MY GOD!

What the hell Liora?

You kissed Jasper but like the other 2 as well.

Fuck. Maybe mom was right when she said I was a whore.

How can I like more than one guy at a time?

What will this do to their friendship?

Nope. Nope, it's time to go home. These guys are turning me into a puddle of mush.

Jasper slowly pushes himself off of me before standing and holding a hand out to help me up. Taking his outstretched hand, I let him pull me up and stand next to him.

Looking around I see that Ryder and Malrik are looking at us with different expressions. Ryder looks like he was turned on and Malrik just looks indifferent or at least that is what he is going for.

The tent in his pants says otherwise. Looking back at Jasper I see the tent he is sporting and dayum if it doesn't make me want to rub my thighs together at the thought of being plowed into with their dicks.

Chapter 49

Jasper

Kissing Liora is like nothing I could have ever dreamed up. The feel of her lips and the way she reacted and let me in is hands down one of the best moments of my life.

Groaning into her mouth because how the fuck does she taste so sweet? It had to have been from the snacks she had earlier. I will let her have any sweets she wants as long as I can kiss the sweet taste back off of her.

I probe her with my tongue and can't help the way my eyes try to roll back at her letting me explore her mouth. I don't intend to nick her with my teeth however the moan she lets loose at it has my cock tightening to a painful size in my jeans.

I'm about to rock into her to make her make that delicious sound again when a throat clearing has us stopping. Me from frustration at the jealous asshole and her I'm sure in shock of what just happened.

I get off of her and help her up not even trying to hide my erection that she elicited from me. Malrik however is trying and failing to show his indifference at the reaction she causes.

I smirk at him and go to open my mouth to retort something when he says, "I didn't realize she would allow something like that in front of an audience. What happened to the shy girl now or was it all a show?"

My smirk drops and I can't help the anger that builds in me. Just because he isn't sure of whether or not he wants to complete the bond with her doesn't mean he can say such hurtful things.

Neither Ryder nor I get a chance to say anything because she pushes at Malrik and gets in his face.

"What the hell is your problem? Huh? No one said you had to stand there and watch." she states and damn if she doesn't look hot standing up to him.

"It's my house. And you're stinking it up with your smell and how you keep throwing yourself at them princess." Malrik snarks.

"Jasper lives here too, you overgrown lizard. Besides you were the pervert that stared and got hard. So, I don't think what you said is true." she says back sassily.

"I'm a dude, of course it gets hard when there's even a half decent girl around and panting like a bitch in heat. So don't flatter yourself princess." he says smirking.

"I AM NOT A FUCKING PRINCESS!!" she screams before lifting her hand and the open can of dr pepper flies at his face before he can stop it.

"Okay that's enough." Ryder says, trying to diffuse the situation.

No one is prepared for when she sniffles and turns running out of the house. Ah damn he made her cry. He wasn't the one that used to make her cry when we were kids. He was the one she would run to with all of her problems or when picked on her too much or Ryder and her argued.

"Dude what the fuck." I exclaim at him.

"Fuck." he sighs, shoulders drooping at the way he says it.

"You made her cry. We were trying to convince her to stay here longer with us." I say.

"Y'all kissing sent me over the edge and for whatever reason I can't help but argue and be a dick to her." he says, throwing his hands up.

"Who gives a damn who she was kissing! There was no reason for you to say those things and make her cry." Ryder says.

"Fuck I made her cry?" Malrik asks.

"Yes, you asshole. She ran from the house crying because of you." Ryder states.

"I didn't mean to make her cry. I just... Fuck I just get so conflicted around her I can't think straight." Malrik says softly.

"Yea, well if you don't fix things with our mate I'm going to kick your ass. Friendship be damned." Ryder says stalking through the house.

Malrik grumbles before heading out the back door to go for a fly. I'm assuming to clear his mind from our sweet-smelling mate and the way Ryder basically said fix it or else.

I wonder how much of what she feels can he feel? Or is it more of an echo? I know they have to be fully bonded for him to be able to pinpoint her location and anything going on in her head when her shields are down.

Walking up the steps to ask for more clarification from him on everything, I just hope he isn't in too much of a pissy mood.

Chapter 50
Liora

Fuck him. God why is he such an asshole? What did I ever do to him for him to treat me like this? Malrik was supposed to be my savior. He was the one that no matter what I could run to with any problems, and he promised to slay my bullies.

But now he is the bully, and I don't know how to change him in my mind to the new Malrik. He's nothing like he used to be. I knew I couldn't just come running to him and all would be better but the utter disdain he has for me is jarring.

Slamming into the dorm I share with Trixie I can't help but be glad she doesn't appear to be here. Running into my room and shutting the door I can't help the overwhelming sadness at the way Malrik has treated me.

I've tried not to let it get to me and for the most part he brings out the worst in me, and I can't help going toe to toe with him. However, his words hit way too close to home today and brought up memories I would rather forget than relive.

Hiding under my blankets and pillows I just want to disappear for a while. I wish I had my stuff so I could at least work on the schoolwork I have missed. Ugh stupid boys.

I slowly doze off my tears just sticking to my face but no longer streaming down my face. I'm not sure how much time has passed when Trixie gets home and knocks on my door.

"Hey, you doing, okay? I thought we were supposed to meet at the guy's house but when I got there, they said you left earlier." she asks through the door.

I don't want to answer or get up to answer her. It feels as though my body weighs a ton. I just want to go back to sleep and forget everything that happened today.

Disappear no one will care, a voice whispers in my head. They don't need you or your drama, another one says.

Knock, Knock

"Do you wanna watch an anime?" Trixie says in a singsongy voice matching the tune of do you wanna build a snowman.

I can't help the smile that graces my face or the joy at how her voice banished the voices in my head. Getting up I trudge to the door and pull it open causing a surprised Trixie to squeak as she falls in the room.

Laughing at her because what the hell? To be fair the same thing probably would've happened to me if roles were reversed. And bet your ass she would've laughed at me too.

When she gets off the floor, she gives me a mock glare before saying, "How rude I could've gotten hurt, and you laugh at me?"

"Oh, you're fine and you would have done the same if it had been me." I say rolling my eyes at her.

"That's true anyways, you didn't answer my question, are you okay?" she asks, while leading me to the kitchen.

I ponder her question trying to decipher how I'm feeling and if she would judge me for how I reacted. While I'm figuring out what to say she rummages through the cabinets pulling out the stuff to make margaritas for us.

She also orders us some tacos because that's what every sad girl night needs. I shrug and go along with it because what do I know she is my first real girlfriend in my life.

"I knew something happened because you would've told me you were coming home otherwise, and I never got a text." Trixie says handing me my drink.

"Yea well I did run out of their house in a hurry, so I didn't think to text you and let you know what was going on." I reply.

"Why did you rush out? Or is that not something you are ready to talk about?" she asks.

I don't say anything at first in confusion at my feelings towards the guys. Despite everything I still want to be around them almost like something is pulling me to be with them but that would just be straight up weird right?

"I have some news if you want me to go first?" she offers.

Nodding in relief at her because I'm still all confused about my feelings. Are they genuine feelings or just attraction because it's been so long? No, I think they are genuine because I used to always gravitate towards the guys. They are my safe place.
Were Li. Were.

Shaking my head I look back at Trixie but see her already looking at me waiting for me to pay attention. Sorry I mumble to her sheepishly hoping she isn't mad.

"Girl, it's all good. I space out a lot too when my thoughts become too much." she tells me honestly.

Breathing a sigh in relief as if I didn't know Trixie is one of the most reliable and kind people I know.

"Anyways my news is that Aurelius and I–" she starts but I cut her off.

"Are dating? I kind of figured with all the looks you two were sharing and how close you seemed." I finish for her.

She nods excitedly. I'm so happy for her. The two of them complement each other very well. They would make such cute babies. Trixie with being a smidge all over the place and Aurelius being like a steady post in a storm.

"I'm so fucking happy for you babe" I tell her getting up and wrapping my arms around her.

"Thank you. So don't be surprised if you see him around more often, okay?" she says giggling like a girl in love.

Oh, she has it bad for him. I think he will treat her well. Plus added bonus that they are both my friends. Okay I think she could help me untangle my feelings when it comes to the guys.

"Okay. I need your help. I can't figure out how I feel." I tell her honestly.

"About?" she questions.

"The guys." I reply.

"Which guys are we talking about? Malrik, Jasper, and Ryder or are we talking about Daemous and someone else?" she asks me.

"Malrik, Jasper and Ryder." I tell her.

"Ok let's start with each one. What do they make you feel?" she asks.

"They're all so different. It feels as though I yearn to be near them. They make me feel safe but conflicted. I feel warm tingles when we touch a pull to be around them, but Malrik is such an ass." I tell her.

"He's always been like that." she replies, rolling her eyes.

"But at the same time, Malrik used to be the one I could run to and count on to help me solve my problems or at least the one I could go to when I was seeking emotional comfort. Jasper used to be the one that was the best at making me laugh as long as we didn't end up fighting each other. He could always turn my cloudy days into sunny ones. Then there is Ryder, he used to be the one I argued with the most because he was a possessive overbearing asshole, but he always put me first and protected me when danger was near any of us. Ryder was the one who used to be the best to sleep next to." I reply with a smile on my face as I think about when we were kids.

"It sounds like you are attracted to all 3 of them. But what do they make you feel now as an adult?" she asks softly.

"Is it wrong to like all 3 of them?" I ask unsure.

"There isn't anything wrong with it. In the supe world it isn't uncommon for multiple men to be with one girl because there are more men than women. However, if anyone is rude or makes it seem like a big issue I will zap their asses into next year." she states.

"You're crazy." I tell her.

"The best people are. Now answer the question." she pushes.

"Um well, Jasper and I kissed today, and he elicited feelings in me I wasn't sure I was capable of feeling. Plus, the way he always tries to make everyone happy is something I need after a lifetime of sadness and pain. Then, there is Ryder and the fact that I could hear him in my head. I've never had someone do that before and I was able to fall asleep next to him as easily as I used to as kids." I trail off thinking.

"Uh huh and Malrik?" she pushes.

"He is a giant twatwaffle. I don't know what his fucking problem is with me, but he needs to choke on a dick. I didn't think Malrik would ever be the one to make me run away crying but today his words hit way too close to home. " I say after ranting.

She looks at me expectantly and I know she wants me to elaborate on the whole thing between us.

"He kept calling me a princess and basically said I was a whore for kissing Jasper like that in the living room and not taking it somewhere more private, so he didn't have to witness it." I explain starting to feel the overwhelming sadness at the thought again.

"Wow what an asshole. But you still haven't explained how you feel about Malrik now." she questions.

"He.. he makes me want to come out of my shell and not get walked all over. But so far it is just him I push back on when feeling like I'm being treated unfairly. He makes me feel strong enough to speak my mind and behave the way I used to. But the conflicting thing is even after the way he has treated me a part of me still yearns for him and his protection and his friendship again. It's very confusing and today makes me question everything I've felt or thought about." I tell her honestly.

"No, I understand that, but you are also more than okay feeling the way you do about the whole situation. Malrik definitely needs to apologize for what he said because it wasn't okay. It isn't like you have been all over every other guy in school and besides he used to do a lot worse with Lilthe in public spaces. He just needs reality check or to face his own feelings about everything." she starts.

"What do you mean used to do with Lilthe? I know they used to go out but I didn't think it was serious, serious." I say confused.

"Oh, they used to be touchy feely but more in the way of constant PDA and Lilthe constantly getting guys to flirt with her just to make Malrik mad enough to fly off the handles. And then they had a huge fight about something Lilthe had done to make him like her." she explains.

"Like a love potion?" I ask.

"Yeah, but a more serious version that she should have been charged and taken to jail for, but her daddy is rich and managed to get her off the hook by making her do community service." Trixie explains with a bite in her voice.

"WHAT???" I shout at her.

"Shhhh shhh someone is going to hear you." she says, covering my mouth.

"Smorry" I mumble out behind her hand.

She chuckles slightly and let's go of me before sitting back down in her seat. We watch tv in silence for a few just stewing over everything that was said today. I can't believe Lilthe would do something like that to my dragon. No wonder he hates me he has probably sworn off all girls thanks to her.

The way he talks and acts makes a little bit more sense but I still don't understand what I did to warrant all the hostility he shows me. Screw Lilthe for taking advantage of Malrik. I wonder what the extent of what she did was. I don't think a love potion could warrant jail, but who knows maybe she used like a strong dose or somehting I'm not sure.

Oh how I wish I had dredged through her brain that day. If I had known I most certainly would have. I open my mouth to ask her more about her and Aurelius when there's a loud knock on the door.

Chapter 51
Malrik

Walking down the corridor of Liora's dorm room with her bag of things and trying to decide how to apologize when I decide no, I'll just leave it at her door.

As I'm setting her bag down my shifter hearing picks up voices from inside her dorm. I hear Liora tell Trixie that I help her feel more comfortable to step out of her shell. That has me smiling.

My smile immediately drops when she tells her friend how she never thought I would be the one she ran from crying. Shit. I really screwed up, didn't I?

Raising my hand to knock, I stall when I hear Lilthe's name come out of Trixie's mouth. What would they be talking about her? Pressing my ear to the door to get a better vantage to listen.

Trixie tells Liora how me and Lilthe used to be together and did more than just harmless kissing in public. I let out a quiet groan at that. Liora doesn't need to know any details about any of those things.

I'm not expecting Liora's reaction when Trixie inadvertently tells her that Lilthe essentially used magic to mimic a bond with me. Well, she doesn't say those exact words just that Lilthe did something worse than a love potion and should've gone to jail. Liora's shout of anger has even me wincing and stepping away from the door.

She used to be such a firecracker and was one of the fiercest people when it comes to who she is loyal to. God forbid someone did something to upset one of the other girls or guy she was protective of then she was ready to square up.

Although we normally had to step in and fight the guy because we would never allow a guy to hurt her physically or verbally and we refused to hit girls she would take on that.

Is that why I have been so adamant about her being fake? She isn't as outspoken as she used to be and is more shy and reserved than she used to be which isn't at all what I'm used to.

Deciding I have stood outside the door long enough that I probably look like a creeper I knock loudly on the door and wait.

Trixie opens the door glaring at me.

"What do you want?" she snarls.

"Can I talk to Liora?" I ask as politely as I can.

"She's not here right now." she says acting like I couldn't hear both girls' voices inside.

"I know she's in there. I heard y'all talking." I say.

"Wow creeper. Who knew you were such a stalker." she says haughtily.

"I'm not a stalker besides you both were talking loudly. So please let me talk to her." I try again.

"She doesn't want to see or talk to you. And if you don't go away, I'm going to electrocute you with purple lightning until your dick falls off." she tells me menacingly while purple sparks adorn her hands.

"Fine, whatever. I brought her stuff and wanted to apologize." I say kicking the bag towards her and stalking away.

Making it back to the house the guys are in the kitchen eating and look up when I come in.

"Did you apologize?" Ryder asks.

"No, her guard dog tried to say she wasn't there and then said she didn't want to see me, so I just left." I explain.

"Did you even try to see her and apologize? Or did you do what you normally do and give a half assed attempt at apologizing and walking away thinking everything was okay?" Ryder snarks.

"Hey, I tried asshole." I attempt.

"Fix things with our mate." Ryder growls.

"I don't even know if I want her." I snarl back at him.

"FINE. then you can't get mad when we pursue our relationship with her and you will stop with all the harsh words, or you can leave. Don't make me get momma Rose involved." he says, stalking away.

"You wouldn't dare." I snarl at his back, but he ignores me.

"Are you really not sure about being her mate?" Jasper asks.

"I don't know man. Some things are becoming clearer in regard to her but I'm still unsure. Plus, I never want to be the reason she runs away crying. I'm supposed to be the one she runs to. So now I don't know what I want to do." I explain.

Chapter 52
Liora

When Trixie shuts the door after grabbing my bag off the floor, I can't help the delirious laugh that escapes from me. Wow, that was a terrible attempt at an apology.

"Wow he didn't try very hard at that apology, did he?" she muses.

Shaking my head at her. I can't believe he attempted to even if it was half assed. I do deserve an apology but at the same time isn't it the thought that counts?

Plus, everything makes a little bit more sense on why he has been treating me the way he has. Knowing what Lilthe did to him is horrible and no wonder he is so fucking pissed off at the opposite sex.

Ugh boys are so stupid. I'm nothing like Lilthe and if he can't see that then he doesn't deserve a second of my time. Whatever. I'm going to just relax and spend time with my bestie.

"Hey, why don't we go out Friday to celebrate you being okay and needing a break from stupid ass guys?" she suggests.

"Yea that would be fun. I've never gone out like that, but I would love to go out with you." I reply honestly.

"Ooo yes girls' night! We can dance, drink and forget about guy drama for a little while." she says, ticking what we're going to do off of her fingers.

I can't wait. I could really use a good night of relaxation with Trixie. Only a couple more days until our fun night out. Ugh I don't want to go back to classes tomorrow and see everyone.

"Alright well we should get to bed so we can get a good night's sleep before school." she says standing up and stretching.

"Yeah, you're right I am starting to get tired." I tell her.

We go our separate ways and get ready for bed. Ugh, how am I going to sleep tonight without Ryder? No. I'm a big girl who doesn't need a man to help her sleep at night.

I'm not sure how long I lay in bed scrolling through my homework and notifications on my phone before I slowly doze off.

The guy's family has taken me to the fair in town to get a break from my mom and dad's fighting and for me to have some fun before the holidays come and go. They tell the guys to keep an eye on me but make sure we have fun.

We ride so many rides. Me never getting sick but the guys however getting an upset stomach. I want to go on another ride but feel bad that the guys have kept up with me and my steel stomach for rides. So, I relent and say we can go grab some food and maybe do the other stuff.

"Ooo can we get a funnel cake?" I ask them when we get in line for food.

"I don't know you should probably eat some real food before something like that." Jasper says.

Sticking my tongue out at Jasper I turn to the one I know can't resist me or my wants especially a sweet treat want.

"Mally please, please, pretty please." I give Malrik my best puppy dog eye look, getting some tears to form.

"Yeah, Ra I'll get you some whatever you want just please don't cry." he says giving me a hug.

"Thank you Mally." I say leaning up, giving him a kiss on the cheek.

"Whatever" he says, turning away to order.

Jasper and Ryder argue over what they are going to eat and how it's unfair that Malrik always gives into me and my wants. I can't help but smile at their antics because I do know Mally gives in to me easily especially if I cry.

I'm happily munching away at my funnel cake as we walk through the stalls of games because they have decided to have a contest on who can win the most games and what favors they want in exchange.

I almost drop my funnel cake when I spot it hanging on one of the stalls. I immediately know I have to have it. It's a bright blue bunny with rainbow polka dots and floppy ears. I just know it will be the softest thing ever.

I run over and see that the game is a one of the ones where you have to slam the hammer down to hit a certain number and win.

"Well, hello pretty lady, do you want a chance to win a prize?" the carni asks.

"Yes please, I really want that bunny." I tell him.

I attempt a try at the game but barely make it to the first line on the tower. My face falls at the horrible attempt.

"Well shucks. You didn't win anything that time. However, I'll give you whichever prize you want. You can come to the back to pick out a super special prize." he tells me.

I follow because I'm not going to turn down a super special prize. Just as I'm about to disappear through the back of the stall with the carni. I'm pulled back into a pair of arms. Looking up I gasp at the sight of the guys who all look murderous. Oh no did I run off and not make sure anyone was coming with me.

"Liora you weren't supposed to run off." Ryder states in an angry voice.

"I'm sorry RyRy, I just really want that bunny." I say sadly, trying not to cry in front of them.

"It's okay to know what you want but you can't wander around without us something could happen." Jasper explains.

I nod because yea duh that makes sense.

"I didn't win when I tried so he was going to take me in the back so that I could pick a super special prize." I tell them.

"He what?!" they shout.

"Here I'll win her prize." Malrik says slamming some money in the carni guys hand,

He swings the hammer thing down and it shoots way up. He hits the bell, and it makes a loud horn noise signaling a winner. Ryder grabs my prize, and him and Jasper walk me away from the booth.

Looking back, I see Malrik say something to the carni and whatever it is makes him look like he is scared shitless. When Malrik walks away the carni shoots me a terrified look and now I'm curious on why he looks so scared.

"Happy now?" Malrik asks.

"Yes, thank you so much I'm going to cherish this forever. I really am sorry I just got distracted by the bunny." I tell him honestly.

"It's okay Ra but you can't just run off on us. We worry about you. Alright dad says it is time to go. So let's go meet them towards the front of the gates." Malrik says.

I'm skipping along next to the guys with my bunny firmly against me when I spot my mom. What is she doing here? Should I go over to her to go home with her and not the guy's parents?

"Hey, my mom is over there. "I tell them pointing at where she is.

"I don't see her bunny. Come on let's go before Mr. Rose gets worried or upset at us." Ryder says, ushering me away.

Waking up I see that the sun is starting to come up so I guess it is a good time as any to get up and get ready. I get ready and decide to go ahead and go into the kitchen and grab my drink and something to eat. When was the last time I ate?

Shit no I had breakfast at the guy's house but other than some candy and the margaritas last night I haven't eaten real food since then. Going in the freezer I grab a microwavable breakfast sandwich to cook and eat afterwards.

As the microwaves beeps Trixie comes out of her room dressed and refreshed. I wish I looked that good in the morning. I'm dressed in some cargo sweats and a cropped tee.

I just have no motivation to get cutesy today, so I opted for comfy clothes. Plus, I'm pretty sure aunt flo is about to make an appearance. It isn't always on track and stress makes it worse.

"Good morning girlie, how are you doing today?" she asks while she basically dances into the kitchen.

She prances to the fridge and grabs her drink out before starting to make herself a breakfast sandwich. Great minds think alike. I'm busy eating my sandwich when I realize she is looking at me expectantly like she is waiting for me to answer.

Oh, yea I didn't answer her question. I started thinking about why I decided to dress comfy instead of putting effort in and completely disregarded her question.

"I'm ok but I have a feeling aunt flo is coming soon." I reply to her.

"Ohh I'm sorry girl. Hopefully it doesn't hit during classes." she says.

"Fingers crossed. Come on, let's head to class." I tell her to grab my backpack from the floor.

Chapter 53
Liora

Friday comes before we know it. We rush into the dorm to get changed and ready to go out. I decide to just put on a pair of ripped jeans and a nice blouse because let's be honest, I don't have clothes like that to go out for the night.

I'm redoing my make up when Trixie comes through the bathroom into my room. She's wearing a baby pink body con style dress that glitters when she moves. She's wearing some white heels that make her look taller and her wrists have some bracelets adorning them.

"That's what you're wearing?" she asks.

"Yea? I don't have any other clothes to go out in." I tell her.

"I have the perfect thing for you. Hold on, I'll be right back." she says rushing back to her room.

She comes back in with a deep blue dress almost similar to hers, but it looks shorter and has what looks like a deep v down it.

"There is no way my fatass is going to fit in that." I tell her.

"Oh, come on, just try it on okay." she pushes.

"Fine." I saw taking the dress and walking into the bathroom to change. Slipping it on I have to adjust my boobs, so they don't pop out and flash someone. Looking in the mirror at first glance I really like the way it looks. It makes me feel powerful and that isn't something I'm used to.

But the longer I look the more flaws I find. I'm just about to say fuck it and take it off when Trixie opens the door to get a peak.

"Holy smokes. Liora, I mean this is the most respectful way you look bangable. I would totally do you. You know if we weren't such good friends and you swung this way." she says eyes raking up and down my body.

"You really think so?" I ask her.

"Yes. You have to wear this. Please. I will beg, do you want me to beg because I will. Maybe you will get lucky, and someone will take you home tonight. You deserve to have some fun and to let loose for a little while." she says.

"You're right. I do deserve this. I'm not going to change. I feel hot and powerful. Plus, I just want a night of dancing and having fun." I tell her.

"Yes girl! Here, sit down and I will straighten your hair." she says leading me to the vanity in her room.

She goes about straightening my hair and holy fuck it is long. When she's done, I can't help but admire how silky it looks. My hair looks like a pastel waterfall, and I love it.

"Thank you." I tell her honestly.

"No problem. What shoes are you going to wear?" she asks.

"I have a pair of the converse heels I think would go with this perfectly." I tell her running back to my room.

Searching through my closet I find the one pair of converse heels I own and slip them on. They're black and one of my favorite pairs of shoes to wear when I want to be taller than normal.

Heading towards the living room I decide to grab my burgundy lipstick that is called *fuck this* and swipe it on. It gives me a powerful feeling when I see myself.
I feel like a bad bitch.

This is who I wanted to be when I grew up, someone who gave no fucks about anything and anyone else. Being the shy girl hasn't worked out very well for me. I used to be the one who hit first and asked questions later and who was the most loyal person you would ever meet.

Did my mom make me change that much over the years?

Have I forgotten who I am and who I wanted to be?

Have I lost my way that much?

No starting Monday I'm not going to be the one that gets walked all over anymore. I will stand up for myself and dress and act the way I want to.

Who cares what anyone else thinks? If I'm not happy with who I am, how can I expect someone to love me the way I am?

Liora 3.0 coming in tonight.

Meeting Trixie in the living room she gapes at me. Do the shoes not go as well as I thought they did? I'm just about to ask that when her mouth opens.

"How do you manage to pull off sexy but like you're not trying too hard either? Makes me wish I had some shoes like yours." she says with a fake pout.

"Oh whatever. You know you can just buy some or we can go to town for you to get some." I tell her blushing wildly.

"You're so right. Anyways let girls' night commence." she says, striding towards the door.

We make it to the parking lot and get into an uber which I'm thankful for because now we don't have to worry about driving after a night of drinking. Although I've never been able to get drunk so we probably would have been fine.

No, getting an uber is responsible of us. And we'll just have to hope we don't end up a statistic on the evening news. Wow, Li you have got to chill with the horror movies and what you see on Paravine.

"I texted Aurelius we were going out so don't be surprised if you see him at the club. He promised he would steer clear of girls' night but will be there in case we need help." she explains on the ride there.

"Oh, that's fine. He is more than welcome to join us. I don't mind plus I know you would love to dance with him." I tell her honestly.

"Maybe later. Tonight, I just want to dance and have fun with my bestie. I can't wait to see you move your hot body and hypnotize the guys that will be there." she tells me excitedly.

"Ok if, you're sure. But just know that he is more than welcome to join our night. Plus, I may use him as a buffer if I get weirded out by one of the guys in here tonight. Y'all will be my scapegoat." I tell her.

She cackles at me before saying, "we will be your scapegoat from any weirdos anytime of the year don't be afraid to use it. I would rather that than some weirdo kidnapping you."

Getting to the club we get in line to get admittance into the club. The bouncer takes one look at us and lets us in with no fuss. Hmm, that's nice. Makes me feel like royalty that doesn't have to be carded.

Chapter 54
Liora

We have been dancing together for a while when I feel eyes on me. Discreetly trying to look around at who the culprit could be.

Is it the guys?

No, I don't want to see them.

Stop it Liora. You're supposed to be enjoying a night out. I need a drink.

"Hey, I'm going to go and get a drink." I tell Trixie.

"I'll come with you. I could use another drink." she replies.

We walk towards the bar and wait for our turn to order. The bartender that helps us is actually kind of cute. When he leans down and asks what we would like I can't help the blush that blooms from the way he is looking me up and down.

"What can I get started for you beautiful ladies?" he says with a smirk.

"Um two rum sunsets and 6 shots of watermelon schnapps please." Trixie orders without missing a beat.

"You got it gorgeous if you can get your friend to save me a dance after my shift." he says back to her.

"Deal." She tells him with a smile.

The fact that they just planned all this while I am standing here is crazy to me but at least he is really cute in a boy next door kind of way.

Getting out drinks we slam the shots back, one after another like they are juice. Then we sip on our drinks while we take a break from dancing. It is really nice to not have to worry about anything and just relax and enjoy our night out.

I swear I caught a glimpse of Malrik but there's no way, right? He doesn't seem like the kind to come to somewhere like this. The bun that I thought was his turned out to be someone else.

I finish my drink and wait for Trixie to finish hers so we can go back out and dance. She's drinking her drink while making eyes at someone behind me.

Turning I should have known when I see Aurelius smirking at her. Smiling, I wave him over to come hang with us. I don't mind him because I know he won't be an asshole. Plus, he is also my friend as well.

He joins us and gives Trixie a quick kiss
on the cheek and gives me a smile in hello. I
wonder how everything is going on between
them anyways. They seem close.

"I see y'all met my roommate Lykos,"
he says.

"Roommate? Who's Lykos?" I ask.

"Yea Lykos, he was the bartender that
helped y'all" he explains.

"Oooh, wow what a small world. He
asked Trixie to agree to me saving him a
dance." I say smiling.

"He has talked about you for a while
and even asked me if I knew you. When I said
yes, he tried to get me to talk him up to you. I
told him no, if he wanted a chance, he would
have to figure it out himself. That you would
prefer a forward and honest guy rather than
me talking him up to you. He is a really sweet
guy." he explains.

"Why hasn't he approached me
before?" I ask.

"Because he is a dumbass who doesn't
always know how to talk to pretty girls," he
says.

"I don't think I have any classes with
him so how would he know me? Unless he has
stalked me." I say questioningly.

"No, no nothing like that Liora. He saw you in the Nexus on orientation day and thought that you were cute but then when you changed your hair and he saw you in the cafeteria he wouldn't shut up about you. Then when he found out about how we had become friends and in the same class he has been asking about you daily." Aurelius tells me.

Hmm. He has been talking about me? The thought makes a smile grace my lips. He is cute. I wonder if he would be someone who is fun to be around? Would he give me tingles when we touch? I wonder what supe class he is in?

"What's up Aeru? Are you trying to take the girl I have my eyes on?" a voice says coming up behind me.

"No dumbass, meet Trixie, my ma- magical girlfriend and her roommate/ best friend Liora." Aurelius

"Liora, what a magical name. My name is Lykos and yes, I know what it means. My parents thought they were being funny when they named me that." he says smiling cheekily.

"I don't understand? Lykos it sounds nice, is it some inside family joke?" I ask.

He stares at me for a minute before smirking and his eyes lighting up in joy.

"You really are a little ignorant of our world, aren't you?" he asks.

"Um maybe? I mean I am trying to learn more about everyone, but I still don't understand a whole lot of things." I explain.

"Ugh, can you get any more adorable? You're stealing my heart candy girl, well you can ask if you want, I will tell you anything." he says putting his hand on his heart like he is swooning.

"Um, can I know why your family named you Lykos?" I ask.

He leans in close and whispers, "Lykos means werewolf in Greek. So, they thought it would be funny to name their werewolf son Lykos."

"You're a werewolf?" I ask intrigued.

How does the shift work? Does it hurt? Does he shift back naked? Does he shift back with clothes on? Can he shift whenever or only on a full moon? What color is he? Is he still in charge when shifted? Does he knot?

Oh my god Liora why would you think that? Just because we have read it in books doesn't mean it is a real thing that happens.

"Why did you get so red. I can see your mind going a mile a minute. What is your question?" he asks, smirking.

"How does the shift work for you?" I ask.

He leans in close and gets next to my ear before saying, "It would be easier to show you but I have to get naked to do it. Do you think you could handle it?"

"I can handle you, but I don't think you could handle me, big guy." I tell him before patting his chest and walking away to go dance.

I know I have a slight blush, but I couldn't help but rise to the challenge he presented plus I'm not going to be shy Liora who is scared to do things. As I'm dancing, I feel eyes on me. Looking around I can see Lykos looking at me with a smirk, so I smile in what I hope is a welcoming way for him to join me.

I almost sigh in relief when he heads this way. When he makes it to me, he spins me and has my back to his front. A slow sensual song comes on, and he puts his hands on my hopes before leading me to move my body against his.

My skin gets heated when I feel eyes glaring daggers my way. Why do I feel like I know who is looking at me without opening my eyes? Lykos leans down and whispers into my ear, "Why are we being glared at by Ryder Jackson?"

Opening my eyes I see Ryder glaring at me across the dance floor and if he could smite us with his eyes he would. Rolling my eyes at him before putting more sway into my body. Ryder's eyes narrow before he mouths let's go.

Shaking my head in response I start grinding on Lykos. Why does the thought of pissing Ryder off feel so exhilarating? My body is starting to heat from how hot it is getting on the dance floor and I'm pretty sure Lykos is getting turned on.

What the fuck do you think you're doing Liora?

Dancing. Letting loose and I don't need some overbearing asshole hanging around.

Stop grinding on him.

We're just dancing asshole. Get out of my head.

You have 2 choices: you can stop and step away from him now and he doesn't get hurt or I will tear you away and throw you over my shoulders before tying you to my bed.

You're so full of shit. I can do whatever the hell I want. You are not the boss of me Ryder Jackson.

Bunny, you don't understand the things I will do for you.

Tell him to take his fucking hands off.

Ignoring Ryder I turn in Lykos' arms and wrap my arms around his neck as he pulls me closer to him. Why am I wet just thinking of Ryder's threat? Would he really do that? Maybe I have had too much to drink.

My head feels kinda funny. How much have I drunk? Am I a lightweight? As nice as it feels in Lykos' arms I can't but picture Ryder or even one of the others.

Lykos leans down and my eyes are a little unfocused still imagining Ryder so when he kisses me, I can't help but lean into it more. Letting out a little moan that has him squeezing my ass.

Before we can take it any further, I'm ripped away in such a force that has me stumbling. Before I can fall or trip my world flips and pressure hits my stomach.

Opening my eyes up I can see that I am upside down and staring at some dudes back. From the tingles I can only assume it is Ryder who tossed me like a sack of potatoes onto his shoulder.

"Yo, what the fuck Jackson?" Lykos shouts.

Ryder leans real close to him before telling him, "If I ever catch you with your hands on my mate I will shackle you underground and let the rats have their way with you until I decide to pour acid on you to end your misery."

"Woah, I didn't know she was your mate. She didn't say anything. No need to get so hostile dude. I would never attempt to steal someone's mate I swear." Lykos says placatingly.

I try to wiggle away from Ryder when I hear him in my mind.

Keep wiggling like that and you will show everyone your ass and I will have to kill anyone who looks.

Why do you even care RyRy?

I will always care when it comes to you now stop before I spank you into submission in front of everyone here.

My body is swaying from the motion of him walking. Would he really spank me?

Would I like it? Why did he get so mad about me dancing with Lykos? What is a mate?

I slowly drift off hanging upside down on him and I'm not sure if it's from the drinks or the fact that the blood has rushed to my head but either way he doesn't seem to notice. I giggle at the way the world looks and try to make my body swing harder but the dizzy gets worse and I close my eyes.

I wake when he opens the door I was leaning on. When did I get in the car? How long was I asleep? He gets me out of the car when I push against him now that I'm a little bit more awake.

"Let me go asshole." I shout shoving him away.

All it does is make me fall because I have no stability from the drinks and my legs are sore from dancing and wearing my shoes.

"Stop being difficult and let me help you back into the house to sleep off what I'm sure is going to be a hangover in the morning." he growls.

"No, I don't need any help. I can survive just fine on my own and I don't need anyone else." I slur.

"Yes, you can but I'm going to help you tonight, okay?" he says, trying to lower his voice.

"No, I can't depend on anyone because there's never anyone there when I need help. All I have is me. There's never anyone in my corner when I need it." I say stumbling and falling again when I attempt to walk away from their house and head towards my dorm.

I'm so overwhelmed with the way I'm feeling that I can't help the tears that fill my eyes when I fall and scrape my knee. I vaguely hear fuck it before I'm picked up bridal style.

"Let me go." I say pounding on his chest and crying.

"Come on bunny just sleep here where I can know you're safe and not going to asphyxiate on your own vomit. You can leave in the morning if you still want to, okay?" he says holding me tightly to his chest while I cry.

This is so pathetic, but I'm too worked up to care at the moment. The alcohol mixed with all the thoughts running through my head are not a good combination. I can feel myself trying to slip into that dark place again.

Chapter 55
Ryder

This isn't how I pictured tonight going at all. I just wanted her to stop dancing with that jackass. I knew she had drunk quite a bit, but I wasn't expecting all of this.

She wasn't the one to break down easily unless it was because one of us messed with her or her mom did something while her dad was gone. She knew we would always have her back no matter what.

Her breaking down while trying to say she doesn't need anyone and that she can only rely on herself breaks my heart a little bit. When I picked her up, she fought it, but it was futile.

Walking her towards the kitchen so that I can get her a glass of water and some medicine for a hangover I see the guys in the living room. When they see me carrying her, they jump up asking if she is okay.

Nodding I try to get them to shush as I set her down on the chair in the kitchen. When she grabs my shirt, I have to tell her, "Hey now I'm just getting you some water and medicine or you aren't going to like life in the morning."

She reluctantly let's go of me but curls into a ball on the chair and tucks her head into her knees. It physically pains me to see her like this and every now and then I get an echo of her pain and it's enough to have me stumbling.

What happened? Why is she so sad?
She drank too much but I'm not completely understanding why she is so sad.
Did you do something?
No asshole. She was dancing with some jackass and then kissed him after I told her to step away from him. Then she fell asleep before we even made it to the car. She woke up when I was taking her out to bring in the house when she started fighting me saying she didn't need anyone and that she could only rely on herself. There isn't anyone who she can run to then fell and started sobbing so I just picked her up and brought her inside.
Um guys I think she fell asleep again.

Looking away from Malrik, I glance over and see Jasper is watching her concerned.

She is still curled in the chair, but I can't hear her crying anymore.

I finish getting her drink and walk over and right as I'm about to regretfully wake her up she lets out a small cry.

"Please stop it. I just want my guys. Why can't I go to be with them? Please. Mally where'd you go? Why are you so mean now?" her small voice cries before her body starts shuddering with sobs.

I know I got to see some stuff when I went into her mind a week or so ago, but she sounds so small and heartbroken that I'm not sure how to fix it or help her.

Before I can do anything, I'm shoved aside as a body goes to her and picks her up.

Malrik?

Should've known he was never the one who could handle when she cried. I'm pretty sure it has something to do with his dragon and the way he covets Liora. He takes her into the living room and bundles her against his chest while cooing soft words at her.

I'm not sure what he is saying to her, but she stops making small sobs and her body just silently shakes. We all settle in the living room around them to be here if she needs us.

I'll move her when she falls completely asleep again. I watch them and you can see he truly cares for her but I'm not sure who is running the show right now him or his dragon.

"If you are going to freak out and be an asshole about this to her then I'll take her." I whisper to him.

His head snaps up at me before he says lowly, "Try to take her from me and my dragon will be the least of your problems. And I would never use this against her. Her subconscious knows who and where she is safe even if she fights it when she is conscious."

I hold my hands up so he can see I'm not a threat and won't take her from him even if I want to make sure, she is okay. Just when I decide she is asleep and I can safely take her up to one of the rooms upstairs she lets out a whisper, "Safe.. Finally safe."

Chapter 56
Liora

When I wake up in the morning, I have a momentary panic attack when I see I'm not in my dorm. However, seeing the bunny next to me I know I'm at the guy's house.

Why am I at the guy's house? What happened last night?

Slowly it all flashes through my mind. Going dancing with Trixie, drinking and doing shots, dancing with Lykos, Ryder carting me out, and oh my fucking god I sobbed on Malrik?

What the hell drunk Liora? Of the 3 guys it was Malrik?! Wait, whose room am I in? Looking down I see that I'm still wearing my dress sans my shoes thank god.

Looking around the room, I see that I'm in Ryder's. Whew. At least I already know the layout for his. Going to the bathroom I think of how I am going to sneak out so I don't have to see their faces after last night.

Hmm could I just scale down the wall?

Looking out the window, I see that is not an option.

Maybe they're still sleeping?

The other 2 maybe but Ryder? Unlikely knowing my luck he is the kitchen.

Wait. if he is in the kitchen, I should be able to dip out of the house without him seeing me.

Yea, that's what we are going to try. Shit I don't see my shoes in his room.

Creeping down the stairs I try to stay as silent as I can. As I get to the bottom stair I can hear voices.

Dammit they must all be awake.

Peeking around the banister of the stairs. I almost let out a loud sigh when I don't see anyone in the living room. They must be in the kitchen which works for me.

Taking the last step down, I spot my shoes by the couch. Crawling to grab them and crawl back towards the front door I stand when I'm safely by the door.

Opening it up I step outside when I hear, "Where are you going sugar?"

Shit.

How did he hear me?

I didn't make any noise.

Maybe I can pretend like I didn't hear him?

I think he senses I'm about to run because he moves so fast it is like a blur. Before I know it I'm tossed over his shoulder and back in the house. Well damn.

I'm really tired of being tossed on someone's shoulder.

We move so fast I want to hurl. Why is he moving so fast? What the hell?

I don't get the chance to do anything when I'm dropped onto a couch in a room that is definitely not the living room. Where are we?

"Where do you think you were going?" Ryder asks.

"Home. What's it to you?" I snark back.

"You are home." Malrik snarls.

What the hell? He is mental.

"No, I'm not. I live in the dorms with Trixie." I snarl back at him.

"You cried in my arms last night about finally being safe so no you do not you live with us." Malrik says, trying to make me submit.

"I was drunk, you can't hold that against me! Also, why the hell would I want to live with someone who is an absolute asshole to me." I say back getting up.

"Liora!"

"Malrik!"

It was shouted in unison by Ryder and Jasper because we were both about to blow.

"Screw you guys! I will do what I want. You are not my keepers! No one will tell me what I can and can't do!" I shout and go back up the stairs and out the door of the house.

No one follows which is good because I can't be bothered to be with any of them. Walking towards my dorm I'm sure I look like I am doing the walk of shame, but I just don't care.

Chapter 57
Liora

Making it back to my dorm I push the door open just to squeal, cover my eyes and attempt to walk back out. Fate must hate me because instead of walking back out I face plant the door and fall on my ass dazed.

"Liora!" Trixie shouts in a panic.

Shaking my head to attempt to clear the confusion from my head I give her a wobbly smile.

"I'm sorry I didn't know you were preoccupied." I explain.

She starts laughing hysterically at me once she knows I am okay. Every time she tries to calm down and say what happened it sends her into a fit of giggles.

"Come on love it's not that funny," Aurelius says with a smile on his face.

"You're smiling too jerk." I say.

"Oh, come on Li, you would have laughed too if roles were flipped." Trix says.

"That's true. I just can't believe I walked in on that." I shudder.

"Hey, we could have been doing the nasty when you walked in at least it was just some harmless make out session." Trixie says.

"Shirtless make out. My poor eyes. I didn't think I would walk into the dorm with my best friend shirtless and making out with her boyfriend while he had his hands on your breasts." I say dramatically.

"Oh, whatever my dramatic bestie. We weren't expecting you back so soon. Ryder hauled you off and I figured you would still be there." she ponders.

"Yeah, well Malrik was being an ass, so I left and Aurelius still has my phone from where we gave them to him to hold on to." I say.

"Trixie put yours in your room on the charger." Aurelius tells me.

"Ugh I love you." I say to Trixie dashing into my room to retrieve my phone.

Of course, there's multiple messages and for whatever reason I am now in a group chat with the guys.

Aunt Delilah
Hey Sweetness, just checking on you.

Daemous

Hey Liora, just checking on you.
Wanted to see if you wanted to go to
dinner?

Four of A Kind

Jasper
Hey, created a gc so we don't have to relay
everything.

Malrik
This is so stupid.

Malrik has left the chat.
Jasper has added Malrik to the chat.
Malrik has left the chat.
Jasper has added Malrik to the chat.

RyRy
I think it's a great way for all of us to
communicate and get to know Liora again

Malrik is such an asshole. He has me
rolling my eyes in frustration again. I

understand where Jasper and Ryder are coming from, but I don't like that they are trying to boss me around again.

I already want to throw myself off of a cliff because I cried on Malrik. Of all of them it had to be him? I knew he would be a complete asshole about it like he is about everything.

Four of A Kind

Me

Maybe I don't want to be in a gc with you either.

The thought was there Jasper. At least someone wants to talk to me.

Replying back into the group chat I can't help but feel the bitter sting from how Malrik treats me. I honestly don't get it. If he doesn't like me he didn't have to hold me while I cried or whisper the sweet things he said to help calm me down.

I know Lilthe was a bitch but none of that is my fault. He needs to get over it or have a reality check because I can't keep being his verbal punching bag.

I just want to be loved.

Taking a shower to clean off the night of dancing and sleeping in my dress after crying feels amazing. Taking the makeup off of my eyes hurts but feels so much better once it's off.

I shrug on a pair of baggy sweats and a crop before walking back into the bathroom and brushing out my hair. Once brushed I decide what the hell and do double dutch braids in it because I can't be bothered to do anything else with it.

Walking back out I see Trixie on the couch and Aurelius is gone. Frowning because I really didn't mean to interrupt them, I just wanted to come home and change.

"Where'd Aurelius go? I didn't mean to interrupt y'all and scare him off, I'm sorry." I apologize.

"Oh no girl, you are so good. He had to get to practice. It's a good thing you came when you did. We have a tendency to get carried away and lose track of time." Trixie replies.

"Practice?" I ask confused.

"Yeah, he's on the school's Squashball team. Go rumbling buds." she says semi enthusiastically.

Chapter 58
Liora

Squashball? Rumbling buds? What is with all of the puns in this school's buildings and teams?

"Squashball?" I ask in confusion.

"Oh, shit dude I'm sorry I keep forgetting you're still new to all of the things here. Plus, it's not like we have been to any of the games or the pep rallies. Anyways, Squashball is basically paranormal soccer, so no humans play. There are huge holes on either side of the field. The goal is to get the ball down the field to the other side by either running, throwing or kicking it and then you literally squash the ball into the hole. It also gets the name from the way you can squash your opponents on the field. The only rule is not taking flight or transforming into your shifter." she explains.

"Hmm so more like a mix of football and soccer? It sounds intriguing, it must be a fun time." I reply.

"I haven't been to any of the games this year but last year they were a lot of fun." she tells me.

"Hmm we'll have to make it to one." I tell her.

"Yes! I can't wait to take you to one. But anyways, how are you doing? Did you get up to no good last night?" she asks, wiggling her eyebrows.

"No!" I answer quickly.

Great, you answered too quickly Li. now she is going to think something hot and spicy went on when in fact what actually happened was that I bawled like a baby and then ran away essentially.

"Oh really? Do tell. Because my lovely bestie you answered that way too fast.   Did you fuck Ryder? He carried you out all caveman style and I bet you guys had crazy sex." she says.

"No, you have it all wrong. Well yes, he did carry me out like a sack of potatoes but then I fell asleep and when I woke up, I came back to the dorm. So no, no crazy sex." I reply.

"Awe well sad day. If you want to get some, I'm sure Lykos wouldn't mind linking up for that." she tells me.

"I don't know he seemed put off after whatever it was that Ryder had told him." I explain.

"I can always ask Aurelius and see if he can find out if you want me to?" she asks.

"No, it's okay." I reply.

"If you're sure then I won't. Well, I'm beat so I'm going to head to bed and get some sleep." she tells me.

Damn I didn't realize how late it had got but when Trixie yawns not shortly after do I yawn. We giggle at each other before heading to our rooms and going to bed.

Luckily, I had done the homework that was due Monday already, so I don't have to worry about it this weekend. Thank goodness. Brushing out my hair I change into some comfortable clothes so that I can sleep easy tonight.

Before I lay down, I go ahead and tidy up my room a little bit. It isn't dirty but because I couldn't decide what to wear to go dancing there are clothes thrown around my room.

Laying down I check my phone and go ahead check my messages. Rolling my eyes at the group chat and Daemous I close the messages app and open paravine and absently scroll through my feed. Next thing I know my eyes are closing.

I'm back on the dancefloor seeing how far I can push Ryder's buttons before he snaps. It doesn't take long before he is striding over to me and tossing me over his shoulders. Why do I feel like I'm getting wet over something so simple as being man handled over his shoulders.

Wiggling on his shoulder trying to get down or rubbing my thighs together for friction? Who knows maybe Trix was right and I just need to get laid.

Smack. Did he? Did he just spank me? Why does that insanely turn me on but also make me want to yell at him?

"Stop wiggling bunny or I'm going to make sure you can't sit for a week." he growls.

"Did you seriously spank me?" I sputter out.

Smack.

"Yea I did, and I'll keep doing it if you don't stop wiggling." he tells me seriously.

Half of me is tempted to wiggle some more to see how far I can push him while the other half wants to submit and listen to what he says. The two sides war for a little bit.

Before I can make my decision, I am dropped unceremoniously into the passenger seat of his car. He buckles me in like a toddler before shutting my door and walking towards the driver side.

Starting the car he messes with getting the heat going for me before putting the car into drive. He heads towards the guy's house and when my sobering mind catches up, I can't help but snark at him.

"This isn't the way towards my dorm. Where the hell are you taking me Ryder?" I snark.

"I'm taking you home." he replies, not taking his eyes off of the road.

"That is your home not mine. Take me to the dorms." I argue back before crossing my arms over my chest.

"Don't be a brat or else." he answers gruffly.

"Or else what? What are you going to do RyRy. take me home, I don't belong with you three." I sassily state.

"I will pull over and take you over my knee and spank your ass raw. You won't be able to sit down without thinking of me and when I'm done spanking you, I will fuck you so hard you know exactly who you belong to." he says starting right at me.

It's a little unnerving and I can't help wanting him to act on what he said. It sounds like a fun time and getting to see him come undone for me does something to me.

Rubbing my thighs together he doesn't stop the groan when he notices. I decide fuck it and become a brat just to see how far I can push.

"Stop rubbing those pretty little thighs for me or we won't make it home." he growls.

"I'm rubbing them because I'm cold, not because of you or anything. Someone has a big ego." I smirk.

"Oh, really bunny so if I reach over and dip my hand between those thighs you won't be dripping? Are you really going to lie when I can see the reaction my words have done to you?" he asks me.

"Yes, RyRy I don't know what drugs you have been taking but I'm just cold I haven't had any reaction to you." I snark.

I don't realize we are at the guy's house until he gets out of the car. Oh, shit did I push him to his breaking point? Is he going to fuck me? Do I want it? Who am I kidding? Of course I want it.

He yanks me out of the car before pushing me up against it and slamming his mouth down on mine. His kiss is grueling like he is trying to punish me and own me all at once.

The moan escapes before I can swallow it down and he bites down on my lip in response. My hands are roaming before I can stop them and before they can venture beneath his shirt, he rips his lips away and flips me onto my stomach.

Stomach on the hood I can't help but sigh at the coldness of the metal on my heated cheek. Opening my eyes I see two figures in the windows. Is that? Are they watching?

Smack. Smack. Smack.

Ryder delivers those next three slaps in quick procession, and I hardly feel like I have a chance to breathe in between each one. His hand comes down one more time and a moan escapes my lips, a fog of breath in the night air.

He flips me back over and my mind is dizzy with lust. The metal was cold beneath my palms, yet all I could feel was him—his weight, his nearness, the storm in his eyes.

I try to speak, but the words caught in my throat. He leaned in closer, his hand braced against the hood beside her head, caging her in. His breath brushed her cheek, unsteady, hungry, as though he'd been holding back for too long.

"Say the word," he murmured, his voice roughened with restraint. "And I'll stop."

My chest rose and fell, each inhale shallow, betraying the war inside of me—fear of what this meant, and the fierce pull of wanting him anyway. My fingers curled into the fabric of his shirt, drawing him closer when I hadn't consciously meant to.

That was all it took.

He lowered his head, capturing my mouth with a ferocity that made the world tilt. The kiss was searing, urgent, every bit of pent-up longing poured into the space between them. I gasp, but he swallows the sound, one hand sliding to my waist, holding me as if he was afraid, I would vanish if he let go.

My heart thundered. His lips moved against mine with a desperation that left me dizzy, the taste of him lingering, intoxicating. It was wild, reckless, and terrifyingly right. And I never wanted to stop.

Chapter 59
Liora

My alarm wakes me up before I can finish my dream with Ryder and all that was happening. I can't believe I just had a dream like that about him and I swear I saw Jasper and Malrik in the window.

I have a stupid smile on my face as I get up out of the bed to get ready for the day. Going to walk towards the bathroom I notice how wet and sticky my shorts are.
I can't believe I got wet from a dream. It wasn't even a sex dream. We didn't do more than kissing and maybe some heavy petting so why the hell did I get so wet?

Taking a shower to attempt to clear my mind from that dream and a certain trio. Getting out I get dressed for the day. I don't think we have anything going on today so maybe a chill day.

Ooh I wonder if Trixie will take me to the supe shopping district to get a couple things for myself and just to go look around since we haven't been to the one here yet.

Sending her a text because I would hate it if I woke her up. I strip the bedding off of my bed and take it towards the laundry room. Getting that started I make my way into the kitchen and grab one of my drinks.

Before I can head back towards my room Trixie pokes her head out. Stopping and looking at her.

"Good morning bestie. I'm awake, what's up?" she asks.

"Hey, I was just going to see if you had any plans today?" I ask.

"Um no I don't think so why what's up?" she inquires.

"I was going to see if you wanted to go to the supe shopping center today? I wanna go check out some of the shops and pick up some ingredients for some basic spells and potions." I explain.

"Ooo yes, I would love to go. Give me like 30 minutes to get ready, okay?" she asks.

Nodding my head she shuts her door to start getting ready. I head back to my room and slip on a pair of my flare jeans and one of my form sitting shirts. Lastly, we can't forget a pair of my converse. I do opt for a pair of my lifted ones because I'm short and have to wear my lifted converse or heels if I don't want my jeans to drag the floor.

Slipping my card underneath my phone case I walk back out and wait for Trixie to get done. I chill on the couch drinking my life and savior and scrolling paravine.

There's so many funny videos and videos of friends dancing with each other and I wonder how fun it would be to learn some of them.

"Oh that dance looks so cool." Trixie's voice comes from behind me and succeeds in scaring the hell out of me.

"Sorry love. I thought you heard me come in." she says apologetically.

"Lol it's all good. I shouldn't have been so engrossed in what I was watching. That's what happens when you watch too much paravine you become zoned in on it." I explain.

"No, I totally get that! It happens to me all the time. I will mean to just take a quick break and scroll through it and all of a sudden 3 hours have passed." she tells me.

I laugh at her in understanding because that has happened to me one too many times.

"Are you ready?" I ask.

"Yes ma'am let's go do this. Shopping trip and girls' day. We can stop and have some lunch from one of the restaurants in the shopping district." Trixie tells me.

"That sounds amazing to me." I reply.

It's not too long of a trip to get to the shopping district. It's walking distance from the school almost like it is hidden and if you don't realize it is there you won't know where to look.

You walk the path towards the Whisperwood Forest and veer off slightly and bam it's like being transported.

My eyes widened the moment I stepped through the iron archway that is off to the side of the walkway slightly. One second me and Trixie had been walking down an ordinary cobblestone street, and the next, it was as if we had crossed into another world.

Lanterns floated high above the alley, glowing in shades of violet and gold. The air shimmered faintly with magic, carrying scents of cinnamon, magic, smoke, and something sharper—like ozone after a storm.

"Welcome to Moonpetal Row," Trixie announced with a grin, spreading her arms wide. "The one-stop shopping hub for every witch, shifter, and oddball in between."

The first shop we passed had an entire wall of potion bottles, each glowing with a different hue. A tired-looking goblin behind the counter waved a claw. "Mood tonics! Guaranteed to improve your attitude or worsen someone else's!"

I stifle a laugh. "Tempting."

Next door, an herbalist's stall overflowed with bundles of dried flowers and roots. Some were ordinary—lavender, sage, rosemary. Others pulsed faintly with light, as if still alive. Trixie picked up a sprig of something blue and sniffed it. Her hair immediately curled into ringlets. She squealed. "Okay, not buying that one!"

We duck into a jeweler's shop where necklaces dripped with stones that whispered when touched. One pendant leaned close to my ear and murmured; *Secrets look good on you.* I quickly set it back down and sped walked in the other direction.

Talking necklaces?

What kind of secrets could it know?

Further down the lane, a bakery displayed glass cases of enchanted sweets. Cupcakes frosted themselves, donuts floated lazily in the air, and a tray of cookies giggled every time someone walked past. Trixie grabbed two. "Trust me, they're worth the sugar rush."

Taking a nibble, I can't help the groan of satisfaction at the way the flavor explodes in my mouth. I shovel the rest into my mouth not caring in the slightest if I look unladylike.

By the time we reached the end of the row, my arms were full of small treasures: a vial of starlight ink, a pouch of alyssium, a charm shaped like a rose that hummed softly, and—because Trixie insisted—a bag of fortune-telling marshmallows.

"It's like an entire world hidden in plain sight," I breathe, my heart fluttering.

Trixie nudged her shoulder, eyes sparkling. "Welcome to the real fun part of Rosepin life."

We spend the majority of the day just hanging out and continuously walking around the shopping district. We settle down at a restaurant called **Mythic Eats.**

It's got different types of flowers hanging from the ceiling and there are various plants scattered all throughout the place. We place our orders quickly and our server is so nice.

I order a dish called chow down on a bun which is basically a burger but with herbs

to make it taste amazing. Trixie gets
something called swimmingly lucky which
from my understanding is a fried fish plate
with a lemon and some kind of dipping sauce.

Chapter 60
Liora

Once we are done eating, we decide to call it a day and as we are walking out of the restaurant to head back to the dorms Trixie suddenly exclaims.

"Oh, I forgot I need to grab a Starlit Safeguard before we head back to the dorms." she says.

"Starlit Safeguard? What is that?" I ask quizzically.

"It's like a birth control potion. That's the easiest way to explain it. Come on, one of the shops we passed earlier should have some left hopefully anyway." Trixie says pulling me along.

I follow along still starstruck at how amazing everything looks and the way the majority of everyone is super friendly. We pull up in front of the shop I got the alyssium from and I love the way the shopkeeper's eyes light up when she sees us again.

"Well hello dearies. What have you come back for?" she asks us in such a kind voice.

"Do you happen to have any more Starlit Safeguard left?" Trixie asks.

"Let me see, you kids always take the majority of my stock." She walks into the backroom.

Trixie pulls out her phone and starts texting someone. I'm assuming it is Aurelius, and I can't help but feel a little bit jealous that she has someone like that.

I can't stew on my feelings for long because all of a sudden, my phone buzzes. Pulling it out I see that it is the group chat Jasper created.

Four of A Kind

Ryder
Where are you bunny?

Jasper
Come on sugar, tell us where you are or we will come and find you.

Me
Wouldn't you like to know.
How do you know I'm not at my dorm?

Ryder

You're not at the dorm, we've checked. So, I ask again where are you?

Don't make me get Malrik to track you down by scent. You won't like the consequences.

Me
Come find me if you can RyRy.

Powering down my phone I put it in my pocket with a grin. I love pushing his buttons and thinking about my dream and how he may punish me. There is a thrill of excitement racing through me.

Also how did they know I wasn't at my dorm? Maybe we didn't answer because we are sleeping, or I was in the shower. Do they have a key to our place?

Before I can dwell on it too much the shopkeeper comes back out holding 2 vials of shimmering liquid. They're so pretty to look at. I follow Trixie up to the checkout counter and wait.

"Alright, dearies. I have 2 left. I can make some more, or you can purchase the ingredients needed and can make it yourself." she explains to us.

"One should be good for each of us today. We can come back before the three months are up and get our next one. Plus, the ones you make taste good, so they are easier to swallow." Trixie says sweetly.

"Alright dearies will it be together or separate?" she asks.

"Together. Thank you, ma'am." Trixie says.

When we leave the shop, I tell Trixie she didn't have to pay for mine. Besides I haven't been having sex so I'm not sure why I would need one anyways.

"This one was my treat. Her starlit safeguard potions are delicious besides they look like moonlight reflecting off of water. It is so magical that you can't help but want some." Trixie says.

"Oh, wow the freak thinks she needs starlit safeguard. As if anyone would want to fuck her anyways." a voice says from beside us when we leave the shopping district.

"Fuck off Lilthe. You know it's not nice to talk about yourself that way people may think you're depressed." Trixie fires back.

"Everyone knows who the freak is and it's not me Traxie. Besides, don't you play for both sides so please keep your flirting away from me and keep your freak of a friend away from Malrik he's mine and doesn't need her messing with his mind." Lilith huffs.

"Careful now Filthe. You're starting to sound like a scorned lover. Everyone knows you burned the bridge when it comes to Malrik because you got too greedy and wanted anything with a dick." I tell her.

She's nothing but a bully who doesn't understand that Malrik doesn't want her. I watch her perfect facade break before she screams and rushes at me. Her followers shooting spells at Trixie.

Lilthe takes me by surprise, and we go rolling on the ground. She gets a good punch in on my face before I can use my feet and kick her off of me. She goes flying over my head and I pop up to help Trixie.

I'm not sure what I can do to help other than run at one and knock her out. So I do just that. I run at one that is shooting a yellowish magic at Trixie and roundhouse kick her in the head; she drops like a bag of potatoes out cold before she even hits the floor.

"Liora watch out."

Is the only warning I get before I'm blasted in the side with pain numbing magic. It feels like I am freezing on the spot. Lilthe slams into me and we tumble onto the ground again and I swear I hear something snap when we land.

Oh fuck. What was that?

"Get the fuck off of me." I grit out using what little control I have over my telekinesis and shoot Lilthe into the woods.

Scrambling up because I know Trixie needs help. Although looking at them she is holding her own beautifully. I watch in awe as her purple lightning bolts adorn her hands, and she slowly starts to create a ball of it to shoot at the girls.

I go to take a step forward before I'm halted so suddenly that I would've faceplanted the ground. I'm so sick of falling or being rammed into. I attempt to move my foot again when I'm halted again.

What the hell?

Glancing down my body I see what looks like vines crawling up my legs until I'm completely immobile besides my head.

A ball of black and silver magic catches my eye. What is that? I see one of Lilthe's followers focusing so hard that they have sweat dotting down their face. What kind of spell is she casting? Better yet what kind of magic is that?

I don't get a chance to do anything because like a rubber band has snapped that magic shoots towards me. A body throws itself in front of me to shield me from the magic. A gasp of pain leaving them at impact before they slowly fall to the floor.

The vines vanish immediately, and I look down seeing none other than Trixie on the ground. Blood soaking the area around her and a gaping hole in her side.

"NO! TRIXIE!" I scream dropping down beside her.

Not caring that my clothes are being soaked in her blood I try to stench the bleeding by pressing my hands to her side.

"Please, please Trixie. Why did you get in front of me? Why? I'm going to make them pay." I sob as I do everything I can to stop her bleeding.

Looking up I don't see anyone around us. They must have fled once they dealt the damage they wanted. They even took the girl I knocked out with them. Fuck I need to get her help.

"HELP!" I scream pulling Trixie onto my lap.

I plead with anyone who will listen to help me. I don't want to lose the only friend I have. She came into my life and gave me everything I didn't know I ever needed. So, I need her to be okay so she can't die. I need her. What about Aurelius, what is he going to think?

Panic swallows me whole. I press trembling palms against the wound, desperate, helpless.

"Don't you dare leave me," I whispered, tears streaking my cheeks.

Trixie's eyes fluttered open, hazy but defiant. "Don't... cry, Liora. I'm not done fighting yet."

The words broke something inside me. Heat bloomed beneath my skin, my chest aching as if my very soul has cracked open. Light — pure, golden light — spills from my hands, pouring into Trixie's wound.

The golden light erupts from me illuminating the entire area we are in, swirls of something trace up my arms and I stare in shock, my hands still on Trixie. Trixie's breathing steadies, the color returning to her cheeks as the golden glow starts sealing the seared flesh. I stare, stunned, as the last flicker of light faded from my palms. My hands trembling, but not from fear — from power.

I hear shouts from somewhere as the last of the golden light fades and my body slumps before my world goes dark.

Is Trixie okay? Am I okay?

Acknowledgements

Scorned Lover has been something I have always thought about and maybe played with and wrote throughout the years but never actually finished. To have it finally come alive on the page is one of the best feelings in the world. I am both excited and insanely nervous to share it with you all. I really hope you all fall in love with Liora and her randomness, Malrik and his jerkish ways, Ryder and his commanding ways, and Jasper and his golden retriever energy.

this isn't the last you will see of Liora, and her mates so stay tuned on what is yet to come.

Special thanks to my wonderful husband, Isaac and our 2 wild children who I have no idea where I would be without. Fun fact my characters are inspired by the people around me. You're unwavering support and encouragement is what helped me get to this point so thank you and I love you so very much, and to my in- laws thank you for your support and encouragement to help me through this.

Are you ready for Liora and her mates in book 2?

About the Author

Luci O. is a pen name, but I am from west Texas. I met my husband when we were 14 and got together in 2015. we have 2 wild children who keep us on our toes with their shenanigans.

I have a long cherished the power of books, believing that every story holds something worth discovering, no matter the genre. A lifelong reader, Luci found inspiration in the ability of stories to transport, transform, and connect. Becoming an author has always been a dream, and each book is both a fulfillment of that dream and an invitation for readers to share in it. Through her writing, Luci strives to capture the same sense of wonder and meaning that has made books her greatest passion.

Why choose/reverse harems are my favorite tropes to read no matter the genre, and I will typically reread my favorites.

Follow Me for Updates

Join the O. Haven

Follow me on Tiktok @lucio.author

Follow me on instagram @luci.o.author

follow my group on Facebook Luci O. Author

www.ingramcontent.com/pod-product-compliance
Lightning Source LLC
Chambersburg PA
CBHW020647110726
47901CB00001B/83